An

'Tell me honestly that yo... ...ne,' Charles whispered, pressing Gina ... ...otch.

Gina made an effort to ... ...h hand away but she was caught between confli...ing desires. Part of her wanted to slap him around the face for his rudeness but the other part was curiously aroused by his proximity, by his obvious desire for her, and by the feeling of his erection, growing under her touch. She knew that Charles sensed her hesitation. A wonderful spicy aroma hung in the air: the sexual tension was palpable.

An Act of Love

ELLA BROUSSARD

BLACK
lace

Black Lace novels are sexual fantasies.
In real life, make sure you practise safe sex.

First published in 1998 by
Black Lace
332 Ladbroke Grove
London W10 5AH

Typeset by SetSystems Ltd, Saffron Walden, Essex
Printed and bound by Mackays of Chatham PLC

ISBN 0 352 33240 9

Chapter One

The phone rang, jogging Gina out of a ragged sleep. She looked over at the clock: seven thirty on a Saturday morning. Uncoordinated, she fumbled for the receiver and knocked the clock off the bedside table.

'Damn,' she muttered under her breath, as she lifted the receiver to her ear.

'And a good morning to you too. So, are you alone?' a bright voice asked.

'Kirsten, do you know what time it is?'

'Time you were up. You sound a bit crotchety. I'm not disturbing anything, am I?' Kirsten laughed.

'Well, I'm sorry to disappoint you, but I'm on my own, and have been all night.'

Kirsten tutted. 'I can't believe you sometimes. You're at a wild and drunken and debauched party, you have the hunkiest man there following you round like a lost soul all night, and you end up in your own bed, on your own. Unbelievable. So come on, spill the beans.'

Gina smiled to herself. Kirsten always needed to know all the details.

'There's nothing to tell.'

'Don't give me that. I saw what he was like. He wanted you, no mistake. So what happened? Where did you get to last night? And who was he? No one in the

1

cast knew, and none of the backstage crew had invited him either. Hey, I've done my research, believe me.'

'I never found out his name. I suppose he was quite good-looking,' Gina mused.

Kirsten snorted with derision on the other end of the phone. 'That's got to be the understatement of the year. "Quite good-looking"? He was gorgeous, like George Clooney and James Dean and Brad Pitt and a young Marlon all rolled into one, and then some. So don't give me "quite good-looking", eh?'

Gina laughed. 'OK, OK, but there was something about him –'

'Yeah, how about pure sex?' Kirsten interrupted.

'No, not that. He was just a bit too insistent somehow. I was flattered at first, I mean, who wouldn't be? He was charming, and intelligent, and witty and fun. We chatted about this and that; you know, nothing special, just party talk. And then I wanted to move on, talk to some other people, and he wouldn't let me go. Kept following me around. It really started to annoy me after a while.'

'Jeez, I don't understand you sometimes,' Kirsten said. 'You have Mr Unbelievably Sexy at your beck and call and it annoys you? All I can say is give him my name and number instead, will you?'

'And then finally he cornered me in the kitchen.'

'Ah, now we're getting to the interesting bit,' said Kirsten with barely concealed anticipation.

'He literally cornered me. He was pressing me into a corner, blocking my exit, trying to touch me, saying that he could do a lot for me if I'd let him. He tried to kiss me.'

'Oh, don't tell me: you didn't like it.'

'No Kirsten, I did not. I was fed up with his pestering, with his arrogance, fed up that he wouldn't – or couldn't – get the message that I wasn't interested. I pushed him away, a bit too hard I suppose, because he stumbled and fell. I rushed past him out of the kitchen and left the party straight away. I didn't want to see him again.'

'So you went home, and that was that.'

'Yup, that's about the sum of it.'

'But, come on, don't tell me that you weren't just the tiniest bit turned on by all that attention?'

'Well, OK, yes. I was flattered, and he did seem so nice at first, and I was thinking that maybe there might be something there between us. But then his behaviour just spoilt it all for me. I can't be interested in a man who acts like that.'

'Not even for a quickie?'

'Not even for a quickie. So there you have it. My exciting night at the end-of-run party. I think it was a brilliant production, by the way. I wish I could have been part of it. And you were excellent, as ever.'

'Thanks. Don't worry, kiddo: keep looking in *The Stage*. You'll find yourself a part, even if you don't find a man,' Kirsten said encouragingly.

'Well, I hope so. Time is starting to run out a bit.'

'Chin up. It'll be all right. You'll see.' And with a click and a whirr Kirsten was gone.

Gina hung up the phone, and lay back on the pillows. She hadn't been exactly truthful with Kirsten, but that was because she was uncomfortable with the truth herself. She had been more than flattered by her mystery admirer's attentions: she had been aroused by them. Gina knew that men found her attractive, and enjoyed flirting with them, but she had never thought of herself as special enough to warrant the attention that she had received the previous night. He was handsome, and almost exactly her type of man: dark-eyed and dark-haired, with full lips, a long and straight nose, a square jaw-line. He was muscular and masculine; the antithesis of her own blonde, soft beauty.

The urgency of his relentless pursuit of her had been stimulating, and undeniably erotically charged. She had even thought of giving in to his pressure, but then she had got the first inkling of his arrogance and his temper, and she hadn't liked it. And yet, despite her anger with him, she had been strangely excited. It was wonderful to

3

be so openly desired by someone, especially by someone as handsome as him.

As she remembered, her hand slipped over her stomach, slowly stroking the gentle curve around her navel with the palm of her hand. Gina always slept naked, the feel of the cool linen sheets so much better than the constriction of pyjamas or a nightdress; and, besides, it was easier to enjoy her body that way. She was proud of her body, and rightly so. At twenty-nine, she had a body that a woman ten years younger would envy, and she knew the effect that it had on men. Her waist was small, her stomach flat and her legs long and shapely. Her breasts were naturally high and full, and needed no support, so she often went without a bra. She enjoyed her body. She just hadn't had anyone to enjoy it with for a while now.

Gina was brought round from her reverie by the noise of the papers plopping on to the mat. She got up, wrapped herself in her dressing gown, and padded through to the hallway to pick them up. Then she went into the kitchen and switched on the kettle. As she waited for it to boil, she sat at the table and turned first to *The Stage*.

'Here goes nothing,' she said to herself as she opened it at the first page of 'The Call Sheet', the section of notices for casting calls, auditions and theatrical jobs vacant.

She quickly scanned the pages, scouring avidly for suitable advertisements: 'Casting lead and other male roles in *King Lear*'; 'Wanted: Full Cast for *Boys in the Blockhouse*. Apply Now!'; 'Are you our ideal Rosencrantz or our perfect Guildenstern?'; 'We need Seven Brothers. Brides already cast'; 'Uncle Vanya: where are you?' She swore under her breath. It was always the same. There were so many good parts for men, and so few for women. And the roles for women could usually be split into virgin or whore, love interest or damsel in distress, witch or bitch.

The kettle started to bubble, and then clicked itself off.

4

Gina ignored it, her head cradled in one hand, as she scrutinised the last and smallest adverts, pen poised ready to circle likely candidates. When she finished, she sighed, and sat back in the chair. There must be over four hundred parts advertised in this issue, and only three of them were suitable for her. There were other female roles, but she needed a big part. She needed to be noticed. She cursed again. Things were not looking good. She thought back to her interview at The National Academy of Dramatic Arts. They had liked her, and were willing to offer her a place. But there was one condition. It had been detailed to her by the stern-faced woman who headed the interview panel.

'There is one proviso, and you need not fear favouritism, as we make this proviso to all prospective applicants. Between now and the start of the academic year in September, you must have performed in a play somewhere in Britain. You will inform the Academy of the production, and one or more of our tutors will attend a performance, incognito of course, to assess your potential. I cannot stress to you strongly enough that the bigger your part, the better the production and the larger the venue, the greater your chances of acceptance here at the Academy will be. If either your performance or the production as a whole is not of a sufficiently high standard, the offer of a place may be withdrawn. So it is up to you to select the part and the production carefully, and to attain the highest standards possible. Thank you, Miss Stanhope.'

That had been four weeks ago, and in that month there had been the impressive total of five possible parts for her advertised in *The Stage*. Five including the three she had circled that morning.

'Hey ho,' she said to herself, as she poured the boiling water over the leaves in the tea pot.

Later that morning, she completed her three letters of application, and printed out three more copies of her curriculum vitae from the computer in her study. She addressed the envelopes and stamped them, and walked down to the post box. It was a scorching hot June day, the sky almost shimmering with the heat; she was relieved that she had chosen to wear silk that morning: a loose blouse and a cool skirt. She was also glad that she had pinned her shoulder-length hair up on to the back of her head. It meant that what little breeze there was could trace its cooling touch on her neck.

Gina wondered quite what she would do if she could not manage to get a part. Perhaps she had been stupid to give up her job as a buyer for one of the largest and most fashionable clothes stores in the centre of London. It was well paid and she had enjoyed her work. It was just that she had always had an ambition to act, and lately her performances in the local amateur dramatic society's productions had fanned, rather than assuaged, that urge. She felt she had to do this, for better or for worse. And she had a feeling that it was going to get much worse before it got better.

When she got back to her house she saw that Martin, the local window cleaner, was unloading his ladders from his van. She had only met him once previously, but had been instantly attracted to him. He was a quiet, softly spoken man of about thirty-five, with a lean, tanned face. Once she had got past his shyness, she had discovered that he had a sharp sense of humour. Physically, she found him very appealing: muscular but not too well-built. He was wearing jeans and a T-shirt, and Gina felt a quickening sense of lust. He looked wonderful in the tight denim, and she looked at him carefully, trying to figure out whether he had anything on underneath the faded and ripped jeans.

She greeted him as she went into the house, and asked him to start round at the back. She loved her house. It was modern and airy and built on a single-floor plan. Her study and her bedroom both faced out on to the garden at the back of the house; the wall, one great high sheet of glass, was broken only by the large sliding doors for access.

Gina went into her study, and sat at her desk. She switched on the computer, and started to update her job-application records. She could hear Martin moving about in the garden, and then the watery swish of his sponge against the glass. As she sat on the soft office chair, warmed by the sun, she could feel herself gradually becoming aroused by Martin's presence. She knew he would be watching her through the window as he washed it, and it thrilled her to know he was unaware that she sensed his gaze.

Leaning back in her chair and throwing her head back, she slowly unpinned her hair, and then ran her fingers through the waves of her thick, blonde tresses. Then she leant forward over her computer keyboard, allowing her blouse to billow open at the neck and reveal the luscious swell of the top of her breasts. Gina looked at Martin's reflection in the computer monitor, and saw that his gaze was fixed on her. She could hear his breathing, and in the reflection she could make out the bulge in his jeans, surely larger than it had been a few minutes ago.

She got up and walked nonchalantly out through the sliding door, past Martin and into the still, enveloping heat of the garden. Martin turned from his work and watched her intently. Gina knew that the backdrop of bright sunlight would make the outline of her breasts perfectly visible through the thin silk of the blouse. She stretched, lifting her arms above her head, causing the soft fabric to graze her nipples as it slid upward over her breasts. She looked down as she stretched, watching with a soft smile as her nipples puckered and hardened.

She knew that the effect on Martin would be devastating, and she slowly turned to look at him. Gina enjoyed teasing men, knowing that they would react with pre-dictable lust to her body; and to her delight Martin was staring hard at her, making no pretence of politely looking away or avoiding her gaze. She walked up to him, and glanced down at that tempting bulge between his legs. Rock-hard, she knew instinctively. She was about to reach for the buttons on his fly when she heard her doorbell ring.

'Excuse me,' she said to him with a slow, sly smile, and went to answer the door. She knew he was straining for more. That was how she liked her men. She loved the anticipation and the chase almost as much as she enjoyed lovemaking itself, and she knew that she had certainly snared Martin.

The caller at the front door had the wrong address and, as Gina walked back through the house to the garden, she saw Martin through the sliding doors. She was startled by what she saw. She paused, out of his view, and watched.

Martin was leaning back against his ladder, his head thrown back, his T-shirt off in the heat of the garden and his jeans open and pulled down a little. 'Oh Gina,' she heard Martin moan to himself, his eyes shut. His chest was broad and smooth, with smallish nipples which were tightly erect. His thighs were muscular, the sinews bunched under the strain of his urge. A fine down of blondish hairs clustered at the top of his thighs, spreading out from his groin and a small way up his stomach. Nearer to his crotch the hairs became darker and coarser, a densely coiled dark mass which surrounded his stiff penis. His right hand was cupping his balls, holding them close to the base of his cock, while his left was gripped around his penis, slowly massaging it up and down.

'Oh, you tease, you dirty bitch,' he uttered, as he slowly pulled his hand down the length of his shaft, the thick veins bulging against his hand and the tight shiny dome of his prick exposed as the foreskin slid slowly backwards. 'You wanted me to see that, didn't you?' he murmured. She watched in fascination, as his hand worked his penis in long strokes, pulling his foreskin right back, and then sliding it back up again. Martin was whispering, 'I should have bent you over your desk there and then. You know we both want it.' His hand was working faster now, and a small bead of clear, almost silvery liquid appeared at the eye of his prick.

In the shadows, Gina was transfixed. All she was aware of was the sight of Martin in the garden, and of the wanton response of her own body – her lips had parted, her breath was coming faster and shallower now, and her nipples were tingling. She could feel the familiar warmth between her legs radiating out: the moist urgent need at the centre of her. She languidly touched a breast through the light silk of her blouse, feeling its full fleshiness and the taut point of her nipple. She teasingly rolled her nipple between her thumb and forefinger, loving the hardness of it, contrasting so vividly as it did with the plump softness of her breast, revelling in the silky sheerness of the fabric on her flesh. She slowly slid her other hand down her thigh, grasped the hem of her skirt, and pulled it up to her waist. Then she slipped her right hand down her stomach, under the lacy panel of her panties, and towards the source of her heat, until she could feel the wiriness of her pubic hairs against the side of her hand.

Gina shifted slightly, leaning back against the wall now, her back arching a little as she gently moved her fingers closer to her cleft, which was hot and slick with juices. With feather-light touches she stroked her so-sensitive labia, her eyes all the time fixed on Martin. She slowly moved her hand inwards, flicking and stroking with her fingers all the time. She slid her other hand from her breast to down under her panties, now spreading and stretching herself, with fingers on either side. She loved this wide-open feeling, of being exposed, and her clitoris responded by sliding silkily out from under its hood, flushed dark-red and standing erect. She slipped her fingers from her labia, down into the quaking centre of her need: her beloved sex. Her wetness welcomed her, as she slid her middle finger slowly up and down over her moist opening. She felt a need to be filled, but resisted it, delaying the delicious pleasure. She could tease herself as well as she teased men. 'Not yet, baby, not yet,' she murmured to herself.

Outside in the garden, Martin was now bent over slightly, his head and shoulders bowed as he focussed all his attention on his straining prick, which was now shiny and slick with his lubricating juices. His hand was pumping feverishly; the white knuckles of his fist signalled his urgency, his extreme need. His left hand was still cupping his balls, which had tightened and puckered up against the base of his cock. 'Gina, you beautiful bitch,' he moaned, as his cock enlarged for the final rushing moment, so hard and taut that it looked like it might burst. Gina could almost sense his pulsating flood of pleasure and relief as he reached his climax; but it still took her slightly by surprise as she saw a thick spurt of semen explode from his cock, followed by another, then another. Martin slumped back against the ladder, spent and worn.

'Mmm, was I good for you?' whispered Gina, as she continued to gently finger her yearning vagina. She ran her finger slowly up to her clitoris; it was fully roused now and aching for her touch. The first sensation of her finger against her hard button sent a shiver of delicious warmth deep into the pit of her stomach. The lightest of touches was all she needed; a faint fairy pressure on her little pearl, a constant upwards stroking, was enough to bring her to a thundering orgasm every time. The longer she could prolong it the more exquisite the pleasure.

She dipped her finger into her opening again, just enough to moisten her finger, and returned to the gentle but insistent stroking of her clitoris. The image of Martin's cock unloading its spunk was burning into her, intensifying the heat in her clitoris, and bringing her upwards and then over into the free-fall of a crashing climax. She gasped as she came, and threw her head right back against the wall. For a few, wonderful moments, she lost all control over her body: her legs almost buckled under the force of her orgasm and her back arched right up, pressing her mound and her

10

clitoris up against the palm of her hand. Then, as the waves of extreme pleasure ebbed and subsided, her legs gave way, and she slowly slid down the wall, until she rested in a crumpled squatting position, her head still thrown back and her hands still down the front of her knickers.

After a few minutes she looked up, to see that Martin had composed himself. He was fully dressed now and glancing rather sheepishly towards the house as he started to clean the windows again. Gina smiled to herself, got up and went to the bathroom to take a cooling shower. No need to rush things.

Four days later, Gina heard from all three directors. Her applications for the parts of Juliet, and of Blanche DuBois in *A Streetcar Named Desire* had both been turned down, out of hand. She sat at the kitchen table, playing with the third, unopened envelope, unwilling to open it. At least if it was still sealed she wouldn't know for sure that she was a reject. She fiddled with it for a good quarter of an hour, until she sat upright and told herself to stop being so pathetic, and open the bloody thing.

As she unfolded the letter, she started to realise that this wasn't the usual short rejection letter, a couple of lines long. She scanned it quickly, and read the phrases: 'very interested in your application', 'promising', and 'invite you to come for an audition'. Her head swam. She was over the first hurdle at last. She tried not to concern herself with the fact that she had never heard of either the play, the playwright or the director, Charles Sarazan. It didn't matter. She had an audition and, if things went well, maybe a part.

The audition was to be held the next day, in a church hall in Crouch End, north London. She was required to prepare a piece of her choice for the audition, and also to read part of the play, sight unseen. She tried to work out from the advertisement what might be appropriate, but it gave away little in the way of clues: 'New play by young playwright. Five male and three female parts, including strong male and female lead roles.' She thought that, as it was a play by a young playwright, it might be of the gritty school of social realism; and so she prepared a passage from *The Devil Drives*, a play about homelessness and drug abuse that she had had a part in the previous year.

She worked hard at the passage, and later on in the day she called Kirsten and asked her to come over, and comment on her performance. Kirsten arrived at eight o'clock with a bottle of wine, and watched Gina go through her piece.

'Very good, I really like that,' Kirsten said afterwards. 'I think that you're going to be in with a good chance.'

The next morning, Gina arrived at the church hall with plenty of time to spare. There was a notice on the inner door which said QUIET PLEASE: AUDITION IN PROGRESS, so she waited on a bench outside, knowing that she would be called when it was her turn. On the other side of the door, she could hear a man's voice rising, then falling and shouting occasionally. This must be the voice of a fellow auditionee. There was another voice: low, calm and quietly insistent. Gina felt sure that it was the voice of Mr Charles Sarazan, the director.

After about twenty minutes, the door opened and a man came out, grinning broadly. He had lively brown eyes and short cropped dark hair, and she was instantly struck by his good looks. He winked at her and grinned even more broadly. 'Break a leg,' he said to her, and was gone.

'Next,' boomed a voice from inside the hall. 'Miss Gina Stanhope, please.'

Gina coughed to clear her throat, smoothed down the front of her dress, and pushed the swing door open. It was dark inside the hall and it took a while for her eyes to adjust to the light. She could see a man sitting behind a table below the low stage.

'Ah, Miss Stanhope. Come on in.'

Gina walked slowly towards the table, trying to see

12

where to place her feet. When she reached the table, she looked up, and gasped.

'Hello again,' the man said to her from in the shadows. He smiled knowingly.

It was her admirer from the party. Gina's first reaction was to turn and walk straight out of the hall, but something prevented her. Try to be professional, she told herself. She looked at him. 'Hello,' she said icily.

He reached over the table to shake her hand and she took his unwillingly. He gave her hand a quick squeeze as they shook.

'Charles Sarazan. The pleasure is all mine. I was hoping that we would meet again after the other night, and so we have. Now, I hope that you have prepared something for me.'

Gina nodded, her thoughts reeling crazily. She hadn't expected this, and it had thrown her considerably. She couldn't leave though; she had to try to win a part. It might well be her last chance, given her success rate with previous applications.

'Do you mind if I read from the script?' she asked. She knew that she couldn't now remember her monologue, not with that man sitting six feet away from her. Her mind was numb.

'Of course not.'

She mounted the stage, and read through the part. She couldn't concentrate on the script, on the meaning and the emotions of the words, and her accent wavered with her nerves. All she could think of was that night in the kitchen, of pushing him away, and of him stumbling and falling to the ground, all seen as if in slow motion.

Her confusion and discomfort made her reading rather mechanical. Charles seemed to sense this. 'Try to relax,' he said to her. She started to become angry with herself, angry that she was allowing him to affect her again.

He handed her several pages of script. 'It's from the play, *Riding to the Thames*. Read through, please, as Victoria.'

She read through, barely registering what she was

13

saying. She was so aware of his eyes, set on her, unblinking. Her hand trembled as she held the pages. At last she finished, and dismounted unsteadily from the stage.

'That's very good. I'll let you know within a day or so. And thank you, Gina, thank you for coming.' He smiled at her, and put out his hand again. She forced herself to take it, and he gave her another squeeze. In any other circumstances she might have found it comforting.

With head bowed, she pulled the swing door open. She had blown it, she felt sure. She hadn't expected to meet him again; hadn't expected that he would be the director who would make decisions that would shape her future; hadn't expected him to affect her in quite the way he had. She had been so befuddled that she had forgotten to ask him anything about the production, but that didn't really matter now, as she was sure she had not done well enough to get a part.

She shook her head, trying to understand her reactions to him. He was handsome and, she had to admit, strangely charismatic; but he was also arrogant, unpleasantly so. She was attracted and repelled by him in equal measures.

As she left the church hall, her head still bowed in thought, she bumped into an expensively dressed woman. 'Careful,' the woman said tetchily.

Gina looked up, and could not prevent herself from grimacing slightly. It was Persis de Gaury. Now her day was well and truly ruined. Persis, who had stolen past boyfriends, beaten her to parts, and had even managed to gazump her when Gina was trying to buy her previous house. Persis, half Iranian and half French, was unbelievably beautiful and the most incredible bitch. The two women coldly acknowledged each other.

'Which part were you reading for?' Persis asked Gina.

'Victoria,' Gina replied.

'The lead? Well, don't set your hopes too high, darling,' Persis said, as she swanned past and into the hall without waiting to be called. Gina was fuming. If Persis

14

was going to be in this production, she wasn't sure that she wanted anything to do with it. That woman was trouble.

Later that evening, Gina lay in a bubble bath with her eyes closed and a cooling flannel across her forehead. She had been soaking for the past hour, with a large gin and tonic sitting on the side of the bath, but she was finding it very difficult to unwind. She was thinking of Charles and her future. She also knew that she couldn't afford to turn down a part if it was offered to her, Persis or no Persis. The phone rang, and then she heard the answerphone click in. After her message on the machine finished, she heard Charles's voice, and realised with a sudden lurch of foreboding: of course, her curriculum vitae. Thanks to her meticulously prepared résumé, he now knew all about her. He knew where she lived, how old she was, even where she had been to school.

'Hello, Gina, this is Charles. Sarazan. I was very pleased with your reading today, and I'd like to offer you the part of Dominique. Sorry that it's not Victoria, but that's gone to Persis. She tells me that you know each other, so that'll be nice for you.'

Gina grimaced, but at least she had got a part, that was the main thing. Charles's message continued.

'We start rehearsals next Tuesday. I'll send you a letter with all the details and a contract – you should get it tomorrow morning. I just want you to know that I am really looking forward to this.'

Gina pulled a face. Damn. Persis had done it again. And what exactly did Charles think he was looking forward to?

The letter from Charles arrived as promised the next morning. Also included were a copy of the entire script and several information sheets. Everything had been neatly produced on a word processor, and was precisely worded. It struck her as unusual that Charles had even typed his name on the covering letter, rather than sign it

15

by hand. She wondered what that might signify about him.

Gina read through all the notes very thoroughly. It seemed that Charles Sarazan must be an extremely wealthy man. He was producing and directing the play, and funding it entirely with his own money. The rehearsals would be held over two weeks at Digby House, his house in Devon. After that the production would have two and a half days of rehearsal at The Redditch, a 750-seater theatre in Richmond, prior to the commencement of the run there. She was surprised. She knew of The Redditch, a large, plush theatre that had a reputation for putting on impressive productions. It might not be in the West End, but it was still in London. At least she wouldn't be appearing in a theatre out in the middle of nowhere.

Gina looked at the contract. She would be paid £750 a week during rehearsals, and £1,500 a week during the run: an unheard of sum. In addition, all accommodation and food would be provided gratis during the rehearsals. She couldn't believe the amount that she was being paid. It was a ludicrous sum for most professional actors, let alone an amateur. The going rate was more like £250 a week during a run, less for rehearsals. She tried to work out if it was a typing error, but the same amounts were repeated several times in the contract.

Charles must indeed be a wealthy man to afford all this. Still, she felt that she could not afford to refuse. Time was running out, and the kudos of appearing at The Redditch might just sway the Academy tutors, even if she hadn't landed the prize part.

Another sheet listed more prosaic matters, such as how to get to the house. She picked up the script and flicked through it. All she knew of the play was contained in the three pages that she had read during her audition, and in her distracted state that had hardly made much of an impression on her. She wandered through to the garden and lay in the hammock, deter-

16

mined to read the play from cover to cover and then to begin to study it and make notes.

Despite what she had suspected, she was still surprised at the adult content of the play. There was a good deal of strong language, a fair amount of violence, and a sex scene which involved some nudity. She was rather relieved to see that her character did not take part in the sex scene. Much as she loved sex, she found the idea of simulating something so personal in front of an audience acutely embarrassing. She guessed that rampant exhibitionism was not one of her sexual peccadilloes.

I've got plenty of other ones, but not that, she laughed to herself.

It was Monday evening, and Gina was busy packing for the trip. She had laid out all the clothes she had selected on the bed, plus her washing bag, her make-up bag and her shoes. She wandered over to the bookshelf by the bed and selected a couple of books, wondering if she would get any time to read them if the rehearsals were as intensive as the information sheet had promised.

Dusk was falling. Gina gazed out into the garden. She loved the light that flooded in through the large windows during the day; conversely, she loved leaving the blinds open at night and letting the darkness weigh down outside. She wondered if Andy was about that evening.

She smiled as she thought of him. She had first met Andy the previous summer, just after he had finished his A levels. He lived in the large Victorian house which overlooked her garden, and she had often seen him at an upstairs window, staring down at her. He always seemed to be there when she was sunbathing, and one day she had called him over. He had darted down from the window, and came haltingly up to the fence, almost afraid to look at her, semi-naked as she was in her bikini. He was a handsome young man, with blond hair, and deep-blue eyes which darted across her face and over her body before settling on her face again. She noticed

17

the firm muscularity of his lower legs under his baggy knee-length shorts, and guessed that under the T-shirt was a similarly honed torso. He was shy, but not too shy. She found that very appealing. She was also very aware that he had a crush on her, but he was just a bit too boyish for her taste; and so she had been content to flirt and tease, no more.

Then Andy had gone off to college, and Gina hadn't seen him for almost a year. Until that afternoon, that was. Andy was back home for the summer vacation, looking even leaner and fitter than when she had last seen him; all last traces of puppy fat were well and truly banished. He seemed more confident, more of a man now. They had talked over the garden fence about this and that, and during the course of the conversation she had wheedled out of him that no, he didn't have a girlfriend, no, he wasn't gay, and yes, he thought that she was attractive. Amazing how compliant, how malleable young men can be, she thought after he had left. She had just happened to mention that she always slept with her sliding doors slightly open, as she liked the breeze at night during the hot summer weather, and she wasn't afraid of intruders. She knew that an understanding had passed between them.

After finishing her packing, Gina took a long and particularly languorous bath, the water suffused with exotic oils, and the bathroom lit only by candles. Walking naked back into her bedroom, she could feel the heat from the stone paving outside, still radiating upwards despite the lateness of the hour; she knew it would be another hot, still night. The intoxicating perfume from a large vaseful of white lilies by her bed filled the room, mingling sweetly with the drifts of scent from the jasmine and the honeysuckle which twined their way up the pergola outside.

It wasn't long after she had settled into bed and turned her bedside light out that she heard the rustling of grass, and then the knocking, scuffing sound that could only mean that Andy was climbing over the fence. She was lying on her side with one leg pulled up, and the other stretched straight. She tugged the sheet back a bit, arranging it so that it just covered her legs and her buttocks. She rested one arm under her head and the other by her side, so that her breasts were exposed, but not obviously so. She then lay still, her eyes closed, trying to control her breathing so that she could listen to him approaching.

After what seemed like an age, she heard a soft, slow footfall, then another, and then another. She knew that Andy would be able to make out her body through the window: for, although it was a very dark night, she had thought to leave a lamp on in the hall, and had also left her bedroom door ajar just enough to let a crack of light illuminate her. The footfalls stopped, and now she could hear Andy's breathing: fast, shallow breaths which he was trying desperately to control. She murmured, as if in her sleep, and shifted slightly, causing the sheet to slide just a little further down her buttocks. She heard him catch his breath, and knew he was hooked; with that knowledge, she felt the telltale pouting and moistening of her sex.

Andy must have been alarmed by her movement, as he did nothing for a long time. With her eyes shut, she could picture him: pressed up against the sliding door, his straining prick hard against the glass, drinking her in. Then she heard the slow swishing sound as Andy slid the door further back. His breathing was louder now, and she could sense his fumbling concentration as he slid the glass door closed behind him. Now she could almost feel the warmth from his body as he tiptoed, achingly slowly, towards the bed. And then she felt the first touch, not on her body, but as he gently gripped the sheet at the base of the bed. Carefully, so carefully, he started to pull it slowly back. She felt the sheet slide over the curve of her bottom, slipping down more quickly there, and then felt the excruciatingly soft tickling touch of the material as it moved down the back of her thighs, across the backs of her knees and down her calves. Andy

19

didn't stop until he had pulled the sheet right back, clear of her feet. He was breathing much more heavily now. She heard a belt being unbuckled, a zip being undone, and then a ruffling noise: the sound of clothes being taken off and thrown to the floor. There was a muffled thump, and she realised that he had dropped to his knees at the foot of the bed. Then she had to bite hard on her lip as it became clear to her what he was about to do.

Gina felt the warm, wet softness of his tongue, pressing against the underside of her toes. It was all she could do to stop from crying out, from involuntarily moving her foot from that insistent, sensitive tongue, probing now between her toes. The powerfulness of the feeling, as she lay there with her eyes shut, all her nerve endings concentrated on those five small digits, was almost overwhelming. And then, so nearly too much to bear, he took her little toe in his mouth and gently sucked, all the time sweeping its surface with his tongue. Gina knew that if he continued doing this for much longer she would lose control. She was ready for him, moist and open; but he seemed to have other things on his mind. Somehow, she found the strength, the will to lie there and let him do as he pleased.

Without breaking the contact between his mouth and her flesh, he started the slow ascent. He grazed the underside of her foot with his lips, and then she felt his mouth on her ankle, nibbling and kissing it. 'Oh,' she heard him murmur. 'Oh yes, so soft, so slim.' And then she felt with a slight start his two hands closing round her ankle as he kissed it. The warmth of his breath, and the rasping roughness of his face were sending electric jolts of desire up her. As he nuzzled her ankle she felt his two hands slowly sliding up her calf. But where his hands went his mouth was not far behind, and soon she felt a ladder of kisses travelling up her calf, coming to rest on the back of her knee. Here he covered every square centimetre of that tender and painfully sensitive flesh with kisses, nibbles and even, to her surprise, slight nips.

As he pleasured Gina with his mouth, his hands were now caressing the calf of her other leg, encircling it and stroking it with infinite care. And then his mouth was on the move again. Gina felt that she would burst, but the knowledge of the inevitable conclusion of this upward path of kisses made her hold herself in, made her resist the temptation to grab his head and thrust his face into her crotch. Now! Do it! she thought, the urgency of her need almost taking over. It took all her self-control to lie still and passive, to withhold from reaching out to him, or even from touching herself. She was uncertain whether or not Andy thought she was asleep, undisturbed by his unrequested attentions, or if he knew that she was awake, still and silently compliant. Which would he prefer, she wondered, as her breathing quickened. Andy's lips were now grazing, so sweetly, the inner side of her leg just above the knee; then brushing, kissing, sweeping upwards.

This was exquisite. The position she was in meant that her innermost place was open to him, beckoning him as he climbed towards her very centre. As she felt his hair brushing against the upper part of her thigh, Gina knew that the moment she longed for was not far off. His tortuously slow ascent had almost reached its goal. He kissed and nibbled and sucked, his hands all the time caressing her calves, her thighs, but not straying near where she most wanted them. Maddening, frustrating, but so delicious. And then, she felt his hot breath on that tender, soft skin at the very top of her thigh, below the rise of her buttock. His mouth slowly kissed its way across the V of dark curls, searching out her needy sex.

And now, after all the slowness, he was fast: finding his target, and sliding his tongue along her labia and into her vagina, and making her almost quake with lust. The urgency with which his tongue now moved was nearly too much for Gina, and she had to struggle to control herself, to prevent the roaring sweep of her

21

orgasm from rushing over her just yet. Andy licked and kissed her with a greed she had never experienced: his tongue remarkably agile, probing, and lapping at her slick opening. She was willing him to move to her clitoris, and, as if he could read her mind, his mouth moved upwards, to her hard, prominent nub. The moment she felt his wet mouth settle around her clitoris, she let herself go, succumbing to the inevitable, irresistible force that had been building up inside her. She ground her sex into his face, silently urging him to keep caressing her with his mouth as she pulsed with the receding waves of her orgasm.

'Hmm, you liked that, didn't you, my sleeping beauty?' murmured Andy. 'So let's see how you like this.'

Gina held her breath, hardly daring to think about what might be about to happen. And then she felt the pressure, unmistakable, of a hard cock pressing against her labia, sliding inwards towards her throbbing sex. A slight resistance, and then Andy pushed, and gently slid into her. She could feel the tautness of her vagina, stretched by his large cock as he pushed upwards. He slowly sunk his shaft deep into her, filling her right up. She could feel Andy's breath on the back of her neck now, and the warmth of his chest against her back as she lay there passively. His knees were drawn up behind hers, nestling close up to her. He started to move, very unhurriedly at first, his cock almost leaving her before the next stroke pushed it slowly back in again. His balls were brushing against the top of her thighs with a slow, slapping rhythm as he plunged into her. She could feel him thickening within her, and he grasped her more tightly in his arms, rearing his head back. 'Too much, too much. Still,' he whispered, and stopped his thrusting. His cock was twitching inside her, and she knew that the excitement for him was so great that he was balancing on the edge of the precipice. He kissed the back of her neck gently, whispering, 'Still, still,' before kissing her some more.

When the quivering had stopped, and she knew he was back from the brink, Andy started to move inside her again. This time his rhythm had more urgency to it, and she could not help but to push back to meet his thrusts. He gently gripped the back of her neck between his teeth like an animal, and bore into her with long strokes. She felt him thickening again, and this time he speeded up his thrusts, pushing himself up from her with his palms flat on the bed and with his head thrown back. He came with a loud groan, and she could feel his cock contracting, and pumping deep into her.

He lay curled around her, one arm thrown over her, for a long time afterwards. Her eyes were still closed, and she did not need to open them. In the early hours of the morning, he gently moved away from her, and kissed her on the cheek. 'Sweet dreams, my sleeping beauty,' he said, and lowered himself off the bed. She heard him gather up his clothes, pad over to the glass door, and carefully let himself out. Smiling, and sated by sex, Gina knew that sleep would come easily. She drifted off, wondering what the next fortnight might hold in store.

Chapter Two

Gina turned her car between two imposing stone gate pillars: the entranceway to Digby House. The large cast-iron gates were thrown well back, and she drove slowly up the raked gravel drive. The grounds of the house were large and impressive, with immaculately kept lawns and flower beds. In the distance she could see a man bent over a wheelbarrow, forking what she took to be compost on to a bed. The drive brought her up to a large Georgian house, with a beautifully symmetrical façade and a single-storey wing on either side.

She whistled under her breath. 'Wow. I knew he was rich, but we're talking serious money here.'

She parked her car next to a red open-top sports car. Something told her it belonged to Persis, and she suddenly felt even more irritable. She had had a murderous journey: delayed by roadworks on the motorway, being stuck behind tractors and caravans, and then getting hopelessly lost in the small country lanes as she neared the house. She had been fretting about Charles and Persis all the way; in addition, the sun had turned her car into an oven. She felt hot, sticky and cross. It was not an auspicious start.

From the number of cars parked outside, she thought she was probably the last to arrive. The front door was open, but the house seemed deserted. Gina walked into the huge and deliciously cool hallway, her footsteps echoing on the tiled floor. Charles appeared at the top of the stairs in response to her questioning 'Hello?'. He was smiling broadly. Gina smiled back. She had forgotten how handsome he was.

'Ah, Gina. So you're here,' said Charles as he started down the stairs.

'Yes, I'm here, despite the best efforts of the Highways Agency amongst others. This house is fantastic.'

'I'm glad you think so. Parts of it date back to the fifteenth century, and there was a major rebuilding in the Georgian period when the façade and the wings were added. Other parts were altered in Victorian times. It has got quite a history. I've known this house since my childhood, and I've always loved it. But how rude of me, talking on about the house, when you must be feeling frazzled after your journey. I'll show you to your room. Let me get your bags for you.'

Charles was being pleasant and helpful. Perhaps he would behave differently on his home patch, restrained by their professional relationship. Gina gladly stood aside and let him take her two suitcases. She followed him up the stairs, a couple of steps below him, affording her a wonderfully close view of his denim-clad buttocks. He smelt good, too: a mixture of soap and fresh clean clothes and man. She felt that familiar stirring of want, and had to pinch her arm. 'No,' she whispered to herself. 'Remember what he's like.'

They turned into a corridor and Charles pushed a door open.

'Your room. I hope that you'll find it comfortable.'

He placed the suitcases just inside the door, and stood so that Gina had to squeeze past him to enter the room. Annoyed, she flinched slightly as her right breast brushed against him. He looked down at her knowingly.

She looked around the room, and said, 'Thank you, this is lovely,' hoping that her indifferent manner would indicate that she wanted him to leave. But he remained in the doorway, looking at her, and smiling enigmatically.

'You know, I think we're going to have a lot of fun over the next fortnight,' he said to her. She shifted uncomfortably, not knowing what to reply. She wanted him to go.

'I think that I have a lot to teach you,' he continued.

How arrogant, Gina thought, but said nothing.

'Let's hope that you are going to prove open and receptive to new ideas. This rehearsal period is going to be challenging and intensive, but I'm sure that you will be up to it. I picked you for a special reason, and I know that you won't let me down.'

'Well, I'll try not to,' she said. No, it didn't seem that he was going to behave any differently here from how he had been in London. Mr Charles Sarazan certainly had a high opinion of himself, but if he was such a hotshot director, why hadn't she heard of him before?

'Right then. I'll leave you to unpack. I'll give you a tour with the others later on in the day. See you in the rehearsal room in twenty minutes,' he said. 'Bottom of the stairs and turn left.' And with that he left, quietly closing the door behind him.

Gina looked around her. Again, she whistled through her teeth. The room was beautiful, with dark oak linen-fold panelling on the walls. It was lit by a huge bay window which looked out over the grounds, framed by chintz curtains. There was a large oak four-poster bed with heavy embroidered hangings, a walnut chest of drawers and a large oak coffer, an elegant day sofa with wonderfully plump cushions and no fewer than three vases of fresh flowers. In one corner was a small porcelain washbasin, with a set of fluffy white towels and a flannel hanging over a towel rail. All the furniture was antique, and Gina could see that it was undoubtedly of the highest quality.

Gina quickly undressed, freshened herself up and changed her clothes. Then she unpacked the rest of her belongings, before making her way down to the rehearsal room.

The rehearsal room was a vast, light room with a high ceiling. The sea was visible through the large bay window which reached from the floor to the ceiling. The room was completely devoid of furnishings, apart from a table pushed up against one wall and nine plastic chairs. Charles and the rest of the cast were seated on these chairs in a circle near the window. Gina joined them, taking the last chair.

So here they all were: Charles, Gina and seven other actors. The cast of *Riding to the Thames*. Gina gazed around. Sitting next to Charles was Persis, looking stunning as usual. She had an amazing figure, and always knew how to dress to flatter it. Her oval face with its high cheekbones was framed by a mass of glossy curls which coiled down to her shoulders. She had beautiful dark skin, and the largest eyes and longest lashes Gina had ever seen. Persis's voice, husky and rich, was equally beautiful – even though it pained Gina to admit it. Suddenly annoyed, Gina nodded an acknowledgement of Persis's presence.

Opposite Gina was a man who seemed familiar. He looked at Gina and mouthed 'Hello' at her. She realised that he was the man she had met on her way in to the audition. He was as handsome as she had remembered him to be. His hair, cropped fairly short, was brown and, despite its length, obviously curly. His eyes were dark brown, and what she called 'bedroom eyes': there was something gentle and sensual and seductive about them. He grinned at her, causing a fan of fine lines to spread out from the corners of his eyes, and forming deep creases down his cheeks. She felt herself blushing slightly, as she mouthed 'Hello' back. She didn't know any of the others in the circle.

Charles cleared his throat, and spoke.

'Hello, everyone, and welcome. I'm glad you all made it here without any problems. As you know, I'm Charles

27

Sarazan, but this rehearsal period will be run on first-name terms, as formality obviously has no place here.'

The group laughed, a little nervously. Gina slowly scrutinised them as Charles described the living arrangements and the rehearsal programme.

Sitting on Charles's right was a well-built man in jeans and a T-shirt, which stretched tightly across his chest. Gina studied him. She reckoned that he must be in his mid-thirties. His hair was bleached blond and his arms were tanned. They were folded across his chest, and Gina noted with interest the fine muscle definition of the deltoids and biceps of his upper arms, and the sinewy strength of his forearms. He sat with his legs spread far apart, and even under the looseness of his jeans she could see there was a good-sized knot between his legs. She looked up at his face, and realised with a start that he had been watching her, and that he knew she had been studying his groin with special interest. He smiled at her, and moved his legs even further apart. Embarrassed to have been caught, she looked at the ground. But she thought that things were becoming more interesting by the minute.

Charles's voice broke through her reverie. 'Let me fill you in on this production. I am both the director and the producer, and am funding this production myself. I hope that you will all give me and the production your best efforts. Now, the ground rules. There will be six days a week of intensive rehearsal, from 8 a.m. to 6 p.m., with an hour for lunch. Saturdays are your free days. Evenings and free days are your own, but I expect you to be studying the script. There is a ten o'clock curfew, after which time you must be in your rooms, on your own. The curfew is in place every day, including the night before and the night of your day off, as I require you to be fully rested for your work.

'During the entire period that you are involved in this production, both rehearsals and free time, I will allow no sex and no drugs. The only alcohol that I will permit is that which I provide. I need you to be dedicated to this play. No distractions. Purity of mind, body and spirit are essential. I will enforce all these rules strictly, so I advise you to abide by them.'

He looked around at the cast, then reached down, and took a small bell from off the floor by his feet and rang it. The door opened almost instantaneously, and a woman in her late twenties entered. Her dark hair was tightly scraped back in a bun, making her pale face seem sharp and angular. Charles continued.

'This is Sally Tobin, my housekeeper here. If you have any special dietary requirements, or any problems with your domestic arrangements, see her. I am not to be distracted by such trivial matters.'

The woman nodded at Charles, and then left the room without saying a word.

'Right. I think that's enough of my introduction. This is going to be a very intense period, and we will all get to know each other very well. Now we'll go round the circle and introduce ourselves. Very quickly, just our name, what we do and perhaps our hopes for this production.'

Charles turned to Persis with a questioning look, and asked her to introduce herself.

Her composure was absolute. 'My name is Persis de Gaury. I am a professional actress, and have been in many productions, including several which have transferred to the West End. I played Kate in *The Taming of the Shrew*, Lady Macbeth last year, and Hedda Gabler earlier this year.' She smirked and looked at Gina. Gina scowled. She knew why Persis was specifically mentioning these parts. She had auditioned for them, and had lost out to Persis each time. Gina had managed to be cast as one of the witches in the performance of *Macbeth*, and it was during this production that Persis had contrived to spirit away Gina's then-boyfriend.

Persis sat back triumphantly, almost basking, it seemed to Gina, reminding her of a glossy well-fed lizard on a rock. Charles nodded at the man sitting next to Persis. He was a dark-haired young man of about twenty-five with striking green eyes. He wore a black denim jacket and straight black jeans, and Doc Martens boots. 'My name is Daniel Bell, I have been in several productions recently, though I work in a restaurant to pay my way. I'm not a pro like Persis, I'm afraid.' He looked relieved to have said his piece, and sat back into his chair. Persis smirked some more.

'Thank you, Daniel. And the next?' Charles asked. Now Gina's attention was fully caught. This was the man whom she had met at the audition.

'I'm Matt Burton. I'm an amateur, very much so, but even Sir Laurence Olivier had to start somewhere, so I don't let it bother me. When I'm not acting, I'm a secondary school supply teacher.'

Gina listened carefully. Matt. That was a good, solid, masculine name. She mouthed it to herself. It sounded good. His voice was deep but lively, and he seemed to be smiling with his eyes all the time he talked, as if he was amused by the proceedings. There was something about him that she found immediately appealing, and immensely attractive.

The man next to Matt introduced himself as Will Lawrence, and said he too was an amateur, but was hoping that this production might prove to be his big break. Gina didn't really pay much attention to him, as she was still looking at Matt, thinking about what he had said.

Will finished, and turned to the woman on his left. Even though she was seated, she was obviously tall. She had long, straight fine blonde hair, and was wearing a short sleeveless dress.

'Hello. I'm Sarah Kenyon. I'm a swimming instructor, but I hope to become a full-time actress. I'm pleased to be in this play, and pleased to meet you all.' She smiled as she looked around the group.

It was the turn of the man next to Sarah. He was stocky and swarthy, with a pronounced five-o'clock shadow. 'I'm Rory Dickson. I want to be a professional actor, but at the moment I spend most of my time working as a bouncer.'

'Gina. Gina?' Charles was looking straight at her. It was her turn, and she hadn't realised. She was still gazing across at Matt, preoccupied. Charles had noticed, and scowled slightly.

'Oh, yes, my name is Gina Stanhope. I used to work as a fashion buyer, but I've given it up for this. I've always wanted to act, so I'm going to try my hardest to help make this production a success.'

Charles nodded, and looked pleased at her declaration. Finally he turned to the well-built man sitting on his right. 'And you are?'

'David Philby. Yes, you guessed it, I'm also an amateur. I work as an outdoor pursuits instructor when I'm not acting.'

That would explain the fabulous physique, Gina thought to herself.

Charles paused, and then grinned. 'Well, everyone, that's the introductions over with. It's a lovely hot day, so let's all go into the grounds. I've got a few things that I want us to do together, to help us create a good bond among the group as quickly as possible.'

The cast gathered underneath a large Cedar of Lebanon on the lawn in front of the house. The sun was so hot that Gina was glad of the cool shade it afforded, and also glad that she had chosen to change into a long and light cotton dress earlier on.

'Now, I expect you have all done these things before in previous rehearsals, so I won't take forever explaining,' Charles said. 'They're called Trust Falls, and their purpose is to instil a feeling of absolute trust in your fellow cast members. They are also very good at breaking the ice, as you will see. I need someone to demonstrate.' He looked around, and Gina instinctively looked at the ground, trying to avoid his eye. She wanted to deter his attentions at all cost.

'Gina, come and help me, please,' he said, and she cursed under her breath. She walked over to Charles.

'Now, stand with your back to me, hold your body rigid, and then just fall backwards. Don't bend your knees. It's best if you try to dig your heels in and fall on those. I'll catch you.'

Gina didn't want to do it. She didn't want Charles to touch her.

'Come on, we haven't got all day,' he said irritably. Reluctantly, Gina turned her back to him and asked over her shoulder if he was ready. He said that he was. She fell backwards, her body stiff and straight. She thought that she was going to hit the ground, as she had fallen quite far backwards before she felt him catch her under her arms and push her back upright, pivoting her upwards on her heels. The others clapped.

'There, how did that feel?' Charles asked, grinning at her.

'Well, a bit scary. I didn't think you were going to catch me in time.'

Charles laughed. 'But I did, didn't I? Let's do it again.'

'Perhaps someone else should have a go,' Gina suggested.

'No, everyone will get a turn to do this later on. Get ready now.'

Gina straightened her body, her arms tight against her sides, stiff with resentment. She fell backwards, and this time as Charles caught her under her arms she could feel his fingers gently stroking her through the thin cotton material, lightly massaging the soft area below her arms and to the side of her breasts. She looked up to see if any of the others had noticed, and quickly got to her feet, rather than wait to be pushed back upright by Charles.

He could see that she was flustered. 'What's the rush?' he asked her, disingenuously.

'I just think everyone else should have a go now. They've got the idea.' She was furious. She had been forced to place her trust in Charles, she had momentarily been in a vulnerable position, and he had abused that trust.

Charles clapped his hands. 'OK, now everyone pair off. Gina and Persis go together and, Sarah, you do it with Daniel.' Sarah looked alarmed.

Charles was impatient. 'Don't worry, you will be able to catch him. You might not think so, but you will.' Charles was not participating in this activity, and he watched as the group paired off. Gina had hoped that she would be working with Matt, but Charles had thwarted that.

Persis stood with her back to Gina. 'You'd better not drop me,' she said, and almost immediately fell backwards. Gina wasn't ready and only just managed to catch her in time. She pushed Persis back up on to her feet, and Persis turned and looked at her, laughing. 'Always in the supporting role, aren't you, Gina? That's pretty much the story of your life. Oh well. Your turn.'

Gina reluctantly turned and fell backwards. She felt Persis's hands lightly graze her sides and slither by, and then she hit the ground with a jolt.

'Oops. Sorry. You just slipped right through my hands. I wasn't expecting you to be so heavy,' said Persis.

Gina got up from the ground and angrily brushed herself off, glowering at Persis. She had landed hard on her buttocks and had also knocked the back of her head. She rubbed her head, feeling to see if a lump was forming beneath her hair. Charles did not appear to have noticed. He was calling everyone together again. 'This is going really well. Now we'll do the Height Falls.'

'No way,' groaned Gina, but Charles was already organising everyone. 'We'll use the Rose Garden wall over there,' he said, pointing at a six-foot-high brick wall in the distance. As they trooped over to the wall, Charles explained what was required. He then got the group to stand facing each other in a double line away from the wall. He joined them this time, and Gina was thankful that he wasn't opposite her.

'Rory can demonstrate this, as he's the heaviest. It's a

good way of showing group spirit, and group trust. Rory, hop on to that wall, and fall backwards, just as you have been doing before. We'll catch you, I promise.'

Rory grinned and clambered onto the wall. It seemed a fearsome height from where Gina was standing.

'Link arms with the person opposite you,' said Charles. 'OK, Rory, when you're ready.'

Rory stood ramrod stiff, and then fell backwards. Gina closed her eyes at the impact, expecting the weight of his body to break through her flimsy grasp round Will's wrists. But she was surprised. Rory's weight was evenly distributed between the eight of them, and they managed to support him easily. He lay there in their arms, laughing, and they gradually let him down onto the ground.

'That was great,' he said, eyes sparkling. 'I really enjoyed that.'

'Good, because you're all going to have a go,' said Charles.

One by one, they clambered on to the wall and fell backwards into the waiting arms. Gina's stomach was churning. She was afraid of heights, and was hoping desperately that Charles might overlook her. Soon everyone else had had their turn, and Charles turned to her and said, 'Up you go, Gina.'

'I really don't want to,' she said.

'You must,' he ordered, looking at her sharply. He was obviously displeased by her reticence in obeying.

'I don't like heights. I'm scared.'

'That's too bad. This is group participation, and so everyone has to take their part.'

Matt interrupted. 'But if she's really scared of heights, surely you can let her off?'

Charles's head snapped round sharply towards Matt. 'Who is running this, me or you?' he demanded angrily.

'You,' said Matt curtly. 'But that doesn't mean I can't voice an opinion.'

'Get on the wall,' Charles snarled with such ferocity that Gina clambered up. Her legs were shaking as she

stood with her back turned to the others. She willed
herself to relax, and with her eyes screwed sharply shut,
she called out: 'Ready?'

The group replied that they were ready, and she let
herself fall backwards, with a sickening lurch in her
stomach. She landed in a soft bed of arms and, as she lay
there, she looked up and saw Matt grinning down at her.

'Well done. It wasn't that bad was it?' he said.

'Just lie there and relax a bit; try to recover,' said
Charles. 'You're not heavy, and we can support you.'

Gina lay back, and closed her eyes. She could feel
arms under her neck, another set across her back, another
set beneath her buttocks, and a fourth set under her
knees. It was surprisingly pleasant, like lying on a soft,
warm, floating cushion. As she lay there, she could feel
one of the hands moving beneath her. At first it seemed
like a movement purely to adjust the hand-hold with the
partnering person, but it continued longer than an
adjustment would have taken. Fingers were gently stroking the soft flesh of her buttocks through the flimsy
material of her dress. She didn't want to open her eyes,
but she did want to know who was doing this. It was a
gentle circling motion, like a light massage, and it eased
the aching of her bruised flesh where Persis had let her
fall. She looked out secretively from beneath her nearly
closed lids, and saw that the two people supporting her
there were Matt and Will. She wondered whose hand
was caressing her like that, and dearly hoped that it was
Matt's. Neither man's face was registering anything, so
she was none the wiser.

Then she heard Persis saying, 'Can we put her down
now? She's heavy,' and then she felt herself being passed
along the line, ready to be set down. When she was
standing again, she brushed her dress down over her
front and then her bottom, echoing the touch of the
mystery hand.

'Well done, everyone,' said Charles. 'Now I think we'll
have a brief tour of the house and gardens so that you

can familiarise yourselves with all the facilities. Then after lunch we will start the first major rehearsal session.'

Charles led them around outside first, showing them the tennis court, the heated swimming pool and more of the beautiful grounds, including a hothouse. On the ground floor of the house were several reception rooms, the rehearsal room, the dining room, Charles's study, and a library. They walked past a closed door and into a huge and sunny drawing room. They then went through to one of the wings. It contained a games room and a well-equipped gymnasium.

'I won't show you the other wing, as it just contains the kitchen and Sally's living quarters. As for upstairs, it's just bedrooms and bathrooms. And now we're ready for lunch, I think. It's such a lovely day that I've asked Sally to provide a picnic lunch on the lawn at the back of the house. I'll join you there in a few minutes.'

The lunch was a sumptuous meal, hardly a picnic. There were smoked salmon sandwiches, slabs of paté and huge wedges of cheese, individual homemade pizzas, fresh loaves and rolls, salads and dips, cold smoked meats and overflowing bowls of fruit. There were also several bottles of chilled mineral water, with beads of condensation rolling down the glass in the heat. Gina wondered how she was going to manage to keep her figure, if all the food during the fortnight of rehearsals was going to be like this.

She took her plate and napkin and glass of water, and sat on a grassy bank below some terracotta containers filled with a tumbling mass of bright flowers. The sun was blazing; the light was so bright that it bleached the landscape and made the cloudless sky and the sea appear to be a single sheet of pale blue, the horizon indistinguishable. Gina fanned herself with the napkin, closing her eyes in the cooling breeze.

The others came over to join her, except Persis, who wandered off to look at the view. Gina suspected that she was probably more interested in striking a pose than appreciating the scenery.

Daniel was laughing to himself. 'What do you make of it then?' he asked. 'He's more dictator than director, isn't he? Still, shouldn't complain, not with the money he's paying us.'

Matt sat down next to Daniel. 'I don't know what it is about him, but I don't trust him.'

Gina was interested to hear someone else voicing an opinion similar to her own. She was curious to learn more about Matt.

'So, you want to become a professional actor?' she asked.

'Yes, I'm hoping to go to The City Acting School. If I get noticed in this production, that is.'

'Oh, that's funny. I'm under a similar condition of acceptance,' Gina said. To her surprise, the others all nodded and agreed that they were also facing such a condition.

'You mean, we're all trying for drama school this autumn? That's quite a coincidence. I wonder why Charles chose so many non-professionals?' Gina was rather taken aback.

'Probably because he thought he could get away with his bullshitting more easily with amateurs,' said Matt, gruffly.

Gina gazed across at Matt. He was looking very attractive, the sunlight behind him casting a bright halo of light around his hair. The first few buttons of his shirt were open, and Gina could see a few hairs curling out from underneath. She realised that she was staring and that Matt had noticed, and looked away. Matt smiled.

Persis wandered over to join them. Gina suspected that she had become frustrated because no one was paying her any attention. She sat down next to David, and had obviously overheard the tail end of the conversation, because she asked them all which drama schools they were trying for. When she heard which one Gina had applied to, she commented, 'Oh, I went there. I won the T. E. Stark Prize for Outstanding Achievement, of course.'

'Of course,' said Matt dryly. Gina tried not to let her annoyance with Persis show. She couldn't seem to shake free from this bloody woman no matter how hard she tried.

'Do they still have the same conditions of acceptance? They come and see your production?' Persis asked Gina. Gina nodded.

'Well, we'd better hope that they notice you in that part then, hadn't we? Blink and they'll miss it.' Persis looked beyond Gina, to where Charles was approaching. She immediately got up and went over to him.

'What a cow,' said Will, watching her walk away.

'I was in a play with her two years ago,' said Sarah. 'Everyone hated her. The backstage crew all called her Queen Bitch, even to her face.'

'Why is it that the most attractive ones are often the most unpleasant?' Matt asked. Gina was mildly irked that he thought Persis attractive, but at least he'd also said that she was unpleasant. Gina was also annoyed with herself. Her strong attraction to Matt meant that she found it hard to talk to him. It was always the same with men that she really fancied. The stronger the attraction, the more tongue-tied, the more uptight and guarded she became, and the less able she was to relax and truly be herself. Gina was quite surprised, as she had not felt this way about anyone for quite a while. She had indulged in several casual affairs over the past few years, but no great passions had come her way for a long time. These new stirrings, stirrings of more than just lust, were unfamiliar to her.

At intervals through the meal, Gina looked over to where Persis and Charles were sitting on the lawn. They sat close together, deep in conversation with their heads bowed. At one point, Charles rested his hand on Persis's arm. It was a very intimate gesture, and made Gina uncomfortable. What was the story there? she wondered.

* * *

Reassembled back in the rehearsal room after lunch, the cast again sat in a circle, ready to start their first read-through of the play. Persis was preening herself, and flirting outrageously with David. Gina managed to get the seat next to Matt, and felt the *frisson* of his presence, his leg only a few inches from hers. Maybe she might let her leg accidentally brush against his.

Charles told them that he would not interrupt with any comments during this first read-through. 'I don't want to disrupt the flow; I just want to see what you make of it without any direction from me.'

Gina thought this was a good idea, and was surprised to find herself in agreement with him. Her part was not large, but at least it was larger than Sarah's, which was little more than a walk-on role, she had so few lines. Gina listened to her fellow actors. She liked Daniel's reading, but especially Matt's. She felt she could close her eyes and happily listen to him for a long, long time. His voice was deep and rich and warm.

In contrast, Persis was over-acting outrageously, and Gina waited for Charles to correct her. Then she remembered that he was not going to interfere during this read-through. Gina read her own part well. She felt that there was an immediate connection with Matt as she read with him, and at one point she looked up from her script to see him smiling at her.

Later on in the play there was a love scene between Matt and Persis. Gina shifted uncomfortably on her seat as she listened. Persis barely seemed to look at the script as she read, as she was gazing at Matt from under her heavy lids, her dark almond-shaped eyes signalling something that Gina knew only too well. Gina had seen Persis looking at men like that before, and inevitably they ended up in her clutches. And inevitably they were the same men that Gina was interested in. She couldn't believe it was happening again. Did Persis do it to spite her?

The read-through took just over two and a half hours, and Gina guessed that once they were obeying the stage instructions as well, and with the pauses for scene changes and the interval, the performance would probably run for about three hours. As soon as they had finished, Charles told them to start all over again.

'Only this time, I'm going to give you direction.'

'Could we have a break for some tea?' Matt asked. 'I'm parched.'

'No you cannot. This is not a holiday. We are here to work,' Charles said curtly.

Matt got up. 'Well, I'm going to the loo. I don't think you'll deny me that, will you?' he asked Charles, who sat with tightly pursed lips and said nothing.

They all waited in silence until Matt returned, and then Charles asked, 'Are we all ready now? Does anyone else want to delay this?' Nobody spoke. Gina looked over at Matt, who was nonchalantly flicking through the script. The second read-through had not got off to a good start.

Gina soon came to see that Charles was incredibly precise and demanding in what he required from his actors. His criticisms on the second read-through were mostly detailed and thoughtful, but he was unwilling to allow the actors to play the part in their own way. Any interpretation that was suggested by an actor was overruled and replaced with one from Charles. Gina had not worked under such a controlling director before, and she resented the way that he seemed to concentrate his criticisms on her in particular. They finished the second read-through at seven o'clock.

'We've overrun slightly. Never mind. Dinner will be served in the dining room at eight. Please dress appropriately.' Not so much a request as an order from Charles.

Gina saw Matt raising his eyebrows at Rory, exchanging a look of contemptuous disbelief as he left the room. She could understand why. She was about to leave when Charles called her back.

'Gina. What did you think of the second read-through?'

'I think it went well. I didn't like the way you kept picking on me, though.'

'I wasn't picking on you. You need direction. I'm being hard on you for your own good. I feel that there could be a fine actress in there – I have got to be harsh to bring her out. And I can see how you respond to harshness.' He placed a certain emphasis on the word 'harshness' and she looked up at him sharply.

'Rubbish. You're just getting your own back on me for rejecting you at that party.'

'Oh, my dear, how you flatter yourself,' Charles laughed. 'No, I'm doing this for the greater good, not only for your development as an actress but for the production as a whole.'

'Don't give me that,' she snapped. 'I can see what you're about.'

'Temper, temper, Gina. But I like your spirit. That's good. I can use that.'

'Oh, you're impossible,' she said, and turned and left the room.

Gina was so wound up that she decided to go for a walk around the grounds to calm herself down before supper. She wasn't sure if living and working with Charles was going to be bearable. Seeing him over the breakfast table, making polite small talk at dinner: there would be little escape from him. But she was confused too, because no matter how angry she became with him, she still felt herself attracted to him. She angrily swiped at the box hedging in the rose garden as she walked by.

The gardens by the house were linked by pathways, by gates through brick walls, by openings in high yew hedges. As she wandered around the grounds, she could feel the tension ebbing away. The gardens were beautifully kept. The flower beds were a blaze of bright colour, filled with a huge variety of plants; the heady perfume from the roses, the lilies and the night-scented stock calmed and soothed her. Gina knew that she could not remain angry when surrounded by such beauty and experiencing such sensuous delights.

As she wandered, Gina discovered one by one the knot garden; the formal sunken garden with a fountain; the water garden with a long formal pool and beyond it a series of three ponds linked by a small stream; and then the herb garden. The herb garden was by the side of one of the wings of the house, and Gina suspected that it must be close to the kitchen. She wandered over to a clump of lavender growing by the wall of the house, intending to pick some of the flower heads to put in amongst her clothes in the chest of drawers in her room. Her eye was caught by a movement through one of the windows. She automatically froze, not wanting to draw attention to herself. She could see into one of the rooms, and what she saw held her gaze. Her lips gradually reddened and parted as she watched.

In the room, a man was standing with his back against the wall, his hair tousled and his shirt unbuttoned. Sally Tobin was kneeling between his legs, unbuttoning his flies. She was fully dressed, but her hair was loose and spilling down her shoulders. Gina could see the prominent bulge beneath Sally's hands, and watched, transfixed, with that familiar feeling of warmth and wanting spreading over her. The man's eyes were shut. His hands were on Sally's shoulders, and he was kneading them with an insistent urgency. Sally undid the last button, and slowly peeled his jeans back and down over his hips. She let them fall to the floor as she reached for his pants. Gina could see that the man was wearing a thong, which had the effect of bunching together his cock and balls. His cock was enormous now, a long solid ridge under the thin material, straining for release. A small part of her felt that this was wrong, that she should not be watching, but that brief thought was bulldozed aside by her rising want. She tried to control her breathing, worried that she might be heard, that she might give herself away.

Sally hooked her fingers round either side of the man's

thong, and pulled it down in a single, sudden movement. The man's prick sprung out, hard and bulging, standing free. It was thick, and circumcised, which gave it an angry, demanding look. Sally placed her hands on the man's hips, and slowly lowered her head over his cock, and he closed his eyes with anticipation. Gina had never seen another woman doing this before, and she was fascinated. She was torn between the desire to watch, and the desire to throw the window open, climb in, pull Sally away, and pleasure the man herself.

Gina watched as Sally gradually slid her lips down the length of his cock, her mouth filling with his hardness, a few stray strands of hair falling forward across her cheek. The man moaned, and put his hands on the back of Sally's head, as if to push her mouth even further down over his prick, but instead he started to twine her hair around his fingers in an abstracted way. Gina could see his buttocks bunching and then relaxing, as he slowly started to thrust deep into Sally's mouth, moving in and out with a steady rhythm. Without realising what she was doing, Gina moved closer to the window.

Sally's bright-red lipstick had smeared along his cock, visible every time the man drew back from her. His movements became faster and more urgent, and Sally seemed now to be taking the whole length of his rigid manhood into her mouth. The man gave a loud cry, and Gina could see that he was reaching a shuddering climax. His prick was pulsating, and he gave a final lunge and then collapsed back against the wall, Sally straining forward to keep him in her mouth. Gina could see his cock pumping his semen deep into Sally's throat, and she greedily gulped it down.

Neither Sally nor the man had noticed Gina standing outside the window throughout the whole performance, and she quietly turned and walked quickly out of the herb garden. The image of the man with his penis in Sally's red mouth was so strong in her mind, it was as if she could still see it. Flushed, Gina hurried to her room and splashed cold water on her face. She looked at the clock. She still had time for a shower before supper at eight. If Sally would be serving it on time, that was.

The dining room was lit by candlelight. The mahogany dining table was deeply polished, and there was a vase of roses in the centre, gently perfuming the room. The cast were all seated around the table. Gina looked at her place setting, marked by a beautifully written name card. Her name was scribed in precise, controlled, elegant italics. Somehow she knew that Charles had written these cards. The glasses were fine crystal, the cutlery was silver, the napkins were embroidered linen and the plates were porcelain. She thought with a wry smile about her own kitchen, with its stainless-steel cutlery and matching but chipped crockery from Habitat.

Everyone was dressed smartly. In amongst all the information that Charles had sent them, had been an instruction that they would be expected to dress for dinner. Gina wondered how many of them would normally dress up like this. Persis was looking wonderful in a long clinging gown, which she was loudly telling Sarah was a Dolce & Gabbana one-off. Somehow Gina had thought that Matt might turn up for the meal in jeans, but he too had made an effort. She liked the way he looked, in smart trousers and a striped shirt, but she was pleased to see that he had foregone a tie.

Charles entered, and Gina was not surprised to see that he had outdone them all, perhaps bar Persis. He was wearing a dinner jacket and a crisp white shirt with a starched collar. His bow tie was perfectly tied and adjusted, and his gold cufflinks winked in the candlelight. Gina caught a very faint drift of aftershave as he walked past her. He took his place at the head of the table.

'Ah, how civilised,' he said. 'Life as it should be lived, don't you think?'

He reached for the small bell which he had used earlier in the day, and summoned Sally in the same manner. Gina turned to watch her as she came into the

44

room, briskly carrying a large tureen. She was wearing a grey uniform and a pinafore, and her hair was scraped back in her customary tight bun. She wore no make-up. Nothing to indicate that less than an hour ago she had been wild-haired and lipstick-smeared, taking a man's cock deep into her mouth. And who was he? Sally's face was expressionless as she laid the tureen on the table and announced, 'Chilled cucumber and mint soup.' She took two porcelain bowls filled with thin slices of fresh French bread from the mahogany sideboard, placed them on the table, and then left the room.

'Please, help yourself.' Charles gestured both at the soup and at the wine in the cut-glass decanters, and sat back and surveyed the scene.

Gina was thankful that the soup was chilled, as the wilting heat that day had killed her appetite, and the last thing she wanted to eat was hot, heavy food. She looked with trepidation at the three sets of knives and forks in front of her, along with the soup spoon and the pudding spoon and fork. Charles certainly didn't seem to do anything by halves.

When everyone had served themselves and all the wine glasses were full, Charles raised his glass and proposed a toast.

'To us all, and to the success of the performance.'

The cast all raised their glasses and drank, and the gentle lull of conversation started up. Gina was pleased that Matt was sitting on her right, but not so pleased that Persis was sitting to his right. However, Persis was deep in conversation with Charles on her other side.

Matt turned to Gina with a smile. He spoke in a low voice. 'Don't let him get to you. He likes to think of himself as a Svengali-like character, but he's just a second-rater.'

'Have you worked with him before?' Gina whispered.

'No, but I know his type.'

Gina was picking at her bread. 'Do you think he's above board? I mean, it's all a bit strange, this set-up, isn't it?'

'I wouldn't worry about it. My philosophy is to get through this with as much fun and as little stress as possible, and roll on drama school in September. Who needs him after that, anyhow?'

'Excuse me, my dears. Didn't your parents ever teach you that it's rude to whisper?' asked Charles loudly from beyond Persis at the end of the table.

'We were just discussing whether Persis has got any knickers on,' said Matt casually, without missing a beat. Gina almost choked on her soup with stifled laughter, and Persis shot Matt a look of pure venom.

'Ah, in this case whispering is certainly preferable. Hardly a suitable topic of conversation, though, I would have thought,' Charles said tartly.

Gina was still trying to control her giggles, and Matt kicked her gently under the table. They had made contact.

Tired and slightly woozy from all the wine, Gina opened the bedroom windows, and breathed in the sharp smell of sea air. With the night came a gentle sea breeze, but the heat was still oppressive. She pulled back the crisp linen sheets and got into the four-poster bed. She could smell the starch on the sheets and pillows, a comforting smell that reminded her of her childhood. Suddenly taken with another childish notion, she knelt up in the bed and reached round to draw all the hangings on the four-poster, sealing herself in. The hangings were dark and thick, blocking out the light, and muffling Gina into a secret cocoon. As she lay back, she could smell the beeswax polish too, used time and time again over the centuries to polish the intricately carved posts of the bed. She closed her eyes, and soon was drifting off into sleep, smiling with thoughts of Matt and their laughter over the meal. She was very happy. Their talk had been so intimate, so friendly. She felt that a deep chord had been struck between them.

Later, she had no idea how much later, she gradually became aware that there was someone inside the hangings, standing next to the bed in the darkness. Surfacing through the muzzy dislocation of dreams, she felt someone stroking her hair with a quiet, steady rhythm. She lay there, slowly disentangling herself from sleep, enjoying the gentle touch, and thinking of Matt. He had come to her.

As the stroking continued, more persistently now, Gina revelled in the seductiveness of the touch. She had never before thought of her head as being an erogenous zone, but it was proving to be such. The strokes followed her hair, and drifted down her neck now. The lightest touch of his fingers played against the ridge of her collarbone and then along to the hollow at the base of her neck. She shifted slightly, and, unable to help herself, moaned very quietly. And then she heard the voice.

'That's right, you like this, don't you? You just don't realise yet that you want me. But I'm not going to take you by force. That's not my style. I'm going to make you beg me to make love to you. I'll bend you to my will, and you will not be able to resist.'

Charles. She froze, her body suddenly rigid where seconds before she had been relaxed and totally at ease. His hand ceased stroking, and she felt a slight draught as he pulled the hangings back and left. Her eyes still shut, she muttered through gritted teeth, cursing.

'Bastard. Who the bloody hell does he think he is?'

Chapter Three

Gina woke early. She pulled back the hangings round the bed and padded over to the window, which she had left open overnight. Drawing back the curtains, she surveyed the magnificent view from her window: the grounds of Digby House gently falling away, with the still flat blue of the sea beyond. In the distance she could see a couple of small sailboats moving slowly across the calm sea. The sky was a brilliant blue, unbroken by clouds. The sun was still low, casting long shadows across the lawns. Birdsong filtered down from the trees, and Gina drew in a deep breath, taking in the sea air mingled with the scent of the roses that were flowering around her window. This was perfect. She looked across at her clock, and was surprised to see that it was only half past five.

She picked up the script, and settling into the cushioned window seat, started to read through her part once again. She had been pleased to see that she shared a few scenes with Matt, but was less pleased that Persis shared the bulk of hers with him.

After an hour or so, Gina heard other people starting to move about in the house. She had delayed taking a shower so early in case she might wake the others. Now she pinned up her hair, put on her silk robe, gathered up a couple of towels and her washing bag and went out of her room and down the corridor to one of the bathrooms.

The bathroom was as plushly fitted as her bedroom. There was a deep carpet underfoot, and a couple of large porcelain basins were set into a long marble washtop. Gina wondered if the taps were really gold: they certainly looked as if they were. There was a huge old enamelled cast-iron bath, standing on lion's feet, and a large shower stall, as well as the loo and a bidet. There were several piles of fresh fluffy towels positioned around the bathroom, and an elegant wicker chair stood next to the bath. Shelves above the bath bore bottles of perfume, bath crystals and relaxing oils, talcum powders and moisturising lotions. One wall was covered with a large mirror, and as she took off her robe and threw it on to the chair, she glanced over at her reflection and smiled with satisfaction. She hoped that Matt would find it just as pleasing.

Walking back along the corridor after her shower, Gina bumped into Persis as she came out of her room. Persis was elegant as ever, even when casually dressed. She was wearing chinos and a silk T-shirt, and looked stunning. Gina decided that politeness was probably the best policy. The less she allowed herself to be antagonised by Persis, the better.

'Good morning, Persis,' she said cheerily.

Persis looked her up and down, and sniffed. 'Oh, you poor thing. Didn't Charles give you a room with an *en suite* bathroom? Too bad.' She nodded dismissively at Gina, and walked past her and down the corridor to the stairs.

Gina scowled as she watched Persis go. She knew her well enough by now to know that Persis would never miss an opportunity to belittle her. She would just have to make sure that she didn't give Persis the pleasure of seeing her react to her taunts.

She went back into her bedroom and dressed in sloppy clothes – a pair of jogging trousers and a baggy T-shirt. She knew from experience that rehearsals were usually both physically challenging and dirty, so there was no point in putting on smart clothes. She also knew that somehow, inexplicably, Persis would be looking radiant at the end of the day, while everyone else would be sweaty and tired and grubby.

The enticing smell of freshly ground coffee beckoned Gina down into the dining room. Breakfast was almost as sumptuous as the dinner had been the previous evening. The sideboard was laden with food: kedgeree and kippers, bacon, sausages and scrambled eggs waited under covered silver dishes; croissants and brioches, warm in a basket under crisp linen napkins; jugs of freshly squeezed orange and grapefruit juice; loaves of brown and white bread waiting next to a toaster; cut-glass dishes containing marmalades and preserves; and some five or six types of cereals in large bowls. Gina smiled. Nothing as vulgar as a cereal packet could possibly grace Charles's dining room.

Will, Daniel and Matt were already eating, chatting to each other as they worked their way through plates piled high with food. Persis was sitting at the end of the table, reading a newspaper with a cup of black coffee in front of her. Gina helped herself to some coffee and a couple of croissants, and sat next to Daniel. She wanted to sit next to Matt but didn't want to give herself away. She hated being too obvious when she was in pursuit of a man.

'Morning,' Daniel said through a mouthful of bacon and eggs. 'I could get used to this hotel.'

Gina laughed. 'It's not bad, is it?'

'Pity about the proprietor though. Never mind. I don't think I'll be leaving him a tip at the end of my stay here,' whispered Will.

Gina laughed, and Persis looked up sharply and scowled at them. Gina smiled at her warmly. She knew that Persis couldn't have heard, but it was better not to take risks. Persis was not to be trifled with.

* * *

'Right,' said Charles. 'We are not going to tackle this in a linear fashion. It'll help us to keep it fresh. I want to start with the first scene between Victoria and Felix, and then we'll skip to their big love scene in Act Four. Up you get, Persis and Matt. The others – watch and concentrate.'

Gina thought that this was an odd way to approach rehearsals, as it did not allow the sequence of character development within the play to take place, but she said nothing. The cast shuffled their seats back to create a stage area. Persis strutted out to the empty central area, and surveyed the scene and her audience with self-satisfied approval. Matt came up to join her, running his hand through his hair in a distracted way which Gina found appealing. Persis smiled at Matt, and Gina felt herself bristling, an unspoken thought racing across her mind: Hands off, bitch, he's mine. She was dismayed to see Matt grinning back at Persis.

'OK, let's go,' said Charles. 'From the top. Act One, Scene Three.'

Gina's character, Dominique, did not appear in either of these scenes; despite this being the first full day of rehearsals, when her concentration should have been fully focussed, Gina quickly became distracted and resentful. Her reaction was partly because she could not bear to watch Persis preening and overacting so terribly, and partly because she could not bear to watch her in such close proximity to Matt.

Gina sat with her script on her lap and eyes downcast, pretending to follow the text. She could not disguise her lack of interest, and it soon manifested itself in her actions. First she started scuffing her shoes backwards and forwards against the parquet floor; then she fiddled with the script, folding the corners of the pages down and back again. She glanced over at Sarah, who was sitting next to her. Sarah wore a similarly glazed, bored expression. Hardly surprising, as Sarah's part was far smaller than Gina's, and her character only appeared in the third and fourth acts.

As Persis launched into a particularly histrionic interpretation, Sarah glanced up and, catching Gina's eye,
winked at her. Gina smiled, glad that someone else
seemed to find Persis's acting style unbearable. Every
now and then, as Persis's normally attractive voice rose
to a most unattractive screech, the two women
exchanged glances and smirked. Gina wondered why
Charles was not correcting Persis's obvious short-
comings.

Like the other actors, Sarah had brought a pen into the
rehearsals, prepared to make notes in the margins of the
script. Gina watched as Sarah turned to the back cover
of the script and doodled a drawing. She then slyly held
it up for Gina to see. It was instantly recognisable as a
wickedly accurate caricature of Persis, her large eyes and
curling tendrils of hair grossly exaggerated into madly
staring and bulging orbs and Medusa-like snakes of hair.
Gina started to chuckle.

Instantly, Charles threw his copy of the script down
on to the floor and stormed over to Gina. Matt paused in
mid-speech, surprised. Charles stood over Gina, glowering at her. She felt very intimidated by his physical
presence: by both his size as he towered over her, and
by his proximity. She could almost feel the anger bristling like sparks out of him, almost taste his bitterness,
his sharp disapproval.

'I have had about enough of you. I've been watching
you for the last half hour. You have not been paying any
attention to the rehearsals: you've been fiddling, and
fidgeting, and farting about. Sarah too. Get out.'

Gina looked up, surprised. Surely his reaction was out
of all proportion to her misdemeanour?

Charles almost spat his words out. The venom was
undisguised. 'Go on, get out. And you, Sarah. And don't
come back until you can behave like adults. You are here
to do a job, remember.'

Gina put her script down on her chair, and walked out
of the rehearsal room with as much dignity as she could

manage. Her face was burning. Behind her, she heard Sarah starting to speak. 'I'm sorry –'

Charles cut her off. 'OUT.'

Sarah joined Gina in the hall, shutting the rehearsal room door quietly behind her.

'Jesus, what's eating him?' asked Sarah.

Gina shrugged. 'God knows. Sod him. Let's go and explore.'

'Do you think we ought?' Sarah asked.

'Well, he's not going to let us back in there for a bit, is he?'

They walked out through the hall and into the brilliance of another scorchingly hot day. They strolled down across the lawn and over to the ha-ha, the wall in a ditch which marked the boundary between the formal grounds and the parkland beyond. They sat on the edge of the ha-ha, legs dangling down the grassy slope into the ditch, and took in the view. In the distance were a herd of Devon Ruby cows, grazing in the shade of one of the ancient oak trees. The day was perfectly still, and a heat haze shimmered in the distance. Overhead, skylarks were singing.

Sarah reached out and picked a few daisies and started to thread them into a daisy chain. 'It's perfect here, isn't it?' she said, sighing contentedly.

'Well, almost, apart from a certain director and his leading lady,' Gina replied. 'But, no, I mustn't be negative. You're right, it is so incredibly beautiful. I used to come on holiday to Devon when I was a kid: I love it here.'

The two women sighed, almost in unison, and surveyed the quivering, trembling horizon.

'I hardly know anything about you, Sarah,' said Gina. 'Where do you come from?'

'Manchester. I live right in the centre of the city, so I don't get to see sights like this very often.' Sarah proceeded to tell Gina about her life in Manchester, about her recent break-up with her boyfriend, about her hopes of making it as an actress. Gina liked Sarah. She was friendly and open, honest and unpretentious – almost the exact opposite of Persis, in fact.

After a while, Sarah got up and brushed the daisies from her lap. 'I think we ought to be getting back.'

'Not me,' said Gina. 'I don't think he'll want to see me just yet, and I'm not sure I want to see him either. You go on back. He was mad at me, not you.'

'Well, if you're sure.' Sarah shrugged.

Gina decided to to go for a walk in the woods that she could see beyond the parkland. The sun was now so hot that she wanted to find some shade. She gingerly stepped down the slope into the ditch of the ha-ha, and then clambered up the five-foot-high brick revetment wall on the other side. Luckily the wall wasn't too well maintained, and she found easy footholds where some of the bricks had crumbled away. The grass of the parkland, growing in tussocky hummocks, was much rougher than the manicured lawns of the grounds, and Gina had to keep an eye on where she was treading. She plucked a long stem of grass, and chewed it thoughtfully as she walked past the cows. Their red coats were almost glowing in the bright light. There was a rusty barbed wire fence at the boundary of the park and the woodland beyond, and she managed to wriggle her way safely through it without catching either her clothes or hair.

The cool of the woods was welcome after the dry, searing heat. The undergrowth was thick, and Gina glimpsed a path through the trees in the distance and pushed her way through the ferns to reach it. There was a lush damp smell, a smell of decay and regrowth. As Gina followed the path she looked all around her, taking in her surroundings: the bracket fungi growing on fallen trees, the soft mouldering leaves underfoot, the dappled sunlight filtering through the green canopy overhead.

She paused when she heard a dog bark. It sounded fairly close by. It barked again, and she scanned the direction from which the noise had come. She saw a movement between the trees, and suddenly a greyhound scurried out and past her, sniffing the ground as it went.

Following the dog, a woman walked towards her along the path. Gina guessed that the woman was about thirty-five or so. She was tall and elegantly beautiful, with her long blonde hair piled wildly on top of her head, fixed roughly in place with what looked from a distance like a couple of chopsticks. She was wearing an ankle-length cotton dress, a moth-holed cardigan and sandals. A long necklace of amber and silver beads swung from her neck, and heavy silver bangles clinked and rattled on her wrists. She walked with long, easy strides, and smiled in greeting as she noticed Gina in her path.

'Hello there. You're not from round here, are you?' she asked when she reached Gina. Her voice was warm, cultured, friendly.

Gina smiled back, amused. They were chopsticks after all, and not even a matching pair at that. The woman had keen, alert eyes, the colour of aquamarines, and a kind face that immediately put Gina at ease. It was a face that made her feel she could tell this stranger the most secret things about herself.

'I don't often meet people on my walks,' the woman continued.

'Oh dear. Is this private property?' asked Gina.

'Well, yes, actually it is. But please, feel free to enjoy it. Beauty like this shouldn't be reserved for the lucky few, should it?'

'Is it yours?' asked Gina, immediately surprised by her own forthrightness. It wasn't really any of her business.

The woman did not reply to the question, neither affirming nor denying it. She smiled at Gina again. Then the woman looked beyond Gina, and called for her dog. There was no response. 'Oh Lord, she's probably after rabbits in the parkland, in amongst the cattle. Now I can expect a snotty phone call from Charles.' Something about the woman's tone suggested that relations between her and Charles were not good. 'Do you know Charles Sarazan?' the woman asked.

'Yes, I'm employed by him at the moment. He's putting on a play, and I'm in it.'

'Oh, he is, is he? How very entrepreneurial of him. I would never have had him down as a lover of the arts.' The woman was going to say something else, but then checked herself. She smiled. 'Dear me, how rude of me, I haven't introduced myself. Helena Burckhardt. Pleased to meet you.'

She held out her hand, and Gina shook it. 'Gina Stanhope.'

'Well, Gina, I am delighted by this chance meeting. An actress. How wonderful. Tell me, Gina, how do you find Charles?'

Gina was surprised by the question, but something about Helena's manner compelled her to answer truthfully.

'I'm not sure I like him.'

'You're not sure?' said Helena, obviously amused. 'That's an interesting reaction to a man who usually provokes the strongest of feelings in people.'

'It's hard to explain. I don't quite trust him.'

'Gina. Even though we have only just met and barely know each other, allow me to give you a word of advice. I know Charles of old. He is a very clever, very cunning man. He likes to play with other people, without regard for the consequences. He needs to control all who come into his sphere. And he is ruthless in achieving his desires. Be careful. Please be careful. Charles can be a very dangerous man.'

Gina wasn't sure what to make of Helena's warning: it seemed wildly improbable and far-fetched. She was about to ask Helena how she knew all this, when a high screaming cry came from the direction in which the dog had disappeared.

'I must go,' called Helena, starting to run off. 'Fern has caught a rabbit. Goodbye, Gina.'

Gina watched her go, and then sat down heavily on a moss-covered stump. She thought over her conversation with Helena. Gina was perplexed, but also curious. She knew that Charles was domineering, but to hear him called dangerous was disconcerting and worrying. Something told her that she should believe Helena, and that she should be even more on her guard than she had been before.

'Gina. You have decided to rejoin us. How delightful.' Charles smiled at Gina, and gestured to her to take a seat with the others. There was no sarcasm in his words, and he seemed genuinely pleased to see her. It was as if he had completely forgotten the events earlier that morning. Charles certainly had the capacity to surprise.

'We're about to start on the third act. It's the fight scene. Will, Daniel, Rory and David, come up here and join Persis and Sarah. Now, let's get into this. You're in a pub, it's closing time, you've all had too much to drink, and Persis – that is, Victoria – is about to provoke the fight.'

How appropriate, thought Gina.

Charles was busy with his instructions. 'We'll just improvise with the chairs and tables for now, and these plastic water bottles. We'll have balsa-wood furniture come the actual performance, and sugar-glass bottles, so it will be very realistic.'

Gina was pleased that only she and Matt were watching. Pretending to adjust her chair position, she managed to shift it a bit closer to Matt. He was looking even more attractive than he had done yesterday. He was wearing baggy jogging shorts which came to just below his knees and, while pretending to look down at the script, Gina sneaked a few looks at his legs. She liked what she saw. His tanned legs were covered with a downy fuzz of blondish hairs. His calf muscles were firm and toned, but not too pronounced for her liking, and they indicated a wiry strength. She liked athletic, fit bodies. All the better for sex.

Charles was involved in choreographing the fight scene, his attention fully taken up with positioning the actors and showing them how to use the props effectively.

While Charles's back was turned, Matt leant over to Gina and whispered to her.

'You had the right idea going for a walk. He's been bloody impossible this morning. I'm not sure that I agree with Daniel's description at breakfast of Digby House as a hotel. This place is getting more like a prison camp every minute. I might try your escape route if it gets any worse.'

Gina tried to suppress her laughter. She didn't want to provoke Charles into a repeat of the morning's episode. She whispered in Matt's ear, her mouth so close that his hair tickled her lips. 'The entrance to the tunnel is by the Cedar of Lebanon. You'll need to know the pass code: "Trapdoors and greasepaint". Don't forget your identity papers and emergency rations. We rendezvous at The Redditch in a fortnight. Best of luck, old chap.'

Matt grinned at her. 'Don't you think it would be easier going over the top? You know, brave the barbed-wire fences and guard dogs and sentry towers and all that?' he asked.

'I think the only thing that's over the top here is Persis's acting,' sniggered Gina.

'I couldn't agree more,' Matt whispered. 'Christ knows why Charles gave her the female lead rather than you. You're by far the better actress. But, on second thoughts, I think I know exactly why. Something to do with the old casting couch, do you reckon?'

Gina nodded, but she wasn't really thinking about Persis. She was going over what Matt had just said about her acting. That meant that he had been watching her, and had noticed her during the read-throughs. She wondered what else he had noticed about her.

'An excellent day's progress. I am very pleased with you all. Given the weather, I think that we will have our evening meal on the terrace. There will therefore be no need to dress quite as formally as last night. Casual wear will be acceptable, but make sure that it is not too casual.

58

We do have standards to maintain here,' Charles said at the end of the day's rehearsals.

Later, Rory leant towards Gina as they stood side by side helping themselves to the buffet meal laid out on the dining-room table. 'Don't eat too much of that,' he whispered.

She looked up at him. Did he mean that she was too fat? 'Excuse me?'

Rory realised that she had misunderstood him. 'No, not that, you've got a lovely figure, believe me. We're going for a few beers and a swim on the beach later on. Don't want you getting cramp.'

Gina wondered where the beers had come from. She was about to ask when Rory shushed her. Persis joined them at the table.

'Let's go outside,' Rory said to Gina, glancing across at Persis and raising his eyebrows in a meaningful way. They wandered out through the French windows and on to the terrace. Several teak garden tables and chairs were spaced around the terrace, giving it an almost café-like appearance.

'So, what's going on?' asked Gina, smiling. Anything that contravened Charles's wishes was all right by her.

Rory leant conspiratorially across towards Gina. 'All this "no alcohol" business. What a load of bollocks. David and I both brought a bootload of beers: emergency rations, know what I mean? We've stuck them in one of the big ponds in the garden to keep them cool, and tonight it's party time, down on the beach, right after supper. Are you on for it?'

'You bet.'

'Excellent. Not surprisingly, we are not extending the invitation to Svengali or Queen Bitch. We'll have to sneak out. We'll get the beers down to the beach. You just bring yourself.'

The others joined Gina and Rory on the terrace, and all through the meal they were exchanging glances and knowing looks. Persis seemed oblivious to it all. She was talking to Charles in the dining room.

After the meal, Gina went up to her room to get ready. She had brought a selection of swimming costumes and bikinis with her, and she spent a few minutes trying each on in turn, trying to decide which one would make Matt notice her the most. She settled for an orange one-piece bathing costume, with high-cut legs and a low, scooped back. The colour set off her tan beautifully. Then she put her clothes back on over the costume, and stuffed a towel and a pair of spare knickers into her shoulder bag. She heard a sharp rattling noise against the glass of her window, and then another. She looked out to see David standing below, beckoning her down.

'Come on, let's go,' he hissed, as he dropped some gravel pebbles back on to the path.

The others were standing in the shadows of a large yew tree, giggling like mischievous schoolchildren. Each of the men was carrying a pallet of beer cans. The group made its way across the grounds and down the steep steps cut into the cliffside down to the beach.

The beach was within a small cove, an expanse of white sand emphasising the blue of the water. The sea was so clear that Gina could see shells and pieces of seaweed lying on the sand beneath the swell.

Daniel and Will disappeared off to look for wood: 'Can't have a beach party without a bonfire,' said Daniel.

Despite the late hour, it was still hot, and the sand was warm underfoot. Gina helped the others move the pallets of beer down into the water, to keep them cool. Daniel reappeared, bearing a large unwieldy armful of twigs and sticks; Will followed, dragging a long, bleached branch behind him.

'There's loads of driftwood up at the high-water line,' he said, and so Gina and Sarah went up to bring some more down for the fire.

Soon the bonfire was lit and the first cans of beer already emptied. Gina had kicked off her sandals and was playing in the warm sand with her feet.

'He won't find us down here, will he?' asked Sarah, pouring a fistful of sand from one hand to the other.

'No chance,' said Matt. 'I overheard him tell Persis that he would be working in his study all evening. Something to do with his direction – reading Stanislavsky, I think he said.'

'I know where I would rather be, given the choice,' laughed David.

They lounged around the fire, chatting and laughing, drinking and joking. Even though they had known each other for barely thirty-six hours, they were already learning a lot about each other. Friendships were developing, and they were quickly bonding as a group. And the more alcohol consumed, the freer the conversation became, turning to questions about partners and attraction, and then to sex, pure and simple.

David asked Sarah where she had lost her virginity. She laughed, drunkenly. 'It was in the science lab in my sixth-form college, up on one of the work benches – after school of course. We were thrashing about so much we broke a few of the test tubes.'

'Who was it with?' asked Rory.

'My teacher,' giggled Sarah. 'He was thirty-four and I was seventeen.'

David whistled. 'Lucky man.'

'OK, Matt, now it's your turn,' laughed Gina. 'Where and when did you lose yours?' She hoped that she wasn't betraying her interest in him with the question.

'I was nineteen,' he said.

'Ooh, a late developer,' Sarah giggled.

Matt continued. 'It was on the floor of the living room in my parents' house; it was with my first girlfriend, and it was a complete disaster.' Everyone laughed at Matt's honesty.

Gina felt so relaxed and happy. The sound of the waves beat out a calming, hypnotic rhythm over the gentle lull of the conversation. As they talked, the light slowly faded over the horizon and night fell. The moon came up, and its reflection rippled and danced on the dark surface of the sea. The stars appeared, a few at first, and then more and more until the whole arc of the sky looked as if it had been speckled with fine spots of paint.

Gina poked the fire with a stick, sending up showers of sparks from the embers. The firelight reflected in the faces of her friends: a warm orange light, flickering and dancing. Rory sighed and lay back on the sand, his arms behind his head. Everyone was feeling mellow and relaxed, and extremely drunk.

Suddenly Sarah jumped up. The alcohol had emboldened her.

'Right. Last one in is a sissy.' She rapidly stripped off her T-shirt and shorts, and to Gina's surprise she was naked underneath. Gina noticed that all five men, Matt included, were watching Sarah. Her body was magnificent. It was full and voluptuous, a classic hour-glass figure, but there was a hardness under the soft flesh, a muscularity which Gina supposed must be the result of Sarah's profession. Her skin was pale, and her breasts were tipped with small pink areolas around the nipples. The swell of her hips after the inwards curve of her waist was so pleasing to the eye, her legs so strong and athletic, that Gina could not help but study her. She was surprised to find that she wanted to look, and also embarrassed by the realisation that she enjoyed gazing at Sarah. Below Sarah's gently rounded stomach, so in keeping with the glorious abundance of the rest of her body, her blonde pubic hair was clipped into a neat inverted triangle. Gina felt her cheeks flushing, as she realised that she could see the hood of Sarah's clitoris through the short cropped hairs. She looked away quickly.

'Skinny dip,' Sarah yelled as she dashed towards the water, her long blonde hair swinging from side to side.

At this, Daniel, David, Rory and Will suddenly became mobilised, scrabbling up and pulling off their clothes. Gina saw with satisfaction that Matt was not in such an unseemly rush to join Sarah in the water. David hurriedly threw his clothes to the ground. Gina remembered the way she had regarded him as the cast were introducing themselves in the rehearsal room, and his body was as muscular as she had expected it to be. She looked, fascinated, at his broad chest narrowing to his stomach, which was hard and marked by the small knots of his abdominal muscles. Gina blushed slightly on glimpsing his cock, semi-rigid and standing free from his balls, before he turned and ran down the beach after Sarah. Gina followed him with her eyes, taking in the details of his back, the way the muscles moved as he ran and the tautness of the cheeks of his arse. Very nice.

'So you like that, eh?' Surprised, Gina turned, and Will was facing her, naked and smiling.

She reddened slightly, taken aback by his closeness. His body was lithe, with good muscle definition; firm but not over-developed. He too was becoming aroused, she could see, and his eyes were tracing over her body in an overfamiliar manner. Then he too turned and headed for the sea. His tan was all-over, she noted. Rory gave chase, trying to rugby tackle Will to the ground, but Will was too fast for him, and ran laughing into the sea. Rory had a fit, blocky body, like that of a body-builder. Gina was interested to see that his shoulders and upper arms were almost as black with fuzz as his chest, legs and forearms. She liked hairy men.

Daniel was laughing and hollering drunkenly as he took his clothes off, and Matt shushed him, telling him to be careful not to make too much noise, as they didn't want to risk rousing Charles. Gina saw with interest that Daniel, too, possessed a fine, lean body. This evening was turning out even better than she had hoped: four fit, naked men in front of her. But, most of all, she wanted to see Matt naked. He, however, appeared to be in no hurry to disrobe. She guessed that she would have to make the first move.

Gina felt a warm flush of anticipation. She knew she looked good in her swimming costume, but she would look even more stunning naked, lit by the moonlight. Affecting a false modesty, she turned her back to Matt. She stepped out of her clothes, slipped off her swimming costume, and walked slowly to the sea. The soft wet sand gave slightly under her feet. She hoped that Matt was watching her, and so gave her hips an extra little swing as she walked. She knew her rear view was good, her buttocks pert below her narrow waist, her beautifully rounded behind rolling enticingly from side to side. She was aroused and she wanted Matt to know it.

It felt so good to be naked in the open air: the freedom and freshness of it all was invigorating. She reached the sea and felt the temperature with her toes. The dark water was warm and inviting. The others had gone out until the sea was at about waist height, and were laughing and splashing about. Sarah was in the middle, her statuesque body glistening in the moonlight, tiny droplets of water rolling down her body as she splashed water at the four men. She was obviously enjoying being the centre of their attention.

Gina slowly waded out towards the others, the water gradually lapping over her calves, then her thighs. She felt a slight chill as the water came in contact with her crotch, the contrast emphasised by her mounting heat. She dived smoothly into the water, and approached the others with a few strong strokes under the water. She surfaced next to Daniel, who started to splash her. Gina saw Matt join the group, but she continued to splash Daniel. She must not seem too obvious.

'Last one to the buoy's a Sarazan,' shouted David, and the five men started to swim out, frantically racing each other. The dark water was churned into a white foamy froth as they made their way out to the buoy.

'This is a challenge I can't resist,' said Sarah, and swam off strongly in pursuit, leaving Gina to watch. She saw Sarah quickly catch up and then overtake the men. When she reached the buoy, Sarah clambered on to it, and waved wildly at Gina. The men reached the buoy and started to rock it, forcing Sarah to slip off again into the water. Gina could hear the calls and shrieks, and felt jealous again, not so much that Sarah was surrounded by five eager admirers, but that one of them was Matt.

Gina slowly lowered herself under the water, and floated on her back with her arms thrown out. She felt herself moving on the gentle swell of the waves, and also felt a sense of total abandon. She looked up at the stars. A shooting star shot across the sky, and she made a silent wish: Make Matt want me as much as I want him.

Then she heard Sarah shout out again, but couldn't make out the words. The group started to swim back to the shore, at a more leisurely pace this time, and Gina waited patiently for them to join her again. As they approached, she lowered her body under the surface and trod water, so that just her head and shoulders were visible above the water. She didn't want to flaunt herself too much. Matt might be one of those men who prefer their women modest.

Matt swam up to her, and trod water by her. 'I think you were very sensible to stay behind. It's much further than it looks,' he said, in between breaths. The race had taken it out of him. The others joined them, laughing and whooping.

A water fight broke out, Sarah falling back on to her back and splashing up water in their faces with her feet. Will started to splash water into Gina's face and, before she could retaliate, she felt a pressure against her ankles, and suddenly her feet were pulled away from the sand and she was unceremoniously dunked under the surface. She struggled round in the water, and pushed against a warm muscular bulk that she guessed was Matt. Her ankles were gripped together under one of his arms and, as Gina thrashed about, pretending to try to escape his clutches, her hand accidentally brushed against his groin. She felt his hardness, and knew he was aroused. She surfaced, coughing and spluttering and laughing all at once, pretending that she had not noticed anything unusual. Matt surfaced next to her, and then dived under the water again, and dunked Sarah in the same manner. Gina felt another prick of jealousy. She had hoped that Matt had sought her out in particular. Sarah

65

surfaced, laughing and screaming, splashing Matt in an attempt to stop him from repeating the dunking.

Gina decided that blatancy might be the answer after all. It was time to take action. Taking a deep breath, she dived under the water to where Matt was standing, and grabbed one of his legs, encircling his ankle with her hands. She tried to pull him over, but wasn't strong enough. As he struggled to try to free himself from her grip, and partially as a result of her buoyancy, her hands gradually slid up his leg as she rose to nearer the surface of the water. She felt the hardness of his calf, the muscles moving as he twisted in the water. She could sense that he could easily free himself if he so wished, and that the gentle struggling was all part of the game.

Then her hands were encircling his knee and, as she drifted upwards, they were forced apart by the girth of his thigh. She could feel the hard, tensed muscles under her hands. Her right hand was now around his inner thigh, and she gave a shiver of delight as she felt what she realised was the soft buoyancy of his balls against the back of her hand. Her breath was running out, but she didn't want to break the contact and surface. However, she had no option.

As she rose next to him, gasping for breath, he called out, 'Come on, everyone, let's have some more beers.' He smiled at Gina, his face mischievous and full of fun, but it wasn't quite the knowing smile of complicity that she expected. Matt swam off towards the beach, and the others followed.

Gina felt a keen pang of rejection. However gently done, it was still a rebuff, she felt sure.

The others were already back on the beach, scrambling into their clothes. Gina stayed in the water for a while, wondering how to handle this blow to her morale. Then she walked out of the water, very slowly. She knew that, much as all eyes had been on Sarah as she went into the sea, now all would be on her as she rose from the waves, a moonlit Venus. She approached the others and stood before them, allowing the firelight to play over her body,

66

before bending to pick up her towel. She noticed that Matt was watching.

'Come and sit next to me, Gina,' said Will, and Gina gladly complied with his request. As the evening wore on, she laughed and chatted with Will. She knew that she was flirting, and she also knew that she wasn't doing it because she was attracted to Will, but rather because she hoped that it might make Matt jealous. He, however, seemed to be deep in conversation with Rory and Daniel. She realised that Matt was going to prove a greater challenge than she had expected.

Chapter Four

*A*t last, after spending the whole of the previous day watching the others, it was Gina's turn to rehearse properly. She felt that the delay in rehearsing any of the scenes in which she appeared was more than fortuitous, and more likely part of Charles's plan to discipline her for her transgressions, such as they were. She was learning to add 'petty' to the list of adjectives that she could use to describe him.

The heatwave continued. The windows in the rehearsal room were thrown open, but still the heat was oppressive. Gina was glad that she had chosen to wear a light loose linen skirt and a long cotton blouse that morning. She wore the blouse loose, rather than tucked in to her skirt, and could feel delicious wafts of refreshingly cool air around her body as she moved. But even this could not help calm her nerves. In the scene that the cast were about to rehearse, Gina would be centre stage for most of the time. She was worried about the scene, as it involved some long monologues. She hoped that she would remember her lines perfectly. Gina was worried that the heat combined with the strain, both physical and mental, would take their effect on her. Please let me get through this OK, she willed silently.

Charles called her on to the central stage area, and indicated to her to begin.

An hour later, Gina was close to tears with frustration. She was used to being pushed by directors, and she was no wimp; she could take criticism. But this was something different. This constant needling, this nit-picking and fault-finding, which seemed to be exclusively directed at her, was all getting to be too much. It wouldn't be so bad if it were constructive criticism, but it was too barbed and personal. Worst of all, Charles seemed to enjoy baiting her, and seemed to get more animated the more distressed she became. In addition, she was still smarting from Matt's apparent rejection of her the previous night, a rejection that seemed all the keener as she had earlier seen that he had been aroused. She just didn't understand him.

'Acting is life lived at the limits, Gina,' Charles ranted at her. 'I need you to feel these things, all these extreme emotions. Let it out – shout, scream, whatever. You're not giving me enough.'

Each time she started to go through a passage, Charles would interrupt. Gina could feel the frustration mounting, and she knew that it was inevitable that something was going to give. She couldn't take much more of this.

Gina mentally counted to ten very slowly, and then started on a long and difficult monologue, which she had to deliver whilst undertaking some complicated actions: making an origami swan out of thin, easily torn tissue paper, putting it inside a box, and then gift wrapping the box. This last action involved a nightmarish amount of fiddling about with scissors and sticky tape and ribbons.

She finished the speech, word perfect, and she had handled the props faultlessly. The rest of the cast broke into appreciative applause. Charles was quiet for a moment; knowing that she had performed well, Gina waited for his praise. There was nothing he could criticise her for this time, she knew.

'Let's try that again, only this time, Gina, can you tie the box with a bow rather than making a rosette with the ribbon? I think that would be much better.'

That was it. The proverbial straw. Gina looked at him, seething, and hissed through gritted teeth: 'No.'

'I'm sorry?' Charles looked at her coldly.

'I said "No".'

'Did I hear you correctly? You are refusing me?'

Gina exploded. 'You bet I'm refusing, you pompous prat. There was nothing wrong with that, and you know it.'

Charles appeared unmoved by this outburst. 'How temperamental. Still, I suppose it is only to be expected from members of the acting fraternity. And especially from a female member.'

'Stop patronising me. My sex has got nothing to do with it,' Gina snapped at him.

'*Au contraire*, my dear Gina. Your sex has got everything to do with it.' Charles placed a careful emphasis on the last sentence, and Gina knew that he was playing another of his games with her: a game of double meanings. He was staring at her, his gaze hard and angry and challenging.

Gina knew that trying to argue would be futile. She started to walk to the door.

'Come back here, Gina. I will not permit you to leave these rehearsals.'

'Just you try to stop me,' she shouted, throwing the door open and storming out of the room.

She heard rapid footfalls behind her, and felt a hand grip her firmly, almost painfully, round her upper arm.

'Come with me,' Charles hissed, eyes flashing and nostrils flaring with anger.

'Let go of me,' Gina shouted, trying to shake her arm free of his grip. Charles was walking quickly, steering her towards his study. He pushed the door open with his free hand, and shut it behind him before releasing her. She stood in front of him, glowering and rubbing her arm.

He leant back against the door and tilted his head to one side, looking at her from under hooded eyes. He was breathing rapidly from his exertions.

'A proper little firebrand, aren't you, Gina?' he said eventually.

'Cut the crap and open that door,' said Gina. She wanted to get as far away from him as she could, but he was blocking her exit.

'I will open the door, but not just yet. You and I need to sort a few things out first. I am the director of this production. I am your employer and I must be obeyed. You not only undermine my authority, you undermine the whole project when you question or disobey me.'

'Well, why don't you stop picking on me then? I don't see you criticising your precious Persis, and she needs direction ten times more than I do, God knows. You must be able to see how bad she is. So why are you carping on at me all the time?'

Charles shook his head. 'Gina, Gina. How you misunderstand me. I am concentrating on you because I know you will respond to my direction. I am well aware of Persis's strengths and weaknesses, but she is too set in her ways now to pay any attention to me. You, on the other hand, can still be . . . moulded, shall we say?'

Gina snorted. 'Moulded? You think I'm malleable, do you? Keep on picking on me, and I'll leave this bloody production. That's how malleable I am.'

Gina knew that calling Charles's bluff was a gamble. There was no way that she could afford to quit the production. To her intense annoyance, Charles merely laughed. 'Oh, I don't think that you will be leaving us, Gina. I know that you need to be in this production as a condition of acceptance for drama school, and I assume that you're not about to jeopardise your place there.'

Gina looked up sharply. How did Charles know this? She certainly hadn't told him, and had made no mention of her offer from the National Academy on her curriculum vitae. Then, with a juddering realisation, it dawned on her. Of course. Persis. His little spy. Persis had been around when Gina and the others had been discussing their places at drama school, and she must have passed the information on to Charles. What else had she told him? Gina's mind was racing, trying to work out what else Persis might know. Had she found out about their evening on the beach?

And, after the realisation of Persis's treachery, came another awful realisation. Now that Charles knew that she could not afford to quit the production, he had leverage over her. He could carry on behaving like this towards her and she had no comeback, no armament against him. She felt suddenly deflated, all the fight in her now dissipated. Her head sank on to her chest.

Charles took a step towards her and, seeing that she did not move or flinch, came and stood by her.

'There, there,' he said, soothingly. He took her arm, and she offered no resistance. 'Did I hurt you? Let me see.' He pushed up her sleeve, and bent closer to her to inspect her arm. She caught a faint aroma, spicy and slightly exotic, wafting up from his hair, which was glossy and well cut. He tutted as he saw the redness of her skin where he had grasped her.

'Oh my goodness, Gina. I do apologise. Come and sit over here, let me see to it.'

Gina allowed him to lead her to the leather chesterfield sofa. He sat down and patted the seat next to him, gently pulling her down by the wrist. Then he took her arm and lightly massaged it with both hands. Gina was surprised by the gentleness of his touch, and by the apparent genuineness of his concern. He started to talk, his voice low, with a softness she had not heard before. It was a softness she would not have believed him capable of.

'You're a very special woman, Gina. I knew that the minute I met you at the party. You're beautiful and sensual, and the audition showed me that you are by far and away the best actress I have had experience of.' He placed another special emphasis on the last five words. More double meanings.

72

Gina was lulled by his low insistent voice, but not by what he was saying. She rolled her eyes heavenwards as he bent over her arm, massaging and talking on. If he thought that she would fall for that old baloney, he would have to think again.

Charles continued, his voice gently hypnotic, 'I honestly believe that it is necessary for me to treat you like this. You need me to be cruel to be kind, for your development as an actress. And for your development as a woman.' Charles looked up, his face so close to hers that Gina could feel his breath on her face. Again, that last sentence was loaded with another layer of meaning.

'Christ, Charles. You're doing it again. I don't need you or your cod philosophies.' Suddenly angered again, Gina moved to get away from him. Charles held her firm, his eyes flashing with a new vigour.

'Tell me honestly that you aren't attracted to me,' Charles whispered. He took her hand and, to her shock, placed it on his groin.

Gina tried to pull her hand away, but he pinioned it there with his own, firmly pressing down into his crotch so that she could feel his hardness beneath the soft looseness of the material of his trousers. She looked at him, caught between suddenly conflicting desires, much as she had been that night at the party. Part of her wanted to swing round with her other arm and slap him sharply across the face for his rudeness, but the other part was curiously aroused by his proximity, by his obvious desire for her, by the feeling of his growing erection under her hand. She also knew that Charles sensed her hesitation, and realised that the absence of an instant angry response to his forwardness meant that an angry response probably would not be forthcoming at all.

She saw him smile to himself, pleased at his success. Gina looked at him, confused. Why was she allowing him to do this to her? Before, she would have slapped him, got up and run away. But now, she felt something else. The irresistible pang of sexual attraction. He was,

73

after all, an undeniably handsome man. His dark eyes were challenging her, holding her gaze. That wonderful spicy aroma hung in the air. The sexual tension was palpable.

'Don't try to fight it, Gina. Feel how hard I am for you. And you want me, too.'

Charles reached over and gently stroked Gina's cheek with the back of his other hand, drifting his fingers over her skin in lazy strokes. Gina sat rigid, upright, transfixed. She was paralysed like a fly trapped in a spider's web, unable or unwilling to protest. Gradually Charles traced a pattern down Gina's throat, playing gently with the hollow at the base of her neck. His touch was electrifying.

As he moved his hand still lower, something made Gina suddenly come to her senses and see reason. This could not happen. She could not allow Charles to seduce her. It was unthinkable.

Gina abruptly stood up and walked towards the study door. Charles was taken by surprise. He had obviously thought that he had won her over.

'I'm going back to the rehearsal room. The others are waiting and we've got work to do,' she said as she opened the door and left.

After Charles and Gina had returned to the rehearsal room, the cast worked on a very complicated scene towards the end of the play, when all of them were on stage together. Gina was relieved, as this meant that Charles's attention would not be focussed exclusively on her. It was another very physical scene, involving a violent argument between five of the characters, with the other three attempting to restrain them. The rehearsal went very well, and the cast were tired after their efforts. They sighed with relief when Charles clapped his hands together and announced that lunch would be served on the terrace.

Gina grabbed her towel and walked outside and round to the terrace, rubbing her neck to dry off the sweat. The heat was cloying now, and its stifling closeness was draining her energy. Sarah ran to catch her up, and walked beside her.

'Are you OK? What went on back there?' Charles's pursuit of Gina out of the rehearsal room, and their subsequent absence for some time had obviously worried Sarah.

'Oh, it's fine. We've sorted out our little misunderstanding, I think.'

Another extravagant meal was laid out on a long table which had been brought on to the terrace. The two women stood side by side, filling their plates with a variety of wonderful salads and cheeses and slices of freshly baked bread. David came up behind Sarah and put his hands round her waist and gave her a friendly squeeze; laughing, Sarah turned and hit him lightly over the head with her rolled-up napkin. Gina wondered whether more had gone on during the skinny dip than she had been aware of. She walked over to the low balustrade at the edge of the terrace, with its views over the grounds, and perched on the worn, lichen-covered stone. To her pleasure, Matt came and sat next to her.

'Were you all right in there with our friendly neighbourhood control freak?' he asked, nodding over to Charles, who was talking to Daniel.

'Yes, fine, thanks.'

'We were all cheering you on. He has definitely got it in for you, and it was excellent that you gave him as good as you got.'

'I don't think that will stop him, though,' Gina said, fanning herself with her napkin. Fortunately, Matt would think that it was the heat that was affecting her.

'Here, let me do that,' he said, taking her napkin from her and gently wafting it in front of her face and neck. The fresh breeze it created was such a relief. Gina closed her eyes and leant her head back, equally enjoying the coolness and Matt's attentions.

'You know, I really enjoyed our chat at supper the other evening,' he said.

She opened her eyes and looked at him. Was this just a pleasantry, or did he mean more?

'Me too.' But before Gina could say anything else, a familiar husky voice spoke behind her.

'My, this all looks very cosy. Mind if I join you?'

It was Persis, holding a plate which bore a few endive leaves and half a tomato, and nothing more. She was smiling down at Gina and Matt and, without waiting for a response, she walked around to sit at Matt's other side.

Gina cursed silently. That woman had done it on purpose. She had seen what was happening and just couldn't bear it. She would never let Gina get near to a man without throwing herself at him as well.

Gina became even more annoyed when Matt turned and started to talk to Persis. Gina stared glumly down at her plate and moodily played with her food, stabbing a slice of brie with her fork, and watching the soft yellow cheese ooze out of the white rind. She could think of someone else she'd like to give a hearty prod with a fork as well. But she wasn't going to look over at them. Persis would like nothing more than to hold court with Matt while Gina looked on, deliberately excluded. Gina wasn't going to give Persis that satisfaction. However, as she gazed off in the other direction, she couldn't stop herself from listening as Matt chatted with Persis.

'Are you sure you've got enough on that plate?' he was asking, laughing.

'I have to watch my figure, you know,' Persis said coyly. 'That's if someone else isn't watching it for me already.'

'You don't need to lose weight, surely?' asked Matt.

Persis laughed. 'Oh, I'm flattered that you'd noticed. No, I don't, but I don't want to risk putting any weight on either.'

To her relief, Matt then turned to Gina. She knew that he was sensitive enough to realise that she might be feeling left out.

'What is it with women and diets? Most of them don't need to diet. A well-rounded, full body is a woman's natural shape. I just don't understand why they fight against it, and try to look like those anorexic-looking skinny beanpole models. God, being in bed with one of them must be like trying to make love to a skeleton: all ribs and bones, angles where there should be curves. We men like something to get hold of, do you know what I mean?'

Persis laughed, commanding Matt's attention again. 'Oh, Gina knows all about that. "Well upholstered", one of the directors called her. She's been on a constant diet for as long as I've known her.'

Gina's mouth fell open, and she drew in a sharp breath of disbelief at what she heard. Every word was completely untrue. The depths to which Persis would sink in her quest to scupper Gina's chances with men never failed to amaze her. But before Gina could deny Persis's outrageous claims, she saw that Persis had put her hand on Matt's thigh and was lazily rubbing it up and down as she spoke to him in an even lower, even huskier voice. Gina knew this voice, as she had heard it plenty of times before. It was Persis's seduction voice.

'Of course, you're so fit you must work out regularly, I'm sure. Ooh, I can feel the muscles in your thigh. Go on, tense them for me.'

Matt laughed, and Gina was appalled to see that he complied with Persis's wishes. Oh, honestly, that woman is so transparent. He's not going to fall for that old crap, is he? Gina thought angrily.

'Rock solid. That's so sexy, you know,' Persis was saying, looking up at Matt with those irresistible big brown eyes.

Gina got up. She knew that Persis wanted her to be around to witness this, and that it was all part of Persis's plan to humiliate her. But it was too much: she couldn't bear it. Matt didn't seem to notice as she walked away, and this annoyed her even more.

Will was standing at the table, helping himself to more food. He glanced up at Gina as she approached, and smiled. 'God, this is all a bit healthy. A man needs his

77

pie and chips, you know. I've got to get my full lard quota somehow.'

Gina laughed. Will always seemed able to cheer up the proceedings. 'I should think the only chips allowed around here are the ones on the roulette table in the games room,' she replied. 'Mind you, call them *pommes frites* and they might just be allowed – but only in the servants' quarters, and when Charles is away.'

Will ate a mouthful of food. 'God, this stuff's disgusting. Bloody rabbit food. What's in it? No meat, that's for sure.'

'I think it's a spinach-and-tomato terrine, and that's a rocket-and-chicory salad,' said Gina.

Will frowned and pushed the plate on to the table, his food unfinished. He jerked his head over in the direction of Matt and Persis. 'I see the shark is circling her prey.'

Gina grimaced. 'Ugh, I had to leave; I just couldn't bear it. Talk about flaunting herself. She's not exactly subtle, is she?'

'No, but remarkably effective,' said Will. Gina looked at him. She was curious. What did he mean?

He understood her questioning look. 'Mademoiselle Persis de Gaury. Voracious carnivore, devourer of unfortunates, or, if you like it in plain English, a man-eater. I should know. I've been there.'

Gina laughed, an embarrassed laugh of disbelief. 'What? You and Persis?'

Will nodded his head gravely, and then grinned at Gina. 'Yes, I know what you're thinking. But, believe me, it's a mistake you only make once.'

'So how . . . ?' Gina was bemused. Somehow it seemed a very unlikely pairing.

'We were in a production together last year.' Will looked at Gina. 'Look, it's a lovely day, and we've got another half-hour for lunch. Why don't we go for a walk in the grounds? I don't exactly want this overheard, if you know what I mean. It's not something I'm proud of.'

Gina nodded, and they walked down the steps in the

centre of the terrace and out into the vast expanse of lawns and gardens.

'So go on then, we're far enough away now. Spill the beans,' said Gina.

'Well, I was seeing this other girl in the cast, Justine. Nothing serious – we were having an affair because it suited both of us. We knew that it probably wouldn't last past the end of the production, but it was fun, and we went really well together. "Made a good couple", as the stage manager told us. Well, Persis walked in one day and caught us making love in the Green Room. I guess it was rather a public place, but you know how it is – lust knows no common sense, and the thrill of the possibility of being caught is all part of it. Persis didn't say anything, just turned and walked out again, and I didn't think anymore of it. I mean, we all know what a randy lot actors are, and there's always something like that going on during a production, isn't there?' He looked across to Gina, and she nodded, because she knew it full well.

'So, it all started later that night, after the performance. Justine had already gone home, and I was having a few drinks in the bar with some of the others to unwind. Persis came up to me and was being really attentive: offering to get me a drink in the bar, being incredibly flattering about my acting, telling me that I was too good-looking and too talented to stay an amateur for long. God, we men can be such suckers at times. I knew she was trouble – her reputation had gone before her – but I couldn't resist.'

Gina was becoming more and more interested. She had never heard a man talk so openly about desire and sex before, and the effect on her was quite electrifying. Whereas only ten minutes earlier she had regarded Will as a friend and nothing more, now she was looking at him through new eyes. Even though he was not what she would normally call her type, there was a rough, basic attraction there; she knew that this was largely because she was aroused to hear him describing his

79

sexual desires. And, if he was talking about sex, maybe he was also thinking about sex – with her.

'Why couldn't you resist?' she asked leadingly.

'Picture it. There I was, young, horny and stupid. And next to me was a beautiful woman with a fantastic body, wearing a virtually transparent dress, throwing all sorts of wild and unearned compliments at me. What was I to do? I defy any man to resist. That sort of thing tends to turn a man's head, as well as other parts of his anatomy. I wanted her, there and then, no question. And no thoughts of Justine. I finished my drink in one gulp, and we went off to one of the dressing rooms.'

Gina and Will had reached the formal sunken garden, and Gina walked over to the fountain and trailed her hand in the cooling water.

'What happened then?' she asked, without looking up at Will. She knew that he had sensed her interest, her arousal.

'Well, I started to touch her.' Will moved closer to Gina, and she leant back against the surround of the fountain. Wordlessly, their mutual desire had communicated itself.

'I touched her, a bit like this,' said Will, facing her and placing his hand on Gina's thigh. He slowly started to slide it upwards. Caught between his hand and her flesh, the light material of her skirt started to move upwards as well. Gina swallowed. This was all so unexpected, but exactly what she wanted.

'And then I did this,' Will whispered. He buried his face in her neck, kissing and nibbling. He pushed her skirt further up, and his fingers started massaging the soft skin of her inner thigh. He kneaded her flesh with a maddening slowness.

All thoughts of Matt had gone. All that mattered to Gina right now was the closeness, the hardness of Will. 'And then, I did that,' he said, running his fingers over the cotton-covered mound of her pubis. She willed his fingers to slide under the elastic of her panties, to find their target. But to her disappointment he removed them, and let her skirt fall back down.

'That's enough for now. We don't want Uncle Charles to see, do we?' he said, half serious, half teasing: challenging her to disagree with him, to beg him to finish what he had started.

'More,' she whispered.

He put his hands on her waist, spun her round so that she was facing the fountain, and pulled her back against him. His hands reached round her, stroking her stomach through the light cotton of her blouse, and moving in small, swirling trails further up her body. She could feel his muscular chest through the cushioning soft material of their clothes, and his stiffness pressed against her, hard against the cleft of her bottom and the base of her back.

She leant her head back against him, feeling his lips dance over her shoulder and neck. Her breathing quickened, and he responded by slipping his hands beneath the bottom of her blouse and lightly grazing his hands further and further up her naked flesh. Her breasts, so full and firm, were aching to be touched, and her nipples were hard and pink with desire. He slowly slid his hands up her until he reached the base of her breasts. He paused for a tantalising second. No, don't stop, don't tease me, not now, she was thinking, and then he cupped both her breasts in his hands. She moaned, and pushed back against him. He whispered in her ear as he slowly squeezed and massaged her, catching her nipples between his fingers.

'You have the sexiest breasts. I've been wanting to do this since the first moment I saw you. You looked so good on the beach, and I could tell this morning that you didn't have anything on underneath your blouse. You're such a tease.'

Gina smiled. She couldn't deny that she often went without a bra more for other people's benefit than for her own. Reaching both her hands behind her, she felt the firmness of Will's thighs. His cock was throbbing against her lower back, and she shifted slightly, pressing into him.

She was surprised by her wantonness, by her total and overwhelming carnality. All thoughts of propriety, of who might be watching, of the fact that she had only met Will a few days previously: all these thoughts were cast far away as her body responded to the primal urges he had unleashed in her.

'You're hot for it, aren't you?' Will whispered into her ear. 'I knew that right away.' He moved his right hand from her breast, and she heard the sound of a zip, as he released his prick from the confines of his trousers. Closing her eyes, she pictured it as she had seen it on the beach the previous night, only thicker, longer, and much harder. She heard a tearing sound, and then the slippery, rubbery noise of a condom being rolled on. Then she felt Will reaching around and behind her, pushing her skirt up around her waist, lifting and adjusting. She knew that he was positioning her over his cock.

'Yes,' she moaned. 'Come into me, Will.' Nothing else existed right now, just her and Will.

He pulled her panties to one side and slowly pushed and probed at her moist vagina with his prick, trying to find the right angle so that he could slide easily into her. She went up on tiptoe and bent forward slightly from her waist, keeping her balance with her hands on the low wall of the fountain, looking down to see his left hand cupping her breast under her blouse and his right holding her at the waist. A moment's resistance and then he slid sweetly into her. She gasped: he was very big, much bigger than Andy, much bigger than Martin, and she felt she would not be able to take him all. She closed her eyes, revelling in all the sensations that were pulsing through her body.

'Slowly, Gina, I'm going to screw you really slowly,' he whispered.

He was moving steadily now behind her, his legs bent at the knees so that he could drive his penis right up into her. She straightened slightly, still on tiptoe, and started to move with him, feeling his manhood filling her up. His right hand moved from her waist, down under the waistband of her skirt and panties and on to her mound. She felt him sliding his finger into the upper part of her furrow, and then meet the rigid button of her clitoris. He started to rub her, slowly and deliberately, while gently pumping into her.

Gina's lips parted with desire; she felt a mounting heat as Will thrust deeper into her, and his hand brought her clitoris to a throbbing climax that she could not hold back. She moaned with pleasure as the waves of her orgasm pulsed through her. Will was not far behind; she felt his stomach muscles contract against her back and his thighs go rigid as he came with slow, juddering thrusts. When his orgasm had abated, he flopped forward against her; she could feel his lips on her neck and his hot breath as he tried to control his ragged breathing.

Suddenly, to Gina's horror, she heard the sound of someone approaching. They quickly disengaged themselves, and Gina pulled down her skirt and her blouse, while Will made himself decent. Gina leant down to splash some water from the fountain on to her burning face.

'What's going on here, then?' asked Charles as he stepped down into the garden.

Gina prayed that Charles had arrived too late to witness their coupling.

'I was just telling Gina about a production I was in last year,' said Will, hand in pocket and cool as a cucumber.

Gina looked up at Charles, hoping that her flushed face would not betray her. He was scowling, and she knew at once that he suspected them. Yet the absence of instant fury also told her that Charles could not prove what he suspected. Mercifully, he had not seen.

'Get back to the rehearsal room, both of you,' he snapped. 'You're late.'

* * *

It was half past nine in the evening and Gina was in her bedroom. She had been trying to read one of the books that she had brought with her, but her thoughts kept drifting back to the day's events. The afternoon's rehearsals had gone fairly well, although Charles had seemed distant and peevish. He had placed Gina on the other side of the room from Will, which she was sure was supposed to be some kind of punishment. Will had caught Gina's eye across the room a couple of times and winked at her, but she had pretended not to notice. This was largely because Will was sitting next to Matt, and now that she saw them together, she knew that what she had done with Will in the garden would not happen again. He was good-looking, but paled in comparison beside Matt; besides, he did not affect her in the way that Matt did. But then she reasoned that it had been pure lust with Will, and that she had responded to a bodily need. With Matt it was something more. She felt there was a connection – emotional, spiritual, whatever – she wasn't sure. What she was sure of was that it existed, even if she couldn't name it or classify it.

Her thoughts were interrupted by a tentative knock at her door. Worried that it might be Charles, she opened it cautiously and peered round. Standing in the corridor were Daniel, Sarah and Rory, with their fingers to their lips. Rory gestured over to Persis's room; Gina knew immediately what he meant. Whatever secret adventure they were going to have this evening, Persis was to have no part in it. And if it again contravened Charles's edicts, so much the better.

Sarah whispered, 'We're going down to the pub. Come on!'

Gina nodded, and signalled for them to wait. She dipped back into her room and picked up a light cotton jumper and her purse, which she slipped into a pocket in her jeans. Then she rejoined the others and they tiptoed out along the corridor and silently down the grand sweeping staircase, into the hall and quietly out of the front door. Outside, David, Will and Matt were waiting for them. David was holding a map and a torch.

'Wow, you're well prepared. First the beers and now this,' whispered Gina.

'I wasn't a Boy Scout for nothing, you know.' He grinned. '"Be Prepared", and all that. Follow me, troops.'

They hurried off, walking on the lawn rather than the gravel drive to keep the noise down. Once through the gates, they were able to start talking more normally.

'This is such fun. Like naughty schoolkids bunking off from school,' giggled Sarah.

'How far is it to the pub?' asked Daniel.

'Depends on how good my map-reading is,' replied David. 'It's about a mile and a half to the pub. If I get it right, it should take us about half an hour. If I balls it up, we could be walking all night, who knows?' David chuckled, and the infectious good humour spread amongst the seven friends.

'Does anyone know anything about the pub?' asked Matt. 'I hope it serves real ale.'

'I don't know anything apart from the PH marked on the map at Lower Combeworthy,' said David. 'No great surprise that Charles didn't tell us about it, given his ban on alcohol.'

'PH. Surely the two most important initials to any drinking man. Public house, inn, bar, pub, boozer, hostelry, tavern. All such beautiful words, and like music to my ears,' said Daniel.

'Anyone would think you haven't had a drink for months, the way you're carrying on,' said Rory.

'It feels like it, believe me,' replied Daniel with feeling.

They followed the road for a bit, and then David swung them to the right, over a stile and into a field of ripening wheat, the heads reaching almost up to Gina's waist. There was a footpath trampled straight across the middle of the field.

'Are you sure this is the way?' Sarah asked nervously. 'Aren't we trespassing?'

David was quite adamant. 'No, this is a right of way all right. Come on, I can almost smell the beer from here.'

They walked on through some more fields, then through the edge of a wood. There, at the bottom of the valley opening up in front of them, they could see a small hamlet of some six or seven cottages. As they walked down towards the hamlet, laughing and chatting, Will fell into step beside Gina.

'I noticed that you were ignoring me this afternoon.'

Gina started to try to explain, but Will shushed her.

'All I want to say is it's OK; I really don't mind if you just want it to be a one-off and no more. It was fun, and now it's finished. That's fine by me, if that's what you want.'

Gina whispered quietly, 'Yes, that is what I want, Will.'

'That's fine. I won't hassle you. But I did want you to know that I enjoyed it.'

'So did I,' whispered Gina.

'That's great then. All sorted.' Will kissed her on the cheek, then ran ahead to join Rory and David.

The pub was a very old building, with cob walls bulging under a thatched roof. Over the wide, studded, oak door, a sign swung creakily in the light breeze: THE THREE HORSESHOES. The low murmur of voices drifted out from behind the door. The group went in to be greeted by the warm, smoky fug of a country pub, the sound of clinking glasses and wooden stools scuffing on stone flagstones. The pub was split into two bars, both with low, beamed ceilings. Old oak settles were pushed up against the walls, and clusters of chairs and tables stood scattered about.

Some of the locals at the bar looked across, and smiled at the newcomers. As they approached, the landlord glanced up from the pint pot he was drying with a rather tatty teatowel.

'Good evening, ladies, gents. What can I get you?'

'I'll get this round,' said Will. He took their orders and passed them on to the landlord, while the others went over to a table by the big inglenook fireplace. Soon they were settled and supping.

'God, you can really feel how different the atmosphere is when Poisonous Persis and Charles aren't around,' Daniel said. 'What a shame it can't be like this all the time.'

The conversation ranged over various topics, and Gina sat back contentedly, enjoying the rapport between her new friends. If her fellow cast members had not been so likeable and supportive, she felt that she would not have made it through the past couple of days.

After a while, the beer glasses were almost emptied. 'My round,' piped up Gina. 'I think I owe it to all of you after the disruption I caused this morning.'

She peeled the back off a beer mat and wrote the order down. Rory started to laugh. She looked across at him, unsure what it was that he found so funny.

'Christ on a bike, Gina, you're an actress. If you can memorise a whole play, you should be able to remember an order for seven drinks.'

Struck by both the truth and the absurdity of what he had said, Gina laughed.

Smiling at two of the men at the bar in order to ease her passage, she squeezed between them to give her order to the landlord.

'So, are you on holiday down here, then?' one of the men asked genially. He was old, with a lined face and a full white beard. An unlit pipe was clamped between his teeth.

'Not exactly. We're staying with Charles Sarazan at Digby House, rehearsing a play.'

There was a distinct intake of breath from several of the men standing round the bar. The landlord leant over confidentially towards Gina. 'Don't mind them. Look, you'll find out sooner or later, so I figure that it's best you know now. Then you won't be surprised by what people say.'

Gina looked at him, hoping that he would explain what he meant a bit more clearly.

'Don't take this the wrong way, if he's a friend of yours. It's just that Mr Sarazan isn't too popular round these parts.'

Gina was intrigued. First there was her meeting with Helena Burckhardt in the woods, and now this. What had Charles managed to do to antagonise a whole village?

'To tell you the truth, there's a rumour going round the village about you lot, too,' said the landlord. 'Something about Mr Sarazan having a group of sex slaves staying with him.' The locals and the landlord all started to chuckle at the idea.

Gina blushed. Surely no one could have known about her and Will that lunchtime? But it was a very odd rumour to have started up so soon. Still, small isolated villages were odd places.

Gina was pleased to see that, when she returned from her final trip from the bar with the last of the drinks, Matt had saved her a space next to him.

Later, after more talk and more drinks, the evening was climaxing in an alcohol-fuelled silliness. Will demonstrated various tricks involving beer and coins, boxes of matches and beermats. Then Rory and Daniel started to tell some ribald jokes. They hardly noticed the time pass, and so were surprised when the landlord rang a bell. 'Time, please,' he called out. 'Sup up, good people.'

'Goodnight, ladies and gents,' he said as they trooped past on their way out some fifteen minutes later, beer glasses empty and stacked on the bar at last. 'Come again.'

As Gina passed by the old man with the white beard, she stopped to say goodnight. The man grasped her arm, in the same place where Charles had grasped her earlier in the day. She winced slightly.

'Watch out for Charles Sarazan. He's a no-good. That house used to be owned by his uncle.'

Gina was rather confused by the apparent *non sequitur*. She didn't understand what he meant.

'I'm sorry?' she said. But the man just shook his head and drew his fingers across his mouth, as if fastening a zip.

Chapter Five

Charles rapped his knife smartly against the side of his glass. The orange juice inside it swirled slightly with the movement. 'Cast, your attention, please. Today our rehearsals will be slightly interrupted by sessions with the costume designer. And I am pleased to be able to tell you that we are very fortunate in having Miss Mariangela Abruzzi as our costume designer.'

Gina looked across the breakfast table at Sarah and grinned. Mariangela Abruzzi was one of the top theatrical costume designers in Europe. She was renowned for her beautiful creations. Her dresses, worked with stunning detail, were so beautiful and stylish that they could easily be the work of a famous couturier from a French or Italian fashion house.

'I have worked out a timetable so that the rehearsals will be able to continue while you are seen in turn by Miss Abruzzi.' He passed around a sheaf of papers, with names and times precisely listed. 'Make sure you stick to these times, for Miss Abruzzi will not be kept waiting, and I am not going to nursemaid you by reminding you. That is all. Rehearsals commence in fifteen minutes.'

Charles got up from his place at the head of the table and left the room. As usual, Persis followed him out.

David whistled. 'Bloody hell. How much is it costing

him to employ Mariangela Abruzzi? It's crazy, the amount of money he's spending on this production.'

'I'm not complaining,' said Sarah. 'God, I just love her costumes. We're so lucky.' She looked at the paper. 'Hey, I'm first in, at nine o'clock. Fantastic.'

After breakfast, Gina went back to her room to clean her teeth and collect her things. She then went down to the rehearsal room. Apart from Charles and Persis, who were standing by the window with their backs to her, she was the first to arrive.

Persis was gesticulating angrily as she spoke. 'I can't believe you're sending Sarah in first to see Mariangela Abruzzi. It should have been me. It's not right. I am the principal lady; I should have gone in first.'

Charles patted her on the arm, as one might try to calm an angry child. 'Look, you have got the last session with her. Save the best until last, no? And look at the times. I've timetabled you in for twice as long as any of the others. Surely that's a mark of my regard for you?'

Persis snorted. 'Well, all I can say is that the costumes had better be bloody good. I'm not wearing just any old tat, you know. If it doesn't suit me, it's out.'

Gina coughed quietly. Persis spun round angrily and, seeing Gina, shouted at her, 'How long have you been standing there snooping?'

'I wasn't snooping. I am merely here, as I should be, ready to start the day's work. If you want to hold a private conversation, I would suggest that the rehearsal room is not the place to choose. OK?' Gina was ready to give as good as she got from Persis.

Persis looked at Charles angrily, then turned her back on Gina and stared out of the window. Charles walked over to Gina. 'She's such a prima donna,' he whispered. But she knew what he was trying to do; his attempt at playing her and Persis off against each other was not going to work.

One by one the others came into the rehearsal room. Charles checked his watch at each arrival. Daniel was the last in, wandering into the room with his hair still unbrushed and messy, and with white smears of toothpaste at either corner of his mouth.

'Sorry I'm late,' he said breathlessly. 'Bit of toilet trauma, if you know what I mean.'

Charles almost growled. 'That is no excuse. Rehearsals begin at eight prompt. I will not tolerate this laxness. Drop and give me fifty push-ups.'

'What?' said Daniel, incredulous.

'You heard me. Do it.'

'Hang on. This is a rehearsal, not a boot camp,' said Daniel.

'And I am your employer. Do it or you're off the production.'

Daniel shrugged, realising that he had no alternative. He dropped to the ground and started to do the push-ups, scowling up at Charles as he did so. Charles responded by walking over to him and placing his foot on the small of Daniel's back, pushing him down, and making the push-ups even harder.

'Hey, that's not on,' said Matt.

'Do you want to join him?' snarled Charles.

'Not particularly, but –'

'But nothing,' Charles interrupted. 'Come on, Daniel, you're not trying hard enough.' Charles applied yet more pressure to Daniel's back, his mouth twisted into a kind of crooked half-smile, half-sneer. Daniel was grunting with the exertion, and the sweat was dripping from his forehead on to the floor.

As Gina watched Charles, she felt uneasy. He was enjoying this: his eyes were bright, his nostrils flared, his breathing faster than normal. She thought that it was almost as if his enjoyment were something, well, sexual. She shifted from one foot to the other, wincing at Daniel's discomfort, not wanting to watch his humiliation.

Daniel finally finished the push-ups and collapsed on to his stomach. Charles left his foot on Daniel's back, standing over him like a proud hunter posing over the body of his prey.

'Very good, Daniel. I didn't think you had it in you, but you have proved me wrong.' Charles finally removed his foot. Gina could see a dusty footprint in the middle of Daniel's white T-shirt.

Daniel scrabbled up, turning away from Charles. Gina saw him mouth the word 'Bastard'.

'And now, another warm-up. We're going to play Simon Says. Only this is my version, Charles Says. Gather round in a circle.' The group complied.

'Now, Charles says . . . touch your nose.'

Looking askance at each other, puzzled and curious about the purpose of this exercise, everyone did as he said. Daniel was the last to comply. Gina could see that he was very angry.

Charles nodded his satisfaction. 'Charles says . . . lick your lips lasciviously.'

The cast followed Charles's order. Sarah started giggling, and Gina prayed that this would not provoke another of Charles's outbursts.

'Charles says . . . touch your left nipple.'

The cast looked around to each other, amused and mystified. Giggling even more, Sarah followed suit with the others.

'Charles says . . . touch someone else's left nipple.'

Most of the group paused, surprised, and Charles seemed to relish their hesitation. The exception was Persis, who marched straight up to Matt and raised her hand to his chest; she thought again, and slid it up under his T-shirt. She smiled up at him coyly. Matt looked back at her coldly.

Gina and Sarah hesitated, feeling uncomfortable about carrying out this command. Charles noticed this; Gina could see that he was enjoying their unease. Gina walked over to Sarah.

'Come on,' she whispered. 'You and me. It's easier this way. After all, we've both got boobs, so what's the big deal?'

The two women reached out and placed a finger on the other's left nipple. Gina could feel the point of Sarah's nipple under her T-shirt, tight and hard; she felt her own nipples contract and harden at the light touch of Sarah's finger. Gina smiled. Another new experience. She had never touched another woman there before.

'Come on, Matt. You must obey what Charles says.'

Gina looked round to see why Charles was addressing Matt in particular. She scowled when she saw Persis, and what Persis was doing to Matt, and what Persis was expectantly waiting for Matt to do to her in return. Gina could not conceal her irritation. Persis noticed; smiling even more broadly, she thrust her chest up so that her left breast was proffered to Matt.

'Do you like the idea of a hundred push-ups, Matt?' Charles asked.

Matt said nothing, while lifting a finger and pressing it briefly against Persis's nipple, as if pressing a doorbell.

'That's not very seductive, Matt,' Persis purred at him.

'It's not supposed to be,' he hissed back at her with barely concealed distaste.

Charles looked round with approval. 'Oh, I am enjoying this. Now, let me see. Charles says . . . kiss the person you most desire.'

Gina had had enough. 'No. Stop this,' she said. 'This is infantile, and I don't see how it's contributing to our rehearsals.'

Matt walked away from Persis, just as she was about to clamp her arms round his neck, and stood beside Gina. 'I'm with Gina. This is ridiculous. And I think the others are with us. Am I right?' he asked, looking round. Will, David, Daniel, Sarah and Rory all went to stand by Matt and Gina. Persis walked over to stand next to Charles. The lines were drawn.

'You would disobey me?' asked Charles, taken aback by this sudden revolt.

'What are you going to do? Sack the lot of us? Your production would be scuppered if you did that. You would never find replacements in time,' Gina said. She

94

knew that the balance of power had shifted impercept-
ibly, that Charles was not invincible. A feeling of sweet
relief swept over her.

Charles looked angrily at them. Gina could see that he
was thinking quickly, trying to find a counter-argument.
Then his attitude changed. Suddenly conciliatory, he
spoke.

'Of course I'm not going to sack you all. Maybe I was
acting out of turn, if you'll excuse my little pun. Right.
Act Four, Scene Two. Unstack the chairs and put them
in a circle. Let's get to it.'

Gina suspected that no more would be said of this
little episode, because they had scored a minor victory
against Charles. If there was one thing Charles could not
tolerate, it was defeat. She smiled happily, as the cast
assumed their positions.

At lunch, both Charles and Persis were absent. Gina
suspected that Charles was still smarting from that
morning's insurrection. The others were gathered in a
huddle in the dining room, talking about the events of
that morning.

'Talk about unhinged. I think he's lost it, I mean
seriously. He's not all there, is he? A couple of cans short
of a six pack, don't you think?' Will was asking.

'More like a couple of sausages short of a barbecue,'
Rory chuckled.

'That boy ain't rowing with both oars in the water,'
added David. Everyone laughed.

'No, seriously,' butted in Matt. 'I think we might have
problems with him. We've got to watch out – for
ourselves and for each other. And I don't think he's
finished with us yet, not by a long way. He's bound to
have other tricks up his sleeve, other stupid little mind
games to play with us. Challenge a control freak, and
that will just get him even more worked up. I think that
this might be the calm before the storm. We must be
aware of that.'

Daniel nodded his agreement, grim-faced. He had tasted Charles's fury, and he didn't care for it.

'And I think Gina did us proud this morning, calling a halt to it. Good on you, girl,' said Matt, smiling and raising his glass of mineral water to her. The others agreed, toasting her with feeling. Gina smiled. She hadn't told any of them about her previous problems with Charles. She wasn't about to either. It was personal, between him and her. And she was determined to sort him out, somehow.

She filled her plate and wandered outside on to the terrace, where Sarah was sitting on her own at one of the teak tables. Sarah looked deep in thought.

'Penny for them?' Gina asked

'Oh, nothing,' said Sarah. Whatever it was, she didn't want to share it. Gina thought that maybe the unpleasantness with Charles that morning had upset her.

'How did it go with Mariangela then?' she asked Sarah.

'Oh, fine,' said Sarah.

'Just fine? I thought you'd be raving about it.'

Sarah smiled. 'It wasn't quite what I thought it would be.'

'What's "it"? The costumes? Signorina Abruzzi? The fitting?'

'You'll see,' Sarah said enigmatically, got up, and wandered off to get another helping of food. Gina shrugged her shoulders. As Sarah went in through the French windows to the dining room, Will came out.

'Mind if I join you?' he asked Gina.

She smiled at him. He was such a nice bloke. 'Of course not. Help yourself.'

'As the actress said to the bishop,' Will added as he put his plate on the table. He sat down, as they both laughed.

'So, Will, what happened between you and Persis, I mean, after the sex bit? You never finished off your story yesterday,' Gina said.

'Oh, that's right. I didn't, did I? There was some kind of distraction, but I can't remember what it was,' he said impishly.

'Oh, it was that good, eh?' Gina laughed, poking him gently in the side with her finger.

Will chuckled. 'No, it was very memorable, believe me.' He drew in a deep breath. 'Persis. Hmm. I got well and truly burned there, I can tell you. Still, it was my own stupid bloody fault. I fell for it.'

'Fell for what?'

'The oldest trick in the book. Woman bedazzles man, then humps him and dumps him. Uses her sexual allure to trap him. Call it what you will. The sex was fantastic. I was besotted by her, so I broke up with Justine that same night when I got home. I was such a bastard. Justine was in tears, begging me not to do it, but all I could think of was Persis, of that body. You have to understand that it wasn't a mind thing – I want you to be clear on that. But, at the time, I wasn't aware of just what a calculating bitch she could be.'

'The next day she totally ignored me, treated me like I was some bad smell under her nose, some slimy piece of dogshit she'd stepped in. All she had wanted to do was to split up Justine and me, just because she could. It was like a sport to her. So there I was, no girlfriend, no Persis, and feeling partly like a total bastard because of what I'd done to Justine, and partly like the biggest fool on God's earth because of what I'd allowed Persis to do to me. Never again, I can tell you. So there you are. Now you can see why Miss de Gaury is not exactly flavour of the month with me.'

'Oh, Will, I am sorry,' Gina said. Will nodded in a resigned way. She continued, 'I know this isn't much help to you, but what she did to you doesn't surprise me. She did exactly the same thing to me last year – spirited away my then-boyfriend, only to toy with him and then throw him away. Not surprisingly, I didn't want him back afterwards. I didn't trust him an inch and he was sort of, well, soiled after that.'

Will nodded. 'It looks like she's got her sights set on Matt this time round, which is surprising because he's not attached.'

Gina shifted uncomfortably. She didn't want Will to know of her attraction to Matt. She would find it even more difficult to behave normally with Matt if she knew she was being observed, her progress with him being commented on and rated.

Will hadn't noticed Gina's lack of a response, and carried on. 'She doesn't normally go for single men. If he's on his own, it's not so much of a challenge for her. Still, Matt seems to have the good taste to resist her. So far, at least.'

Gina checked her watch. It was nearly three o'clock: her turn to meet the great Mariangela Abruzzi. She coughed and looked over to Charles, who was busy with a scene with Daniel and Persis. He glanced up at her briefly, and nodded curtly.

Gina made her way to the grandest reception room, which had been assigned as Miss Abruzzi's atelier for the day. The double doors were closed; she leant towards them, trying to hear if Miss Abruzzi was busy inside. There was silence. She knocked tentatively on the door. After a long pause, she heard a summoning voice from the other side of the door: 'Come.'

Opening the door, Gina saw a slim woman dressed in a beautifully tailored black silk suit. Under the jacket she was wearing a scarlet silk camisole. She had shiny black hair cropped into a smart sleek bob. Her eyes were darkly made-up and she was wearing the reddest lipstick that Gina had ever seen. Long jet earrings dangled from her lobes. Mariangela Abruzzi was exactly as Gina had thought she was going to look – stylish and elegant, simply but stunningly dressed. Mariangela gestured her over to where she was standing by one of the large windows.

'So, you are Gina. Very good.' Mariangela was looking her up and down, appraising her. Gina felt slightly disconcerted to be viewed with such a cool and professional regard.

She held out her hand. 'I'm really pleased to meet you, Miss Abruzzi. I've been a fan of your work for a long time, and I'm thrilled that you are involved with this production.' Before meeting Miss Abruzzi, Gina had decided to try not to gush too much but, come the moment, she couldn't help it.

Mariangela smiled, taking Gina's hand and shaking it. Gina noted the large, arty-looking rings which adorned every finger. Mariangela's long red nails were painted in the same shade of red as her lipstick and her camisole.

'Very kind of you, Gina. Now, to business. Your part, Dominique, has three costume changes. Lucky you, that's two more than Sarah gets. She was very disappointed, poor child, but if one's part is that of a drudge one cannot expect silk and chiffon, can one?'

'Um, I suppose not,' agreed Gina. She thought how much sexier English sounded when spoken in lilting Italian tones. Mariangela's accent certainly added to her exotic allure.

'I have prepared sketches for the costumes. They are over there on the desk. You may look at them if you like.' Mariangela seemed pleased that Gina chose to inspect her drawings.

'What do you think? Not that it matters, as I would not change them, but I am interested to know.'

'They're beautiful,' Gina answered truthfully.

'Good. Now I must measure you. Take off your clothes.'

Gina slipped out of her T-shirt and her baggy jogging trousers without a second thought, as her acting experience had made her completely unselfconscious about getting dressed and undressed in front of others. She did not consider modesty a necessary virtue in the hustle and bustle of the backstage area. Mariangela regarded Gina's clothes with some distaste as they dropped to the floor. Then she looked at Gina, and smiled, as Gina stood before her in just her underwear. Gina was vaguely relieved that she had put on what she called her slinkies that morning, rather than her tired-looking cotton bra and knickers.

'Good, you have a nice figure.' Mariangela produced a tape and took several measurements, including Gina's hips, waist and bust, the length of her back and legs, and the distance from her hips to her knees. She scribbled them down on a small notepad, and then went over to the desk and compared them with a piece of paper.

'Excellent. Pretty much as Charles said.'

'Excuse me?' asked Gina.

'Oh, yes, of course. I haven't explained. Because time is somewhat at a premium during this short rehearsal period, it has been necessary to make the costumes in advance without having your exact measurements. Charles gave me an indication of your size. A very close one, if I might say.'

Gina shivered, wondering how he had managed this. She thought back to her late-night visit from him in her bedroom. Had there been other such visits?

'So, this is in effect a first fitting. All the costumes are over there.' Mariangela gestured to a long wheeled clothes rack, draped with a dark plastic cover, which Gina had only just noticed in the corner of the room.

'You will try on all the costumes, and I will make a note of any alterations needed. Not that I think there will be many, thanks to Mr Sarazan. He described you very precisely, all your contours and curves.'

Mariangela pulled back the cover from over the costumes, and took an exquisite hand-painted silk evening dress off a padded satin-covered hanger. The plunging neckline and spaghetti straps of the dress were decorated with tiny freshwater pearls.

'This is my favourite. It's for the scene at the dinner party and afterwards. Do you like it?'

Gina nodded mutely. The dress was gorgeous, and exactly the sort of thing that she would choose for herself, could she afford it.

'Now, you will appreciate that, with the sheerness of

100

the material, you cannot wear any underwear beneath this. It would spoil the line. Take off your bra and panties, and I will help you on with it.'

Gina hesitated for a moment, then unhooked her bra and slipped out of her panties. Mariangela looked on, a slight smile playing on her lips. Gina stood naked in front of Mariangela, and raised her arms. She had done this many times, helping and being helped by her fellow actresses to dress; only once, in the *Macbeth* production, had she been assisted by the luxury of a dresser. She closed her eyes as she felt the soft ruffle of the silk as Mariangela released the dress and it fell over her arms and head, catching at her shoulders and unfurling down her body. She adored silk. Mariangela straightened the dress around her, and then stood back to admire the results.

'Good, very good. I shan't need to do much at all. Maybe just a tiny tuck here, by the waist.' She smoothed down the silk over Gina's stomach, and Gina was suddenly aware of the powerful sensation of being touched: flesh on silk on flesh.

'You are actually a tiny bit smaller round the waist than Charles had told me. Such a lovely slim waist.'

Mariangela smoothed down the material again, and smiled at Gina, her face so close to Gina's own. Gina was struck by the colour of Mariangela's eyes, such a very dark brown that they were almost black. Their eyes met, and the two women held each other's gaze for a moment.

Mariangela looked down. 'I think maybe I could get my hands round your waist, it is so slim. Let me try.'

Gina said nothing as Mariangela slipped a hand to either side of her waist and tried to link them. Mariangela's touch, the intimacy of her gestures, her closeness: all were confusing to Gina. She was vaguely embarrassed by Mariangela's attentions, but also felt something stirring. She hadn't expected to react quite like this.

'No, I cannot reach round you. But it was nice to try.'

She removed her hands but remained standing very

close to Gina. Mariangela was an undeniably beautiful woman. Mariangela looked down again, and Gina knew she was looking at her body, not at the dress. Gina's nipples were showing as two slight nubs through the material, a giveaway sign of her unexpected arousal.

The two women exchanged looks. Mariangela's was questioning, and Gina knew that the Italian woman was measuring whether her advance would be rejected if she tried to touch Gina again, more intimately. Gina's own look was one of confusion and embarrassment. This time she couldn't hold Mariangela's gaze: her cheeks flushed suddenly, and she looked away. She knew exactly what Mariangela was signalling, but she was unsure how to respond. Her body was responding one way and, to a certain extent, so was her mind. But she was unsure. Gina had never been involved with another woman before. She wasn't averse to the idea: in fact she was rather intrigued by it. It was just that the opportunity had never really presented itself before.

Now it was being presented to her. But Mariangela had sensed her hesitation and slight reticence, and had already moved away. She walked over to the rack and lifted off the second costume, a beautifully tailored blouse and a pair of smart crêpe de Chine trousers.

'Here, my beauty, do try these on. But again, please, no underwear. It is all too sheer, you see.'

Gina lifted the dress she was wearing by its hem and swiftly pulled it up over her body. Despite her confusion, she liked the idea of showing herself to Mariangela, and she liked the idea that her body was turning Mariangela on. The Italian woman made no attempt to disguise her interest, and gazed over Gina's body. Gina's nipples were hard and erect now, the areolas puckered with burgeoning arousal.

'It's cold in here,' said Gina. She knew it was a pathetic excuse and that Mariangela would not be duped by it for a single moment.

Mariangela came close again to take the dress, and handed Gina the second costume.

'Well, you had better slip into these then, hadn't you?' she said teasingly.

She watched as Gina pulled on the trousers, then buttoned up the blouse. Mariangela stepped up to her.

'No, I think that it is better with these top buttons undone,' she said, and reached over to undo the mother-of-pearl buttons. As she worked down the row of buttons with deft movements of her fingers, the backs of her hands brushed against Gina's breasts. She looked at Gina, who bit her lip but again said nothing. Then Mariangela stood back and regarded Gina once more.

'Luscious. That's the word that comes to mind when I look at you,' she said. 'You look good enough to eat.' Then she smiled, and Gina flushed at the obviousness of Mariangela's double entendre. Or was it an innocent comment, with nothing meant by it?

'Does this one need any adjustments?' asked Gina limply, hoping to change the subject.

Mariangela laughed, seeming to enjoy Gina's discomfiture. 'No, it's fine. Here, I'll fetch the third costume. Take those off.'

Mariangela went back to the rack and selected another dress, a plain Empire-line dress in a rich purple velvet. She helped Gina into it, brushing down the material, smoothing it over Gina's buttocks and pulling it into place over her breasts. Gina was starting to relax more, and to allow herself to enjoy these ministrations. Mariangela stood back once more and looked Gina over.

'Turn around,' she said, sucking her breath in through her teeth as she regarded her handiwork. 'No adjustments needed for this one either. Charles obviously knows you very well,' she said, mischievously.

'Not as well as he'd like to think he does. In fact, not at all,' replied Gina.

'That seems an odd thing to say about your lover.'

'My lover?' Gina said in disbelief.

'Oh, I hope it isn't a secret. He told me that you are lovers – perhaps I was not supposed to mention it.'

'He said what?' Gina exploded. 'Bloody hell, the nerve

of that man. We most certainly are not lovers, and never will be. God, how arrogant.'

'Oh, dear me, my misunderstanding. I have obviously touched a nerve. Forgive me.' Mariangela looked at her watch, and Gina was not surprised to see that it was a Cartier. 'What a shame. Our time is up. I will get the silk dress adjusted, and we will have another fitting. I cannot tell you how much I have enjoyed this. I look forward to meeting you again, Gina, and to getting to know you better.' Mariangela cocked a finely plucked eyebrow into a knowing arch.

Gina hurried out of her clothes, and put her scruffy T-shirt and jogging pants back on. 'Thank you, Mariangela,' she said as she made for the door. Now she suspected she knew the reason why Sarah had come back from her fitting looking flushed, and why she was out of sorts that lunchtime.

'No, thank you, luscious Gina,' said Mariangela, smiling as she watched her go.

After having taken their meals alfresco for the past couple of days, that evening Charles had decreed that the cast would dine indoors again, despite the fact that the day had been the hottest and stickiest yet. The windows of the dining room were closed and there was a stifling lack of air in the room. As ordered, the cast were dressed in their finery, and were seated around the mahogany dining table again. Despite Charles's sudden change of venue, which Gina was sure was deliberate, and intended to indicate his control over them, Gina was coming to enjoy this nightly ritual more and more. She revelled in the lavishness, the good food and fine wine (albeit meagrely rationed), and the company of her friends: friends who were growing closer every day.

Charles had been silent throughout the meal, and this had had the effect of making the others more talkative and more animated than usual. His obvious displeasure fired them on. Because Charles was silent, so too was Persis. Matt, seated on her other side, was steadfastly ignoring her, his head turned towards Gina all through the meal. Their conversation was bright and lively. Gina felt sure now that there were undertones, a spark, other meanings there. The connection between them was growing greater with each day.

While the others were still finishing their coffee, Charles threw down his napkin, pushed back his chair and stalked out of the room without saying a word. Almost on cue, Persis got up to follow him. Once they had left the room, the others grinned at each other with relief, and Rory got up and went over to the sideboard.

'I had a snoop in here the other day, and guess what I found,' he said, pulling out a heavy-bottomed cut-glass decanter with a large, faceted stopper. The decanter was half-full with a rich red liquid. He pulled out the stopper and sniffed.

'Port. And, if I'm not much mistaken, knowing Charles it will be nothing less than the finest twenty-five-year-old crusted port. Let us drink a toast to our not-so-genial host.'

Rory poured himself a glass and passed the decanter round. Sarah looked anxiously at the door. 'What if he comes back?' she asked.

'He won't,' said Matt. 'He's gone off to lick his wounds, and his favourite she-devil is probably giving him a hand. Yuk. What a disgusting thought.' He laughed, and the others joined in. Gina was pleased with the way that Matt was reacting to Persis. It seemed that Persis would not be able to work her usual spell on him.

'How about another trip to the pub? What do you reckon?' asked David. The others nodded enthusiastically. 'OK, let's see. Time to finish our drinks here, and then get changed – let's say we rendezvous by the main gate in half an hour.'

An hour later, they reached The Three Horseshoes. The landlord greeted them familiarly as they trooped in, and Gina noticed that the old man from the previous night was not there. A pity, as she had been mulling over what

105

he had said, trying to understand it; she wanted to ask him again what Charles's uncle had to do with things. Surely it must signify something, otherwise he wouldn't have bothered to tell her.

There was no one sitting on the stools in front of the bar, so the seven friends ranged themselves along it, leaning on the polished wooden surface as they waited for the landlord to pour their drinks. The lads had decided to try the local scrumpy, but Gina wasn't so sure. She eyed it suspiciously as the landlord put the first pint on the bar top. It was very cloudy, with no head, and it looked lethal.

'Eight per cent. That'll knock your socks off. You won't be able to drink more than a couple of pints of that,' said the landlord, proudly.

'I think I'll have a gin and tonic please,' said Gina. She didn't feel up to the challenge.

'So, are you good folk going to the carnival tomorrow?' asked the landlord.

'We didn't know there was one,' said Sarah.

'Oh, you must go to the carnival. It's over at Huish Salcombe, down by the harbour. It's traditional: been going on for getting on over six centuries now, and it's great fun. There's loads to see and do: there's a procession, and morris dancing, and jugglers, and lots of stalls and sideshows. Goes on all day, and most of the night too. The diehards will still be partying the next morning. I used to be amongst them, but that was in my younger years. I'm not quite up to it any more,' he said, patting his beer gut affectionately.

'That sounds great fun,' said Gina. She relished the idea of getting away from Digby House and the oppressive atmosphere there, and the carnival sounded like the ideal opportunity to let off some steam on their first day off.

'Of course, the ladies enjoy carnival day especially,' said the landlord, winking at Gina.

'Oh yes? And why would that be?' she asked, intrigued.

106

'Well, the first records of the carnival date back to the middle of the fourteenth century, but it's said that it goes back much further: that it has an ancient pagan origin. It's to celebrate fertility, you see, and there's this character called the Pole Man. He's all dressed up in a green costume – a bit like a walking tree if you ask me – and he totters up and down through the street, trying to catch the women and give them a kiss. It's said that if you get kissed by the Pole Man you'll be pregnant within the year. If you're a woman, that is,' the landlord added hastily, and the others laughed.

'You'll notice it tomorrow, but most of the women don't try too hard to get away from the Pole Man. They probably just fancy a quick bit of lip-smackery with another bloke, just to annoy their husbands. And then there's the rule that if any of the men at the carnival can get a woman to say the word "Yes", then they get to steal a kiss off that woman. It's all good fun, watching these poor lasses trying to say things like "I agree" and "Indeed" and "Of course" instead of "Yes", especially when they're being pursued by someone they don't want to kiss. Quite difficult, I imagine, remembering not to say the Y-word. Still, you two ladies will find that out for yourselves tomorrow, won't you?'

'Better make sure we don't get caught by the Pole Man, eh?' Gina asked Sarah. 'Otherwise that'll be our acting careers on hold for a while.'

Walking back from the pub at midnight, Matt and Gina had fallen behind the others. They were deep in conversation about relationships, on a purely philosophical level, although Gina was keen to move it from the abstract to the concrete, and discuss a certain Mr Matt Burton and his love life. She couldn't understand why someone as kind and gentle and funny and attractive as he was unattached, but nevertheless was thankful that he was.

'So, Gina, do you have a boyfriend then?' Matt asked.

'No, there's been no one serious for a while now,' Gina

replied. What she wanted to add was: 'But I think I've found my next Mr Right, and guess what, it's you' but of course she remained silent. She didn't understand herself sometimes. She could be predatory and aggressive and in control when it came to finding a man for a quick fuck, for the gratification of her urges, but when she met a man she was so strongly attracted to, someone she wanted more with – love-making not sex, a relationship not lust – she became quieter and more reserved, almost too scared to give away her attraction, lest she be rejected. She felt that she had been getting some very positive vibes from Matt, but she wasn't certain enough of him, or sure enough of herself, to risk acting on them. And Matt seemed equally reticent.

'How about you?' she asked.

'Same as you. Been on my own for two years now.'

'That's a long time,' said Gina.

They had reached the wheat field, and Matt went ahead of Gina along the narrow footpath beaten through the crop. The ground underfoot was very uneven, and halfway across the field Gina tripped and lost her footing. Matt heard her cry out as she tumbled; he turned and helped her up.

'God, it's so dark, it's really hard to see where to place your feet,' said Gina, brushing the mud off her jeans.

'Here,' said Matt, 'hold my hand. That'll help make you steadier.'

Gina was pleased that it was dark, so that Matt couldn't see her grinning from ear to ear. She felt out for his hand, and he clasped it gently, meshing his fingers between hers, and then helped her on through the field. Her hand felt so small in his. But, most of all, what struck her was the contact, the physicality of this moment. Flesh on flesh – so intimate, even if they were only holding hands. She felt her stomach give a little somersault. It was a start. If only he knew how much these little exchanges meant to her.

Chapter Six

The previous night, Gina had taken great pleasure in setting her alarm clock for two and a half hours later than usual. She was determined to enjoy the one lie-in that she was permitted in the week. At nine o'clock the alarm went off, rousing her from a deep and restful sleep, and she sleepily reached over and flicked it off, before settling back into the cool linen pillows. This was the way she liked to wake, slowly coming round, knowing there was no hurry.

Her hand drifted to her stomach, and then lower. Closing her eyes, she summoned up images of Matt: his lean, firm calves under his baggy shorts; then the rear view of his naked body as he had walked back up the beach to the camp fire; his smiling face; his kindly, laughing eyes. She realised that she had not yet seen that part of him which she desired to experience the most: during the skinny dip her back had been turned to him as he had walked down the beach and into the dark, concealing water. But she had her imagination, and as her fingers moved down to her swollen, aching bud her mind was swirling with visions of how he would look, naked in front of her.

Her passion and her urgency mounted, and she kicked back the sheets to allow herself unimpeded access, so that her fingers could dip and stroke, flick and tease without hindrance. She massaged herself with a slow rhythm, imagining that they were Matt's fingers; that he was on the bed with her, naked and aroused, desiring her and her alone. This image of Matt drove her wild, and as she stroked her clitoris with one hand she pushed the fingers of the other deep inside herself, stretching and thrusting with a desperate need. Her body could not resist the onslaught, and her orgasm built, and then climaxed in an explosive starburst of release as she writhed and thrashed on the sweat-drenched sheets.

She lay back, gasping. Tingling with a tender soreness, she brought her fingers to her mouth and licked them, tasting herself: the slickness of her desire, the salty-sweet taste and the musky scent of her arousal. After a while, Gina slipped out of the bed and into her silk robe. Instead of her usual brisk early morning shower, today she would luxuriate in a relaxing bath.

Gina came down for breakfast just before ten. The others had obviously had the same idea about a lie-in, as they were all just starting to dig into their breakfasts. She flushed slightly on seeing Matt, wondering how he would react if he knew how she had used him in her fantasy not an hour ago.

'Hi,' said Daniel cheerily, looking up from his bowl of cornflakes.

'So, what are you lot up to today?' she asked. 'Coming to the carnival?'

The men exchanged glances, grinning. Rory pulled out a chair next to him for Gina to sit on, patted the seat and said, 'No, the four of us are going to charter a boat, and go out sea fishing. There's a guy at Bartonleigh Sands who does a really good deal, apparently. He provides the rods and lines, all the bait: in fact everything we need except a picnic lunch and beers.'

Gina hoped that the fifth man would be Matt, and that he would be coming to the carnival. But David spoke up. 'I'm coming with you and Sarah. It should be a laugh, don't you think?'

Gina was disappointed, but tried not to let it show. 'That'll be great, won't it, Sarah?' she said.

Persis sniffed from behind her newspaper. 'You're not really going to the carnival, are you? Charles has told me about it. All that Pole Man nonsense, chasing after the women. So undignified. You'd have to be pretty desperate to want to take part in that,' she said witheringly, lowering her paper and looking directly at Gina.

'Oh, don't be such a wet blanket, Persis,' said Will.

'These country pastimes are all very well for the locals and the tourists, but it's all too, too provincial. I cannot for the life of me see the attraction,' Persis continued scathingly.

'So I suppose you'll be going to the opera today? Or is it the ballet? Or perhaps you'll be giving an acting masterclass?' asked Matt, his words and voice barbed with sarcasm.

'Actually, I'm going out for the day with a friend, not that it's any of your business.' Persis snapped the newspaper back up in front of her face, indicating that the conversation was terminated.

'Persis. Friend. Not two words that you expect to hear in the same sentence,' David stage-whispered under his breath, loud enough for the others to hear. There was much stifled giggling.

Sarah reached over and tapped Gina on the arm. 'Rather than take one of our cars, I've rung for a taxi to Huish Salcombe at midday,' she said. 'That way we can have a drink or two.'

'Or ten, from what we heard last night,' added David, laughing.

Huish Salcombe was a picture-postcard pretty town. Even from near the top of the town, where the taxi dropped them off, Gina and David and Sarah could hear the noise of the carnival – music and beating drums, and shouts and screams and laughter. It sounded riotous.

'I can smell the sea,' said Sarah, her excitement almost

111

childlike. 'Where is it? I can't see it; the houses are in the way.'

As they ambled along the steep and narrow cobbled streets that wound their way down to the water, the harbour gradually came into view. It was small, with a high wall enclosing an area about the size of a football pitch, and a narrow opening providing access to the open sea beyond. Fishing boats bobbed idly up and down on the calm water, which glittered and sparkled in the bright sunlight. Seagulls were screaming overhead, whilst others sat on chimney pots regarding the activity below with beady eyes. The briny tang in the air was so strong that Gina could taste the salt on her lips.

'Oh God, this is gorgeous. I love harbours. I used to come to places like this on holiday when I was a kid,' said Sarah excitedly, squinting in the glare of the sun.

They walked past several pubs with OPEN ALL DAY signs chalked on to the blackboards by the doors, and other shops which had CLOSED FOR THE CARNIVAL signs propped up in the windows. The streets were festooned with bunting and flags, pennants and balloons. Hanging from the telephone wires were the papery coils of party poppers which had been fired off by the revellers. Some children ran shouting and yelling up the street past the three friends, almost knocking Sarah over in their haste.

'Wow, I think it's going to be quite a day,' commented Gina.

'As the newspapers might put it: "Phew, what a scorcher",' David said, fanning himself with a flyer he had been handed, describing the various carnival activities.

Gina was glad she had put on her light cotton sundress and her straw hat. Its brim gave her welcome shade from the fierce heat of the sun. Sarah was wearing a white floppy Christopher Robin hat, a crop top and shorts. Not very suitable attire given the paleness of her skin, thought Gina.

As if reading her mind, at that same moment Sarah rummaged in her shoulder bag and pulled out a bottle of suntan lotion. She handed it to David with a smile and asked him to apply the lotion, stepping into the doorway of a shop that was closed for the day. David squeezed some of the white liquid into his palm and started to massage it into Sarah's shoulders. She pulled down the straps of her crop top to allow him better access, and the loosened material exposed the tops of her breasts. 'Could you rub some in there as well, please?' giggled Sarah, looking down at the upper swell of her breasts. 'They're very tender.' David quickly squeezed some more lotion into his palm and hurried to oblige.

Gina decided to leave the two lovebirds together, and walked on ahead. When Sarah and David caught her up, they were holding hands. Underneath the white smears of not-quite-rubbed-in suntan lotion, Gina could see that Sarah's cheeks were blushing.

As they reached the road which curved around the edge of the harbour, they were thrown into the throng. The carnival was in full flow. Ever cautious, Sarah surveyed the mass of people and then said, 'Look, perhaps we'd better agree now that we'll make our own way home if we get split up. We'll never find each other again if we get separated in this lot.'

'Good idea,' said David.

In the distance, amongst the surging mêlée, Gina could see a tall figure in green. 'Look, there's the Pole Man,' she said, nudging Sarah, who giggled.

Gina guessed that the Pole Man must be up on stilts, as he stood a good two feet or so above the heads of everyone else. She mused that perhaps that was how he got his name. Or perhaps not, bearing in mind that this was supposed to be a festival of fertility. She wondered how he managed to reach down to kiss the women, but knew that she wouldn't have to wait long to find out.

'Lovely day, isn't it, girls?' a group of men called out as they passed.

'Oh yes, isn't it?' beamed Sarah, before slapping her hand over her mouth, realising what she had just said. The men cheered and gathered round her.

113

'That's a kiss for each of us, darling,' one of them said. Sarah complied with laughing good grace.

'All right, but just one kiss each, OK?' She moved from one man to the next, kissing each one in turn. One man, the most handsome of the group, slipped his arms round her and pulled her close to him, and Sarah did not struggle. The kiss lasted a long time, while the man's companions cheered them on.

Gina grinned at David. 'Looks like Sarah's enjoying this a bit too much, don't you think?' she asked. 'What's the betting that she accidentally on purpose says "Yes" a few more times before the day is out?'

Sarah finished kissing the last man, and so the group moved on, looking for their next hapless victim. Sarah turned to her friends and grinned. 'Oh God, this is going to be really difficult, you know,' she said.

David looked at her and laughed. 'Come on, you two, let's get some lunch. There's a fish restaurant I've heard a lot about somewhere along the sea front, and you should be safe in there, Sarah.'

Their progress along the harbour road was very slow, blocked by the jostling, laughing mass of people and interrupted as Gina and Sarah stopped to look at the wares offered by street sellers. Eventually the surge of bodies carried them to the restaurant. David dived in through the door, almost in a headlong rugby tackle in an attempt to break away from the crowd, and he pulled Sarah in with him. Gina, however, was unable to work herself free from the mass of bodies and was swept along. She looked helplessly into the restaurant as she was dragged past, and was able to mouth a message at Sarah, who was looking at her through the glass: 'See you later.'

Gina decided that going with the flow was the best policy, given that she didn't appear to have much option in this particular matter; and besides, she was enjoying the hubbub, and the sounds and the smells, and the extravagant good humour of the revellers.

Gradually, the mass of people seemed to slow, and

Gina saw that they had gathered near the harbour wall. A man in a top hat clambered onto the wall and began to speak into a megaphone.

'All right, ladies and gentlemen. Are you having a good time?'

A huge cheer came up from the crowd. Gina could see the Pole Man swaying on his stilts over to her right, and was relieved to see that she was well out of his reach.

'Now it's time for the Birdman of Huish Salcombe competition.' The crowd cheered wildly. The man paused to allow the cheering to subside, and then carried on with his announcement. 'You never believed that human-powered flight was possible, until now. See our brave aviators launch themselves out over the harbour! Watch as they attempt to travel as far as possible! Gasp as they plunge into the sea! This is truly a spectacle to remember. And now, would the competitors step up, please?'

The crowd parted to allow a group of men to pass through. All were in the most ridiculous costumes: among their number was one dressed as a bird, and another as a pig; another man was inside a flimsy balsa-wood construction which bore a vague resemblance to a biplane, and yet another wore just a wetsuit with mask and snorkel, and carried an open umbrella.

The crowd cheered, as one by one the men clambered up on to the harbour wall, made a parting speech and launched themselves into space. Gina couldn't see the sea, squashed as she was in the midst of the crowd, but above the yelling and the laughter she could hear the splashes as the men landed. She realised that the lull in the movement of the crowd would give her a good opportunity to get back to the restaurant. She turned and started to slowly make her way through the mass of bodies, and then cursed her tardiness as she heard the band strike up and the people began to move on again, carrying her with them. She hoped that David and Sarah weren't waiting for her to join them before ordering their food in the restaurant. This could take some time.

115

As she was being carried along, she heard a voice calling out behind her.

'Gina?'

Filled with relief, Gina turned to see who was calling to her. 'Yes?'

There behind her stood Charles, grinning broadly. 'Well, I do believe that you owe me a kiss,' he said.

The people around Gina cheered, and moved slightly backwards to form a clear space around Charles and her. Gina was fuming. She knew that there was no way she could avoid kissing Charles. The people watching would never let her. They wanted to see.

Charles was in his element. He looked round at the group of people, acknowledging their whistles and cat calls and encouragement. He addressed them with that arrogant, confident manner of his, like a lord addressing his vassals.

'Well, I never realised that this was a spectator sport, but that makes it so much more interesting.' He turned to Gina and smiled, enjoying her discomfort. 'Don't you agree, Gina?' Charles could sense Gina's anger and reluctance, and was evidently enjoying it all the more for those very reasons.

Gina stood stock still as Charles moved towards her. As she could not extricate herself from this situation, the best way of showing her displeasure to Charles would be by not responding in any way. Her body language would signal her icy unwillingness. Charles put an arm around her waist, and then the other, and drew her towards him. Ramrod stiff, she stood straight and ungiving in his arms. The crowd's cheering was becoming louder as they anticipated the impending kiss.

Charles slowly brought his face close to hers. Gina looked defiantly into his eyes, which were at once mischievous and coldly arrogant. He put his mouth to one side of her face, and for a moment she thought that he was going to kiss her cheek. Instead, he whispered in her ear, his breath hot and sharp against her skin.

'Give in, Gina. It's the only way.'

116

She said nothing. Her mouth was set into a grimace, and her body taut with anger. The crowd were egging Charles on, slow-clapping, shouting and whistling. They had sensed that this kiss would not be freely given, and that made the spectacle all the more interesting.

Charles removed Gina's straw hat and dropped it to the ground. He stroked the side of Gina's face with a finger, and then tilted her chin upwards. As he lowered his face towards hers, she screwed her eyes shut and clamped her lips tightly together. The crowd's cheering turned into a roar. Then she felt his mouth on hers, warm and soft. He kissed her slowly: a tender, gentle kiss. Breathing through her nose, Gina could smell again the same spicy aroma she had noticed two days previously, that day in his study when he had placed her hand on his groin. Held close against him, Gina could feel that he was hard for her again. All she could think was that, mercifully, this was almost over.

But not yet. The pressure of Charles's mouth increased, covering hers and pressing hard against her. The crowd roared their approval. Gina knew that this was no kiss of passion. This kiss was about power. This kiss was to show her that he could make her do what she did not want to do, that her wishes counted for nothing, that he had control over her.

And then she felt something else: Charles's tongue. Probing and insistent, he was trying to force her lips apart, trying to reach inside her. This she could never allow. Summoning all her force, she broke away from him, and stood glowering angrily at him. The crowd went wild, cheering and shouting. They were enjoying this battle of wills.

Charles looked at Gina, calmly casting his eyes up and down her body. Despite how much she despised him, Gina couldn't deny that the kiss had roused something in her: something that she wanted to deny, and something that she couldn't understand why she was feeling. She loathed Charles, and yet she was curiously attracted

117

to him too. He wanted her, and his obvious desire for her had triggered her own. Confused, she looked away.

'Again? Do you want to see more?' Charles asked the crowd. They cheered and shouted their approval, and this jolted Gina into action. Instinctively, she turned and ran, shoving her way past the laughing people. She had to be out of there, away from Charles.

She ran, wildly pushing and jostling the crowd in her attempt to escape, trying to make her way back to the restaurant and to the safety of her friends. She could hear Charles calling her name behind her, but she did not turn to look. She was still so angry and flustered that she did not even recognise Helena as she bumped right into her.

'Hello there, Gina.' Helena smiled, and gently held Gina's arm to halt her flight.

Gina looked up, and the relief on her face was clear. 'Oh, Helena. Am I glad to see you,' she said breathlessly and with feeling.

'Is there a problem?' a deep voice asked. Gina looked round, and saw a tall, distinguished-looking man. He had curly greying hair, a long, aquiline nose, and eyes that signalled intelligence and humour in equal measures. Gina guessed that he was probably in his late thirties. He was dressed in a faded fisherman's smock and corduroy trousers.

'Gina, let me introduce my husband, Marius,' said Helena.

Gina smiled and shook hands with Marius, but her mind was not fully concentrating on this social pleasantry.

'I saw what happened,' said Helena. 'With you and Charles. Are you all right?' Helena's voice was full of concern, and she was gently stroking Gina's arm in a calming, soothing manner.

Gina suddenly felt foolish, as if she were making a mountain out of a molehill. 'Oh, I'm fine. Ignore me, I was being stupid. It's just that Charles has this unerring knack of being able to get to me, to really wind me up.'

118

Helena smiled sympathetically. 'I know exactly what you mean. Try to forget about him. Look, have you had lunch yet?'

Gina shook her head, realising all of a sudden just how hungry she felt.

'Would you like to come back with us for a bite to eat? We were just on our way home. The carnival is great fun, but we can only take it in small doses these days. Either it's getting more hectic or we're getting older, or probably a combination of the two. Anyhow, do say yes.' Then Helena laughed, and added, 'It's all right – unlike Charles, Marius won't hold you to the carnival custom.'

Gina grinned. 'Yes, that would be great. I'd love to have lunch with you,' she said. She knew that she had an ally in Helena.

Helena drove Gina and Marius back to the house in her battered green Range Rover. Gina looked with amusement at the clutter in the back of the vehicle – the dog blankets and wellingtons, raincoats and umbrellas, picnic hampers and rugs. A dented stainless-steel thermos flask rolled about amongst some empty plastic plant pots.

'You'll have to excuse the mess,' said Helena. 'We seem to live our life in a state of perpetual chaos, I'm afraid. But then again, I always console myself by saying that chaos is the natural order of things. When is nature ever neat and orderly?'

Helena turned the vehicle into a rough driveway, marked only by a break in a high stone wall. The drive took them through a profusion of billowing rhododendron shrubs and then some wildflower meadows. Here and there were unexpected pieces of sculpture: a carved stone spiral, a metal sculpture of a group of what looked like icicles, a bronze head. Gina thought with a wry smile of Charles's gardens, with every plant perfectly positioned and neatly staked, tied and clipped, and the gardens decorated with nothing but classical statuary. She felt certain he would tolerate neither plants in such unfettered abundance nor such an idiosyncratic choice of sculpture

'Wow,' Gina whispered as the house came into view. It was a large, ramshackle timbered manor house, covered with rambling roses and flowering clematis. Another piece of modern sculpture was placed just by the front porch, and ivy was starting to grow up its base.

'Do you like the house?' asked Marius, as Helena pulled up the car by it, and they all got out. Gina nodded in dumbstruck awe.

'The oldest part is seven hundred years old. We were on our honeymoon, a walking holiday round these parts, and we got lost and came up here by accident. We fell in love with it the minute we saw it, and Helena just couldn't resist. She marched straight up to the door, asked the owner if he would consider selling it and, amazingly, he agreed. It was his family home, but he couldn't afford the upkeep any longer and he had no children to pass it on to. He admitted that he'd always fancied living in a nice modern bungalow at Seaton, and so was more than happy to accept our offer there and then. It probably was a bit on the generous side, but when you see what you want, you've got to go out and get it, haven't you?' Marius chuckled.

Gina nodded again, thinking how that last statement could be just as easily applied to a certain arrogant egotist of her acquaintance.

'So, we moved in the next month, and we've been here for ten years now. Of course, we go up to London during the week, but sometimes Helena comes down here on her own for longer periods.'

'And what do you do in London?' Gina asked Marius. She realised that she didn't know the first thing about him.

'I'm a banker; I work in the City. Terribly boring job, really, but it pays well.' Marius laughed. 'Bloody well. No, in fact, I'd go as far as to say indecently well. But doing a boring job allows us to indulge our other interests, doesn't it, darling?' He looked over at Helena, who was opening the large studded-oak front door.

'Indeed it does,' she laughed. 'Come on in, Gina, and welcome to Chitherleigh Manor.'

Gina followed Helena into the house, where another surprise awaited her. In the hallway, with its heavily beamed low ceiling and chunkily yet intricately carved Jacobean oak staircase, were pieces of modern sculpture and avant-garde paintings placed amongst the Persian carpets and silk hangings on the walls. Their presence seemed incongruous and yet they somehow belonged, a reflection of their owners' eclectic tastes.

'Would you like a guided tour?' asked Helena, seeing Gina's interest in the building.

Gina nodded enthusiastically, and Helena led her from room to room, through the old parlours and the main hall, up the wide staircase and along sloping-floored corridors into the bedrooms and the other upstairs rooms. Every room was filled with the same individual-istic mixture of antique furniture and modern paintings and sculpture. Any spare surface was covered with objects. Gina saw twisted and bleached pieces of drift-wood, pebbles and pine cones, a bird's skull and some tail feathers from a buzzard. In the corner of one room was a large ceramic pot filled with dried teasels and giant hogweed. A few industrious spiders had draped their webs between the flower spikes. Gina mused on how different this too was from Charles's house, with its neatness: where every piece of furniture was carefully placed for maximum effect, and where every *objet d'art* was undoubtedly chosen for its scarcity and value rather than for the enjoyment it brought.

'I love to think of the lives that have been lived here. Seven centuries. Just think, that's about three generations a century, so that's twenty-one generations of people who have passed their lives here. We're just another in a long line, and there'll be plenty more after us.'

Gina thought of her own house, built barely one generation ago. Somehow there was no comparison.

'Come on down to the kitchen and I'll fix us some lunch,' said Helena. She led Gina down another set of stairs, narrower this time, which brought them down into a large but cosy kitchen. It was painted a warm terracotta colour, and the floor was covered with sea-grass matting and colourful kilims. There was an Aga in the inglenook fireplace, and the room was dominated by a huge oak table, with some eight or ten chairs around it, none of which matched. The table was covered with papers and newspapers, an enormous bowl of fruit and a vase of flowers which were wilting badly, and at one end a cat lay curled up on an old jumper. A dog was sleeping under the table. Gina recognised it as the one that Helena had been walking in the woods the first time that they had met.

Helena swept all the papers up to one end of the table and indicated to Gina to sit down.

'Talk to me while I get the food together. Marius has gone down to the cellar to choose some wine, I expect. That means we won't see him for another hour at least. But I think there's some white wine chilling in the fridge. Would you like a glass of that in the meantime?'

Gina nodded, and watched with bemusement as Helena poured her the most enormous glass of wine, in what seemed a small glass bucket rather than a wine glass. Helena then poured herself another equally large drink, and took a long, thirsty draught.

'Ah, that's better.' Helena smacked her lips together for dramatic effect, and grinned at Gina.

Gina looked around the kitchen. There was so much to look at. The walls were dotted with postcards of Renaissance paintings, of wall friezes from Pompeii, of Clarice Cliff pottery, of arty black-and-white photos of naked men and women. A huge pinboard covered almost all of one wall, and Gina looked at the party invitations, the dried flowers, the wine labels, the photos of Helena and Marius laughing with their friends: the flotsam and jetsam that accumulates in a happily married life.

'I adore your house,' said Gina with feeling, 'I love everything in it. It's so homely. And I adore all these paintings and sculptures.'

Helena looked pleased at this compliment. 'Thanks. We love it here, and the community is so close. We try to take part in as many activities as we can, to support the local life, socially and economically. Marius and I make a point of collecting the work of local artists and sculptors: that's why there's so much of it about the house.'

'Wow. You're the first patrons of the arts I've ever met,' said Gina, mock-seriously. Helena looked uncomfortable. 'Oh, I'm sorry, I didn't mean to offend you,' Gina said hurriedly.

'No, it's OK, really. Look, I'll tell you this as I know I can trust you. Please don't tell anyone else: it's Huish Salcombe's best-kept secret. Marius and I fund the carnival. It's an important tradition, and was in danger of being dropped as the town council couldn't afford to put it on, or so the then-chairman of the council, a certain Mr Charles Sarazan, had convinced everyone. We couldn't let that happen, so we've been bankrolling it for the past few years. I guess that does make us patrons of the arts, even though it sounds a somewhat formal way of describing us.'

'Good for you,' said Gina with feeling. 'That also makes you the first true philanthropists I've ever met.' She was disturbed but strangely unsurprised to hear of Charles's not-so-glorious involvement with the carnival.

Helena laughed. 'Philanthropists! Oh, now you're being overly flattering. But it's very sweet of you to say so. And now, Gina, enough about Marius and me. I want to hear all about you,' she said, as she washed some watercress and baby spinach leaves in the sink. 'How's it going with Charles? Are you bearing up?'

'Oh, Charles,' sighed Gina, glad of the opportunity to talk about her *bête noire*. 'Where do I begin? I just don't understand him.'

'Has he made a pass at you?' asked Helena.

Gina was surprised at Helena's forthrightness, but answered truthfully. 'Yes, well, sort of. I wouldn't actually call it a pass, more like a royal command.'

'Sounds like Charles,' said Helena, shredding the salad leaves into a bowl. 'How did you respond?'

'I turned him down. In fact, I've turned him down quite a few times now, but he doesn't seem to get the message.'

'That's Charles too. He won't take no for an answer. If you do refuse him, it just makes him even more determined to get his way. He relishes a challenge. Oh dear, Gina, I fear that he will make life very difficult for you until he gets what he wants. Believe me, he won't stop until he possesses you completely. And when he does, he won't allow you an original thought in your head, and he won't permit you an unauthorised action. Please be careful.'

Gina thought that Helena was being over-dramatic, but didn't say so. 'Well I'm fed up with it, and with his mind games and his controlling and his interference. All I want is to act in this play, to get on with the job, but he makes it so difficult. The atmosphere in Digby House is terrible. It's a real case of them against us.'

'Them?' Helena asked, as she mixed a dressing and sloshed it over the salad.

'Oh. He's got a little sidekick. Miss Persis de Gaury.'

'Persis,' said Helena thoughtfully.

'You know her?' asked Gina.

'Oh yes. Persis and I go back a long way. Well, I pity you, Gina, if you've got both of them to contend with. They're quite a poisonous pairing.'

'Tell me about it,' laughed Gina.

Helena put the salad on the table, and took some plates and cutlery off the large pine dresser against one wall. 'You must promise us, Gina. Any time it gets too much for you at Digby House, just you come on over here. You're always welcome.'

'Thanks. I really appreciate that,' said Gina.

Helena went to the fridge and got out a huge joint of

124

ham and a bowl of glossy black olives, and then brought a glass dome covering a dish with four different cheeses to the table, along with some fresh small loaves and some butter. She went to a door below the stairs and called down to Marius, who appeared soon afterwards bearing three bottles of wine.

'Let's eat,' Helena said.

'Helena, can I ask you a question?' asked Gina, as she put some salad on to her plate.

'That's an odd thing to ask. Of course you can. Fire away.'

'How do you know so much about Charles?' Gina asked.

Helena looked across at Gina. 'No secrets between friends. That's the best way to carry on, I believe. How do I know so much about Mr Sarazan? Well, I know so much because I had an affair with him.'

Gina almost choked on her food with disbelief. 'What? You and Charles? But . . .' Gina was lost for words.

'But how could I? Well, quite easily, as it turned out. It was a long time ago, some seven years now.'

'But . . .' Gina trailed off again, looking across at Marius.

'Oh, Gina, you are so wonderfully naive sometimes, you know. Marius and I have an open relationship. We sleep with whoever we like, but we only love each other. Our marriage is about love, not sex. Anyhow, the relationship with Charles was short-lived, partly because it didn't take me long to find out what he's like, and partly because Persis appeared on the scene. To be perfectly honest, I was more than happy to leave her to him.'

Gina fell silent, trying to digest this latest piece of information. Marius and Helena exchanged glances over the table, and smiled.

The day had passed swiftly. Gina felt so comfortable with the Burckhardts, it seemed as if she had known them all her life. They had talked some more, and gone for a long walk in the gardens and then into the woods. Then Marius had cooked supper on the Aga, a huge bowl of fresh pasta with a sauce made from wild mushrooms, cream, pesto and toasted pine nuts. The wine flowed as freely as the conversation.

Gina casually glanced at her watch for the first time that day. 'Oh hell, look at the time. I've got to be back by ten,' she said. It was fifteen minutes before curfew. Somehow, she hadn't minded breaking the curfew when she was with the others, but on her own she felt so much more vulnerable. And after the events of that morning, she did not want to give Charles an excuse to single her out for any reason, punishment or otherwise.

'I'll give you a lift home,' said Marius. 'It's not far. Don't worry, we'll get you there in time.'

Seated in the passenger seat of the Jaguar XJS, Gina looked across at Marius as he expertly handled the car down the narrow and twisting single-track lanes. He had a wonderful profile, like a Roman emperor, she thought. Knowing that he had an open relationship, she wondered whether he had looked at her as a potential partner that evening. She could certainly imagine making love with him. The eroticism of this thought as she sat next to him was vivid and appealing, and in an automatic response she shifted slightly in the soft leather seat, contracting the muscles of her sex as she might tense them about a hard prick. She was glad that Marius was not a mind-reader.

Despite her best intentions, Gina began to feel nervous as they approached Digby House. 'It's all right, you don't have to take me right up to the house. You can drop me here if you like,' she said. Seeing her with Marius might stir Charles up even more.

'Nonsense, I won't hear of it,' said Marius. 'I'll take you to the door. Anything less would be improper and ungentlemanly.'

Marius swung the Jaguar through the gates of Digby House and drove up the gravel drive, bringing the car to a halt right outside the front door. The house was lit up, and Gina guessed that everyone else was already back in their rooms.

'Thank you so much for a lovely evening, Marius,' said Gina as she got out of the car. She looked up nervously, half-expecting to see Charles at a window. But there was no one there.

'Any time, Gina,' Marius said. 'We must do this again. Helena said that you were delightful, and she was quite right.'

Gina blushed, said goodbye again and went into the house. As she entered the hallway, Charles was standing at the top of the stairs, looking down at her.

'Out and about with the Burckhardts, I see. Have you had a nice day?' he asked. He made no attempt to disguise his disdain.

'Well, Charles, parts of my day were wonderful, and parts of it were awful. I'll leave you to work out which parts were which,' Gina said casually, as she walked up the stairs and past him, into her bedroom.

Gina was woken by a terrific banging noise coming from along the corridor, and then by shouting. She scrabbled in the dark for her gown and then cautiously opened her bedroom door to see what was going on.

Further down the corridor, Sarah's bedroom door was flung wide open, and bright light streamed out into the darkened corridor. Gina could hear Charles. His voice was shrill and sharp with anger.

'How dare you? You have broken my express commands.'

Gina heard Sarah reply, her voice quiet and low. She sounded terrified. 'I'm sorry –'

Charles interrupted. 'Sorry? Sorry? That's not enough. You think that you can say sorry and that this will all be over? Oh no.'

Then Gina heard another voice, and realised that it was David. 'Come on, Charles, get a grip. We're consenting adults, for Christ's sake.'

Charles's voice rose to another, angrier pitch. 'Not in

my house. Not when you're working for me. I'm the only one who gives any consent here. You knew the rules, and you broke them.'

Gina looked along the corridor, and realised that like her, the others had come out of their rooms to see what was going on. Matt came over to her.

Charles was shouting, his voice high and harsh now. 'This transgression will have to be punished. You knew the rules. You accepted to abide by them, and so now I must discipline you. Come with me.'

'No. We will not,' said David.

Charles spat his words out. 'All right then. Lose your jobs. That is of no concern to me – I have understudies lined up and waiting. They know the script perfectly, and it won't take more than a couple of days to get everything fully rehearsed with your replacements. Don't for a minute think that you are not expendable.'

Gina was certain that this must be a bluff, as it made no sense for the understudies to rehearse separately from the cast. She was convinced that there were no understudies. She was dismayed to hear Sarah say, 'Come on, David. I think he means it.'

'Damn right I do,' growled Charles. David then appeared, pushed near-naked into the corridor. He was wearing boxer shorts and nothing else. Sarah followed, sullen and reluctant, clutching her robe around her. Charles came behind Sarah, and prodded her to move.

'Go downstairs. You others, you come and watch. See what happens when you defy me.' Charles was looking at Gina as he spoke these words.

There was something a bit unhinged, a bit crazed about Charles's behaviour. He licked his lips quickly, and Gina realised that he was behaving as he had the day that he had forced Daniel to do the push-ups.

Charles went ahead of David and Sarah, and led them down the stairs. The others followed, curious and uneasy in equal measures. As she followed the others downstairs, Gina knew that Charles could not have seen her and Will making love in the formal garden that lunchtime. This was how he would have reacted if he had known. Charles halted by a closed door. They had not been shown into this room when Charles had taken them on the tour of the house on their first day. Charles reached into the pocket of his dressing gown and pulled out a key. He turned it in the lock, and opened the door.

'Wait there,' he said, disappearing into the room and closing the door after him.

The group was lost for words. This was so bizarre that they could hardly believe it was happening. Gina thought that she could hear a match being struck, and wondered what Charles was up to. Charles reappeared and gestured David and Sarah into the room, and then indicated that the others should follow.

Gina gasped when she saw inside the room. The rest of the house was decorated in restrained good taste, but this room was like something out of a New Orleans bordello. It was windowless, and the walls were hung with a red brocade-like material. Candle chandeliers were suspended from the ceiling and a plumply upholstered chaise longue was positioned against one wall. A large bed dominated the middle of the room, its ornate brass frame glittering in the candlelight. A wooden sea chest with brass studs stood at the bottom of the bed, pushed up against the bedframe. And then Gina noted another detail. On one of the walls were four metal loops, set at about six feet high, and another group of four set almost at ground level.

'The kinky devil,' Gina heard Matt mutter behind her.

Charles walked over to the loops, and jerked his head angrily at Sarah and David, indicating that they should join him. Sarah hesitated, but David walked straight over to Charles. Sarah followed David's lead unwillingly. Before they had time to react, Charles had deftly handcuffed them together.

'Hey, what's going on?' asked Sarah.

'You'll find out,' said Charles, attaching the padlock and their free arms to three of the loops on the wall, so that they were facing the wall.

Sarah looked at David, but he ignored her. He was looking round at Charles, his breathing rapid.

Charles spoke in a low voice, barely more than a whisper. 'Now, which one shall I punish? Who will be the most receptive to my discipline? Who requires correction the most?' He walked over to the sea chest and threw open the lid. Inside the chest was a curious array of ropes and chains, silk scarves and padded velvet collars, whips and manacles.

Matt let out a low whistle. Somehow, Gina knew that neither she nor any of the others would try to interrupt. There was something hypnotic about Charles's actions. He seemed another person, almost possessed, wild-eyed and driven. And they too were rooted to the spot, waiting to see what he would do.

Gina watched as, straining against her constrictions, Sarah turned her head to see what Charles was up to. When Sarah saw the contents of the box, immediately her body relaxed and she stopped struggling. Her lips parted, and Gina heard her give a soft moan, barely audible.

Charles selected a leather cat-o'-nine-tails from the chest, and swished it playfully through the air. Then he walked slowly and purposefully towards his two captives. Gina could see the sweat on David's brow.

'Charles, punish me. It was my fault. Sarah had already gone to bed and I went to her room. The responsibility is mine.'

'Very well,' said Charles. He turned to the others. 'Persis, come here and assist me.'

Persis stepped forward. She stood next to David and slowly drew down his boxer shorts. He stepped out of them, and she bobbed down to remove them. Gina knew that the lack of instructions, the unspoken understanding between Charles and Persis showed that this was not the first time that Persis had assisted him in this manner.

Now David was naked. His back was exposed to Charles, who was regarding both his prisoners, tapping the whip against his thigh. Despite the surreal nature of what was happening, Gina was interested too. She had seen David nude before, and he had a fine body. However, something about seeing him naked and restrained like this, vulnerable and unable to control what was about to happen to him, made her feel the familiar warmth of desire building inside her.

Gina gazed at David in a reverie. She found the jut of his bottom below his strong back very appealing. His gluteus muscles were toned and, in a moment of fancy, she could imagine how they would appear, contracting and relaxing as he thrust his penis deep into her. She had never thought before that sado-masochism would be sexually arousing to her, and yet she was undeniably turned on by what was about to happen. Was it the sight of a strong, well-muscled man, manacled and helpless? She could step up and fondle him, and he would not be able to resist. Or was it the glowering presence of Charles, whip in hand, powerful and masterful? Or was it the glazed, anticipatory look in David's eyes, the quick flicks of his tongue over his lips, his dilated pupils: all indicating desire rather than fear?

The wait was too much for David. 'Punish me,' he almost begged. 'Please.'

Charles placed the flails of the whip over David's right shoulder, and then slowly trailed them down his back, tracing the line of his spine. He paused when he reached David's buttocks, and then tapped them playfully. David moaned. 'Yes.' From where Gina was standing, she could see the upward tilt of his rigid cock.

Then Charles stood so that he was sideways on to David, and quickly drew back the whip, before giving a deft flick of his forearm. Facing the wall, David closed his eyes. The flails hissed through the air and stung across his buttocks, which he had clenched in anticipation. At the moment of contact, David juddered. Charles drew the whip back and lashed out again. Again, David moaned and shook. As the sixth blow hit his buttocks, David gave a final throaty groan and then fell limply in the manacles. His legs had completely given way. Gina could see a long splash of thick, viscous liquid slowly dribbling down the wall.

Then Charles turned his attention to Sarah.

'I am feeling magnanimous tonight, Sarah. I think that I shall spare you. Let David's punishment be a lesson to you.'

'No, punish me, please,' she begged. 'I deserve it. I've been very bad.'

Charles smiled. 'Very well.' He replaced the cat-o'-nine-tails in the chest, and then approached Sarah. Straining against her restraints, she twisted to see him. He took hold of her robe at her shoulders and, with a single, powerful motion, ripped it apart and pulled it off her.

He surveyed her. 'Good,' he said, stroking a finger down the length of her spine and back up again. Then he went back to the chest and took out a riding crop. It was fashioned out of black leather and glistened in the candlelight.

Charles approached Sarah again, and traced a light, lingering pattern over her buttocks with the tip of the crop. She could not contain her excitement, and moaned with desire. Charles raised his arm and delivered a smart stroke of the crop across her left buttock. Sarah gave a sharp intake of breath, and then relaxed, murmuring, 'Oh yes.' Gina could see a slight red mark rising under the pale white skin. Charles paused, regarding Sarah as she writhed in her manacles. 'Please, Charles,' she whispered.

Charles gave Sarah a single stroke on the other buttock, and then replaced the crop in the chest. Sarah groaned with disappointment when she realised that her punishment was over. Charles approached her and, cupping the palm of his right hand, he took the fleshy globe of her right buttock in it. Gina watched, intrigued and undeniably aroused, as he started to slowly caress Sarah's soft skin, his fingers spread wide over her flesh. Sarah shifted slightly in anticipation.

'Do you like that?' he asked, leaning close behind her

and whispering in her ear. He was directly behind her now, and took her other buttock in his left hand. Gina could tell from the movement of his elbows and forearms that he was continuing the massage, and Sarah's moans became louder. Then Gina saw Charles's arms move differently, and it looked to her as if he was unzipping his flies. At this point, Gina decided that she had seen enough, and quietly slipped out of the room. All the others remained to watch, gripped by the same hypnotised fascination with which David had earlier regarded the cat-o'-nine-tails.

Half an hour later as she lay in the darkness of her room, she heard the others coming to bed. She wondered what else they had witnessed.

Chapter Seven

Rehearsals the next morning had gone very well. Charles was laughing and joking with the cast, and had even gone so far as to praise Gina's performance. Whenever they were not rehearsing, David and Sarah sat next to each other. Gina observed them as they exchanged little looks and smiles. They seemed curiously energised to Gina, and she wondered whether, to them, the punishment that Charles had meted out the previous night had seemed more of a reward.

But despite the good humour and high spirits of the cast, Gina felt a slight uneasiness. Helena's incredible revelation about her affair with Charles was still preying on Gina's mind. She stared at Charles, trying to picture him with Helena, but she could not manage it. They were poles apart: Charles was precise and ordered and neat, with everything in its place and all under his control; Helena was bohemian, with wild clothes, wild hair and wild ideas. She was spirited and impulsive, and Gina could not imagine how they could ever have formed a couple. And Helena had made that enigmatic comment about Persis; what did she know about her?

Then there was Matt. Gina had seen very little of him the previous day, only at breakfast time and later on that night when Charles was demonstrating his prowess as a disciplinarian. They hadn't spoken properly for a while, and she felt that the closeness and the electricity which they had shared only a few days ago had dissipated. She looked across at him as Persis and Rory rehearsed a scene. Matt's head was bowed as he wrote some notes in the margin of his script. It was as if she wasn't there. She had hardly been able to look away from him all morning: he barely seemed to realise that she was in the room.

Charles clapped his hands together. 'Great. We'll break for lunch. You've all been working very hard and I'm pleased with you. I thought that it might be nice to have lunch by the pool. We'll take a longer lunchbreak so that you can swim and relax, and then we'll eat. OK? I have a few things to see to in my study, and then I'll join you by the pool.'

The cast murmured their appreciation for this idea. Gina wasn't so sure. Given that there was only a two-week rehearsal period, she didn't think that they could spare precious rehearsal time to go swimming; besides, she didn't want Charles seeing her near-naked in a swimming costume. She decided that she would give her best friend Kirsten a call instead. She needed to be cheered up a bit, and Kirsten always managed that. Gina had noticed a telephone in the library during their guided tour on the first day, and didn't think that Charles would begrudge her the cost of a phone call, given all his other extravagances. The others had already wandered off to their respective bedrooms to change into their swimming costumes, so this was a perfect opportunity for a quiet and private chat with her friend.

She walked through to the library, pushing open the double doors and breathing in the musty smell of old books and leather armchairs. The library was very much a man's room. The walls were lined with mostly leather-bound antiquarian books which were ranged in mahogany cases, and the small area of bare wall by the door bore a set of four sporting engravings. Over the door was an old flintlock rifle. There were no carpets or rugs on the highly polished wooden floorboards, and no

135

curtains at the large bay window, just the tall internal wooden shutters. A couple of comfortable-looking armchairs were positioned on either side of the window, and in between these was a small mahogany table bearing the telephone and a notepad and pen.

Gina wandered over to the bookcases to see what sort of books Charles read. There were dusty biographies of Victorian worthies, some books about fly fishing, Gibbon's *The Decline and Fall of the Roman Empire*, some volumes of poetry. Nothing very remarkable, and nothing that really reflected Charles's character. Then she noticed a couple of titles by the Marquis de Sade, and smiled. That was more like it.

Outside, she could hear the laughter of the others as they splashed in the pool. Kicking off her shoes and drawing her feet up under her, she settled into one of the armchairs, and dialled Kirsten's number. The line seemed dead for a moment, and then crackled. It must be these rural exchanges, she thought to herself. They were probably not fully computerised yet. And then she heard a familiar voice. It was Charles.

'I tell you, Hugh, it's foolproof. Did you ever see that film, *The Producers*? That's what gave me the idea, and the more I looked into it, the better it got. It can't go wrong. I've set the whole production up to fail.'

Gina froze, unable to believe what she was hearing, scarcely daring to breathe lest she give herself away.

'Ah, but are you sure of failure?' another voice asked. 'Remember what happened in the film. How have you guaranteed failure?'

'Lots of ways, Hugh, lots of ways. The cast is completely made up of amateurs, apart from Persis, of course. But then, she's not far off from being one herself, despite what she might think. I'm throwing enough money at this to make a Cecil B. de Mille production look like cheap amateur dramatics in a village hall. I've got the top set and lighting designers working for me, and Mariangela Abruzzi is doing the costumes. She doesn't come cheap, and I've told her to use the finest materials, no expense spared. I'm paying the actors a ridiculous amount, and I've hired The Redditch, not that we'll be needing it for long. This show is going to bomb on its first night, guaranteed. It's going to be the most enormous tax loss you could imagine and, because I've also persuaded some rich morons to over-invest to the tune of some 400%, I get to keep the extra.'

Hugh whistled. 'Good grief, you're never one to do things by halves, are you, Charles?'

Charles laughed. 'You know me, Hugh. If I'm going to do something, I do it in style. Well, it's been nice talking to you. I must go. I have my charges to oversee. I'll catch up with you when I'm in London. Goodbye.'

Gina heard Charles put his receiver down, followed by the click as Hugh did likewise. She was left holding the phone to her ear, unable to take in what she had just heard. The shrill burr of the dialling tone seemed to drill into her head. Wild thoughts were scrambling and reeling through her mind as she tried to sort things out, to understand the full implications of Charles's words.

So many things were explained now: things which had seemed odd but which she had previously put down to Charles's philanthropy, his desire for the best. Now they were revealed as nothing more than mean-spirited financial transactions. Charles was investing in their failure.

It also explained why Charles had chosen a cast of amateurs, inexperienced and malleable; it explained why his direction had been at times so lax and at others seemingly perverse; why there were no understudies rehearsing with them; why the rehearsal period was so short; and why there were only two and a half days timetabled for rehearsals in the theatre itself. Charles had wanted them to be uncertain of their surroundings, so that, not knowing the set properly, they might fluff their entrances or get in a muddle with the props.

Gina was numb with shock. She could scarcely comprehend the depth of Charles's deceit. It meant nothing to him if their places at drama school were forfeited, if their prospects were ruined. She reflected bitterly that

Charles seemed to make a habit of trying to sabotage cultural events: first the carnival and now this. And what would have happened if it had not been for that fortuitous crossed line? Would she have found out only when it was too late? And how could she prevent it from becoming too late?

Outside she could hear the excited shouts of her colleagues, and then she heard Matt calling her name. She slowly put down the phone and walked, almost as if in a trance, out of the house and round to the swimming pool. Charles was already sitting in a lounger, dressed in knee-length khaki shorts and a T-shirt. She couldn't bear to look at him.

'Hey, why haven't you changed?' asked Sarah.

How ironic, thought Gina. You don't know it yet, but everything has changed. Gina muttered something about not wanting to swim, and went and sat as far away from Charles as she could manage, at one of the tables around the poolside, sheltering from the intense heat under the umbrella. She had to tell the others, as soon as she could. But she didn't know when she would be able to get them away from Charles.

After lunch, work continued. Gina was so preoccupied, she found it difficult to concentrate. The cast were rehearsing the scene that Gina dreaded the most. In it, Daniel had to hit her across the face. Daniel and Gina had spent a long time trying to make the blow seem as realistic as possible without actually making contact, but Charles was still not satisfied.

'Think, Daniel. Tim, your character, is absolutely furious with Gina, and with good reason. She's disobedient. She's treacherous. She's a thoroughly unpleasant woman.' Charles looked at Gina, and she knew that this was more than an analysis of her character's personality. This was what Charles thought of her. 'So, when you hit her, all your loathing for her is concentrated in that blow.'

Daniel nodded, and he and Gina set up the scene

again. Again, Daniel pulled the blow just before he reached Gina's face, and she swung her head violently away to mimic the force of the blow.

'No, no, Daniel,' said Charles, striding up to Gina. 'Like this.' Charles looked at Gina and, to her shock, he slapped her sharply on the cheek. Instantly furious, full of anger and fury and loathing, she acted instinctively. She swung her arm back and slapped him across the face as hard as she could.

Everyone had gone silent, shocked first by Charles's blow and then by Gina's response. Charles put his hand to his reddening cheek, a curious smile half-hidden by his hand.

'Thank you, Gina,' he said. 'You're learning. Very good. I enjoyed that.'

Gina could not tell if he was being sarcastic or serious. After what she had witnessed the previous night, either response seemed equally possible with Charles.

The work continued without further incident and, at five o'clock, Charles announced that the rehearsals were over for the day.

'I need to take Persis for some special instruction,' Charles said, as he left the room. As she followed him, Persis turned and grinned at her fellow actors.

'"Special instruction" my arse,' said Will. 'He's taking her off for a spot of the old horizontal gymnastics, I'll bet.'

Everyone laughed except Gina. Matt saw, and came over to her. 'Are you all right?' he asked. 'You seem a bit strained and out of sorts.' Gina smiled wearily. She was exhausted, both physically and emotionally, and the weight of her knowledge bore heavily on her. She had felt as if she had been sleepwalking through the rehearsals that afternoon. She knew that now was the time to inform her friends about what Charles was up to.

'Look, I've got something to tell you all,' she said, raising her voice to attract everyone's attention. She gestured at them to gather round, and then explained exactly what she had overheard that lunchtime. There was an appalled silence, then Sarah burst into tears. David put his arm round her and tried to comfort her.

'Hell,' was all Rory could say.

Matt looked absolutely furious. 'The bastard. I knew we were fools to trust him.'

'Well, what are we going to do?' asked Will.

'We can't pull out now. It's too late, and we'd never find another production. We'll have to see this one through,' said Daniel angrily.

Gina spoke up. 'Look, even if this is going to be a failure, it's not going to be because of us. We'll do our very best, heads held high. He's banking on us cocking this up. He obviously has no faith in our abilities whatsoever. But we know we can do this, don't we?' she asked, suddenly defiant. It was as if the disappointment and dejection of the others had jolted her out of her own.

'At the actual performances, we'll ignore his direction. It's been all to pot anyhow; we've all known that. We'll go with our own inclinations for the parts, OK? We can't do much about Persis's acting, I'm afraid, but we can help each other: constructive criticism, extra rehearsals. What do you say?'

'I think Gina's right,' said Matt. 'We can't let him get the better of us. This might be a financial failure, but it is going to be a critical success.'

'Why don't we start right now?' asked David. 'We can get in three hours' rehearsal before supper.'

'Right,' said Rory, clearing the chairs to the edge of the room. 'Let's get to it.'

It was two in the morning, and Gina couldn't sleep. She was fretting. The extra rehearsals had gone well, but she didn't know if they would be enough, and time was running out. Her sleeplessness was compounded by the hot and airless fug in the bedroom. She had pulled the hangings around the four-poster bed right back, thrown back the bed covers, and opened the windows as far as they would go, but it seemed to make little difference.

140

The night was so still that she could hear the gentle wash of the waves on to the beach in the distance.

She got up, went over to the basin, and moistened a flannel. Holding her hair up and pressing the flannel against the back of her neck, she stood at the window, hoping to catch any cooling breeze there might be. Nothing stirred. She felt the welcome sensation as the cold water from the flannel dribbled down the back of her neck and down her spine. She leant out of the window and breathed in the fresh damp smell of the dew settling outside, and decided that a walk in the cool grass might help.

She slipped on her silk robe and tied it loosely round her waist. Opening her door, she peered out into the darkness of the corridor. The house was as still and silent as the night outside. She thought that if she turned on the corridor light, she might disturb Charles, so she crept gingerly along to the staircase, her eyes gradually adjusting to the dark. Worried that the stair treads might be squeaky, she leant heavily on the handrail to take her weight as she slowly tiptoed down the stairs. Reaching the bottom, the coolness of the hallway's marble tiles on her bare feet provided some relief. She carefully pulled back the bolts on the front door, turned the key in the lock, and then opened the door, praying that it was well-oiled and would not betray her by squeaking.

The dew-laden, still, night air surrounded her, and she immediately felt herself relaxing. The moonlight was very bright, her way lit almost as clearly as if with a lamp. She tiptoed awkwardly over the gravel drive, wincing slightly as the small chips of stone dug into the soles of her feet, and quickly reached the lawn.

The grass was deliciously cool and damp. Gina swirled first one foot and then the other through the lush grass, feeling the dew drops trickling between her toes. On a sudden whim, she threw off her robe and lay back on the grass, feeling its soothing, cooling touch all over her body. She didn't really care if anyone saw her like this; but then again, who was likely to be about at gone two in the morning? She rolled on to her front, revelling in the sensations. She was reminded of the old country tradition of maidens bathing in the dew. Perhaps they too had slept in hot, airless rooms.

As she lay in the grass, she thought again of the extra rehearsals that evening. The cast had all worked hard, and they had felt a joint energy, a joint will to succeed. The concentration and effort were palpable, and by the end of the rehearsal they all agreed that they had achieved something important. But still Matt had seemed indifferent to her presence.

After a while, when she felt sufficiently cooled off, Gina got up from the grass and put her robe back on. The fine silk clung to the beads of moisture on her body, and moulded itself to her every curve. Her dew bath had fully woken her up, and she did not feel like going back to bed. She would explore the grounds in the bright moonlight.

Gina wandered down to the hothouse. She had not gone into it before. She peered in through the glass panes in the door, and then pushed it open. She was hit by the clinging and sultry heat with an almost physical force, and it felt as if her lungs were constricting as she breathed in the humid air.

The hothouse contained four long bench-like structures, two ranged against the long glass walls and the other two built together in the middle, leaving a path clear on either side. The waist-high benches were built of brick, topped with large marble slabs, and were covered with pots of lush plants, some of which climbed and scrambled up into the elaborate cast-iron girders supporting the roof of the hothouse, and hung down again in jungle-like tendrils.

High above her, Gina saw a swag of perfect pink orchids growing from the trunk of a thick vine-like plant. All around her, the gaudy colours and shapes of the leaves and flowers indicated an exotic origin; despite having closed up for the night, the scent emanating from the flowers was still strong and heady. Mingled with this

142

was another aroma: the smell of damp earth, of rich green mosses, of the tiny ferns which sprouted between the bricks of the path and in the sides of the benches. A fine mist hung in the air, dampening Gina's hair and settling in a light haze on her face.

Gina jumped as she heard a harsh squawk. Looking round, she saw a flash of brilliant colour fly past, then another. To her amazement, she realised that the hothouse was also home to a small flock of parrots. Gina found it hard to believe she was in England. It was as if she had been enveloped by a small part of the Amazonian rainforest.

She wandered up one of the pathways through the verdant plants, which were almost obscene in the fecundity of their growth. Her feet crushed the soft mosses and ferns as she passed, and she lifted one of her hands, allowing it to drift over the top of the plants, feeling the different textures of the leaves. She reached the far end of the hothouse, where a large rectangular pool built of marble was surrounded by yet more ferns and exotic plants. A small arc of water jetted up from the middle of the pool, falling back again on the surface of the water with a gentle pattering sound. Gina felt that she could stand here for hours, listening to the calming, almost hypnotic noise.

Lost in thought, Gina barely heard the creak of the door, and she started when she sensed that a man was standing next to her as she looked over the pool. Gina pulled her gown together across her breasts, suddenly aware of her near-nakedness. She looked at the man, and flushed as she noticed that he was only wearing a pair of cut-off denim shorts. Her embarrassment deepened when she recognised him. He was the man she had last seen with his penis deep in Sally Tobin's hungry mouth. She blushed at the memory, thankful that the man had not looked up and seen her at the window that day.

The man spoke. 'Hello, miss. I'm Steve, the gardener. I saw a movement in here, and wondered who it was. There're some very rare and valuable plants in here, not to mention the birds, and I thought that it might be burglars.' He looked at her with amusement. 'Obviously I was wrong.'

Gina felt foolish. There was no point in trying to explain what she had been doing.

Steve looked her up and down. 'It's a funny time to be looking at the plants, especially with the lights switched off. Couldn't sleep, maybe?' Gina felt the colour in her cheeks rising, and became painfully aware that the combined effect of the dew and then the humidity of the hothouse was making her silk robe near-transparent as it clung to her.

Gina nodded. 'Um, no, I couldn't. It's too hot in my room, really stifling. I came out for a breath of fresh air.'

'Well, I wouldn't exactly call it fresh air in here, would you?'

Gina smiled weakly. Steve continued. 'Mind you, the dew is nice and fresh, isn't it?' He smiled at her knowingly.

'Oh, you saw me,' she stammered, unnerved by the steadiness of his gaze, but tantalised, too.

'Very nice too. Don't get to see sights like that round here very often.' He looked her up and down again, his eyes seeming to devour her body. 'I like to go naked too, when I can. It feels so good, doesn't it? And it's such a shame to keep nature's glories covered up, don't you think?' He ran a hand over his broad tanned chest, over the muscles of his stomach, and let it rest at the waistband of his shorts.

Gina did not reply. Her heartbeat was increasing, and she knew she was at a junction. One path would lead to a good night's sleep; the other to seduction. Despite her tiredness, there was a delicious inevitability about which path her body would choose for her.

'You're looking very tense. Have you had a hard day's rehearsals? Would it help if I massaged you, just here, on the shoulders? I'm told I'm very good at it.' Steve moved to stand behind her, and slowly started to rub and knead her knotted shoulders through the silk. There

144

was no denying it, he had a sure and soothing touch. Gina felt some of the tensions of the day ebb away under his firm hands. She also felt something else – the unmistakable urges growing inside her.

'Oh, you like that, don't you? I can tell. Turn around, and I'll do your front.'

Silently, Gina turned to face Steve. She looked up at him as he raised his hands to her neck. Words were unnecessary. They knew their desire was met, and matched, in the other. With his hands resting on her shoulders, Steve massaged her, stroking her collarbone and neck with gentle but strong, sure sweeps of his thumbs. His hair was bleached by the sun, and his face was tanned to a deep golden-brown colour. Close to, he looked much younger than he had seemed before, when she had glimpsed him through the window.

As he massaged her neck, Gina felt warm relaxation spreading over her. Her eyes gradually drifted downwards, resting first on his neck, then his shoulders. All the digging and barrowing in the garden was obviously good exercise, for he was broad and muscular. She felt small in front of him, and it seemed to her that his closeness and overwhelming masculinity only emphasised her slightness and femininity. She wondered what it would feel like to be held in those arms, crushed close against that firm body.

His hands were stroking and squeezing now, moving along her shoulders and down the upper parts of her arms and then back again. She watched dreamily as the muscles of his shoulders and upper arms worked up and down as he massaged her. Then her gaze travelled down to his chest. Here too, the short hairs which spread across the wide expanse of his pectorals were bleached by the sun. His nipples were small, and a pale brown. Below his nipples, the mat of hair narrowed and continued downwards, centred in the groove of his stomach, between the two groups of pronounced abdominal muscles. She looked down, to see the hair disappear enticingly beyond the waistband of his shorts.

Steve saw where Gina's gaze had settled. He smiled at her.

'You like what you see, don't you?'

Gina swallowed and nodded. There was no point in denying it. Things had already gone too far.

'Would you like to see some more?' he asked. She nodded again. Steve brought his hands to the waistband of his shorts. He undid the first button, teasingly slowly, and then dropped his hands to his sides. The two small flaps of denim at the top of the shorts fell apart, and Gina could see a darker coiled mass of curls spreading out across his lower stomach. Then Steve brought his hands back and undid another button, and again removed his hands so that Gina could see. The second button had concealed the base of his cock, and now Gina could see it: the root of his fleshy shaft, still trapped by the denim. Its thickness showed that he was erect.

Now Gina's rising desire took over, and she brought up her hands to undo the last two buttons. She felt his hardness under her fingers through the material and, as she undid the last button and pulled the fly of his shorts wide apart, his cock slowly sprung up at her. She pushed his shorts down over his hips, and they fell to the ground round his feet. He stepped out of them and kicked them to one side. Then he stood there with his hands on his hips, regarding her almost challengingly, as if to say: Here I am. What are you going to do with me now?

She moved closer towards him, feeling the heat of his arousal emanating from his skin. She could smell him too: that sharp, musky tang of a sexually charged male. She reached out, and with one hand she cupped his balls. They too were covered in a fuzz of dark hair, and they rested with a heavy warm weight in her palm. With her other hand she gripped his penis near the base of his shaft and started to stroke it back and forth, feeling a tremendous surge of combined power and lust as he threw his head back and moaned with desire. She could feel him becoming even harder in her hand, and she knew that it would not be long before he ejaculated if she continued with her deft manipulations. She was not ready for him to come yet. She wanted pleasuring too.

Intuitively, Steve seemed to realise this, as he gently lifted her hand from his cock. He placed a hand on either side of her face and brought her towards him, kissing her softly on the lips. Their kisses were light at first, but then became more ravenous, their tongues meeting and swirling. He pulled her close against him and, with his strong arms about her, she could feel his stiff cock against her stomach through the thin film of silk that separated them. Steve kissed her face, then her neck, then started to work down her body. His hands were busy, finding the opening of her gown and pushing the material aside. The robe fell down, still tied at her waist, so that the top half of her body was exposed to him.

Now he had full access to her breasts. She wanted to feel his hot mouth against them, and she must have communicated her desire to him, as he buried his head against first one breast and then the other, nuzzling and kissing and nibbling. She gasped with surprise as he took a nipple in his mouth and nipped it sharply. Gina could not tell where the pain ended and the pleasure began. She draped her arms loosely around his neck as he caressed her breasts. Then his hands were busy again, feeling for the opening in her robe, hurriedly trying to push the material aside. He raised his mouth to hers once more and, still kissing her passionately, he found the knot of the tie and loosened it. The gown fell down over her hips, and she was at last naked. He stood back to regard her.

'You looked good on the lawn, but you look even better now,' he mumbled thickly, before stepping to one side of her and sweeping the pots off the nearest bench and on to the floor with one strong stroke of his arm. Gina barely registered the crashing and tinkling of the pots, so great was her desire for him. Then he came to her again and, with his lips clamped to hers, lifted her as easily as if she were weightless up and over the broken sherds. Automatically, she wrapped her legs round his waist, and he held her with his hands on her buttocks. He stood, motionless, as they kissed deeply. She could feel his penis throbbing against the groove of her buttocks, and the mixture of his perspiration, the dew which still remained on her, and the humidity of the hothouse made their bodies slick and slippery against each other.

Still locked in their embrace, Steve shuffled towards the bench, and moving his hands to round her waist he placed her so that she was sitting facing him on the edge of the bench, as he stood between her legs. They broke free from their kiss, and Steve put his hands on her thighs and eased them even further apart. He then dropped to his knees. His head was right in front of her vagina, which was now so moist that she could feel her juices trickling down and out of her. She could feel his breath close on her inner thighs and on her sex, and then she heard him breathe in deeply, taking in her scent. The anticipation was too much. She lay back on the marble surface of the bench, which was gloriously cool against her feverish skin, and closed her eyes, waiting for the touch of his hot mouth.

It came soon, the soft dabs of his lips against her thigh, then her lips, and then inward, towards her opening. She felt him spread her labia with his mouth and bury his face deep into her; then she felt his tongue, licking and swirling at the entrance to her vagina. He licked her with long strokes from her opening up to her clitoris and back again. Gina could not help herself. She brought her hands to her breasts, and started to massage her nipples, and then to knead her full, firm globes in her hands. The overwhelming carnality of the moment had taken over, and all she could think of was satiating her desire. She willed him to go right into her with his tongue; but he was in control, teasing and licking, tantalising her to distraction.

She spread her thighs even further apart, and felt down for his head, grasping his bleached curls as she pulled him towards her in an effort to force him deeper into her. He sensed her frustration, and slowly slid his hot, fleshy tongue into her vagina. His hands had been grasping her thighs, but he released his grip and brought one hand up to her hooded clitoris, and slowly started to press with a gentle circling rhythm. He replaced his tongue with his other hand, rising to his feet before her as he slid first two and then three fingers into her.

Gina gasped as he started to move his fingers in and out, twisting and turning them as he did so, with the same rhythm with which he was caressing her clitoris. She opened her eyes and raised her head slightly to look at his face. She saw that he was gazing down between her legs. She knew that what he saw, the sight of his two hands massaging her to a climax, would be almost too stimulating for him to bear. She looked down too, and could see his prick straining against his stomach, a clear bead of semen trembling on the tip.

'Come into me, Steve,' she whispered. Suddenly she needed more than fingers. She needed to be filled, to be stretched, to be possessed by this fit, handsome young man. He needed no further bidding. He grasped his prick round the base and brought it down to level with her vagina. He rubbed its hot, hard tip over her glistening opening several times, still teasing her. Then he put his hands on her hips and, leaning over her, he pushed his penis firmly and slowly into her. She moaned with delight, and wrapped her legs around his waist again.

Gina felt herself being pushed backwards and forwards on the bench as he started to thrust deep inside her. She cried out again, and her cries gradually increased in both volume and frequency as he moved inside her with greater and greater speed. She didn't care now who heard. All she wanted was to reach that blinding climax which had been building for so long. She needed to be released, but Steve wasn't going to let her come. He slowed down again, toying with her, thrusting now in an erratic rhythm so that she could not synchronise her movements with his.

Then he slid his hands below her waist and, their bodies still locked together at the loins, scooped her up

149

off the bench so that she was now sitting on his penis, with her legs around his waist. His legs were partly bent at the knees, allowing him the flexibility to thrust deep into her. She writhed in his grasp, her arms snaking around his neck, grasping his shoulders, then kneading his arms.

Impaled on his hard cock, she felt fuller than she had ever felt before. Steve was so deep inside her it was almost too intense to bear. With his strong arms still round her waist, he was lifting her up and down over his prick, seemingly without effort. Again he speeded up, and this time she could feel that his orgasm was imminent. This realisation triggered off her own, and Gina strained against his hands which he had now moved to the small of her back, arching backwards as she felt the surging pulse of her climax. His followed almost immediately, and he cried out with relief as his orgasm was finally unleashed. Gina wilted in his arms as she recovered from the onslaught. Exhausted, he leant back against the bench and held her close to him as they basked in the after-glow. After a while he gently lowered her to her feet.

As Gina put her robe back on, Steve looked at her and grinned. 'Any time you can't sleep, you know where to come.'

A shape sunk back into the darkness of the shrubbery as first Gina, and then Steve, left the hothouse. Persis waited a few minutes until she was sure that the coast was clear, and then followed Gina back across the lawn and into Digby House. Charles would be very interested to hear of this.

Chapter Eight

'Right, that's rehearsals over for the day. Off you go,' Charles said to the cast. Persis went to the table in the corner of the room to gather up the belongings that she invariably brought to rehearsals every day and never used: a Gucci handbag, a Chanel scarf, and a key-ring with a large and prominent Mercedes fob. Gina knew that all these were for show. Persis hadn't used her car since the day she arrived at Digby House, yet the key-ring was always left on the table rather than in her handbag. Subtlety was not one of Persis's defining characteristics, Gina thought.

Charles repeated himself. 'Off you go. You're free to enjoy yourselves now.'

No one moved. Daniel spoke up quietly. 'We thought we'd do some extra rehearsals, Charles.'

Charles looked surprised. 'May I ask why? Do you feel that rehearsals under me are inadequate?'

'No, it's not that at all,' Matt explained. 'We've all paid close attention to your notes, and want to rehearse with your directions in mind, so that we get everything just right for you.'

Clever Matt, thought Gina. Charles was so conceited and so egotistical that flattery was sure to work with him. Charles nodded, and looked pleased.

'I'm glad to see that you're all taking this so seriously,' he said. Charles was such a good actor that he ought to be in the play, Gina thought bitterly. In truth, he didn't care one jot about how hard they rehearsed, or how good their performances were. As far as he was concerned, they were wasting their time.

'Well, I certainly don't feel that I require any extra rehearsals,' said Persis petulantly. She regarded the other members of the cast. 'Still, maybe you are right. I have noticed that some of you certainly need it.' Persis picked up her things and flounced out of the room. Charles followed.

After late rehearsals and then dinner, Gina decided to go for a walk. It was a lovely evening, not yet dark though the soft twilight was imminent, and at last there was a cooling breeze coming in off the sea. Gina felt a nagging restlessness. It was as if her nervous energy, her intense concentration on the rehearsals and all her concerns about the production were finally bubbling over. She was unable to hold her worries back. She was also fretting about her lack of progress with Matt. If nothing had happened between them by now, surely it never would? She regretted that she had never, in the end, made the phone call to Kirsten, but she couldn't call her now, as there would be little privacy in Digby House. She thought that a solitary walk might help to clear her head a bit, and to put things in perspective.

She made her way down through the woods and on to the deserted beach. The tide was on its way out. She took off her shoes and walked along on the wet sand, where the occasional wave broke over her feet. She looked out to sea, and watched the white-crested waves slowly building and moving towards her in a steady rhythm, before they broke into a frothy spume, bubbled up the beach and then receded again.

Gina heard a dog bark in the distance. Bending over, she picked up a flattish stone and tried to skim it over the waves, but the sea was too choppy and it disappeared in front of a breaking wave. Her reverie was broken by a cold wet touch against her hand. She jumped slightly with surprise and looked down. There was Fern, Helena's greyhound, sniffing and licking her salty hand. She looked round, scanning for her friend, and saw two figures at the far end of the beach, walking towards her, hand in hand. One of the figures raised its arm and waved, and she knew instantly that it was Helena. Marius was with her. Smiling, Gina hurried to meet them. The breeze was sharpening now, and Gina could see the wind whipping Helena's long cotton peasant skirt against her legs, and blowing her loose cotton blouse about her like a flag.

'Hello there,' Helena called above the wind, brushing some strands of hair back from her face. 'What are you doing here all on your own? Not moping, I hope!'

Gina put her arms round first Helena and then Marius, and kissed them in greeting.

'Oh, it's really cheered me up to see you,' she said.

'Ah, so I was right. You were moping,' said Helena.

Gina shrugged her shoulders. 'Well, you know us actresses. Once a drama queen, always a drama queen.'

Marius put his arm around Gina's shoulder and gave her a comforting hug. 'If you've got a problem, don't make light of it, Gina. Would you like to talk about it?'

Gina was touched by their concern. 'Yes, please.'

'Come on home with us then.' Marius proffered Gina his arm, and she took it happily. They walked back along the beach and up through the woods, slowly making their way back to Chitherleigh Manor. Once out of the trees, they followed a narrow path beaten through a meadow full of high grasses and flowers. Gina felt the dew brushing off on her legs, and was momentarily reminded of her dew bath and what had followed. She smiled to herself, wondering what Steve was doing right now.

The path brought them out on to an area of rough lawn, with croquet hoops and mallets lying around on the grass, looking as if they had been dropped only minutes earlier. A hammock was strung between two old apple trees at the side of the lawn. At the far end of the lawn was a wide flower bed and beyond it, the back of the manor house. It looked just as beautiful as it did from its front aspect.

Marius opened a door and led them through the utility room and into the kitchen.

'Don't you lock your doors when you go out?' Gina asked with surprise, thinking of her own front door in London with its Fort-Knox-like number of chains and deadlocks.

'No need to round here,' said Helena casually. 'We don't lock the cars either. Everyone is as honest as the day is long. Well, everyone except you-know-who, that is.'

Gina knew without asking who it was that Helena was referring to.

'You go on through, and I'll bring the drinks,' said Marius, opening a cupboard in the kitchen and getting down three glasses.

Gina followed Helena into the small cosy room which had been one of the parlours in Tudor times. Gina was immediately struck by the scent of fragrant wood smoke. She looked down and was surprised to see a fire burning in the large stone fireplace. A couple of logs were balanced on some cast-iron fire-dogs, straddling a large pile of grey wood ash, and there were glowing embers in the centre of the ash. Gina's surprise at seeing a fire burning in mid-summer prompted Helena to explain. 'We love having fires. It cheers the place up no end because, despite the heat outside, it always stays pretty cool in here, what with the two-foot-thick walls. And also, it's a slight indulgence on my part as I adore the smell of applewood as it burns.' She breathed in deeply to emphasise her point.

Flanking the fireplace and facing each other were two huge, deep and sagging sofas. They were covered with embroidered Middle Eastern textiles and fat cushions which had covers made from old kilims. There was a

154

beautiful Persian silk carpet on the floor between the sofas. Next to each sofa was a small table. Helena kicked off her shoes and threw herself down on one of the sofas, and gestured at Gina to do the same. Marius came in with a tray bearing the three small glasses and several bottles.

'Home-made liqueurs,' he beamed as he put the tray down. 'I'm rather proud of these.' He pointed at the various bottles and described their contents: 'There's damson gin, sloe vodka, this one's made from beech leaves which have been steeped for several months in gin, and this one from hawthorn blossom soaked in brandy. You must try them all.'

As Marius poured the first glassful, Helena closed her eyes and settled back voluptuously into the cushions. She reminded Gina of a portrait of an odalisque in an eastern harem.

Marius handed Gina the small cut-glass liqueur glass. Its contents were a deep ruby-red, almost glowing in the low firelight. She took a sip of the sweet, syrupy liquid, which tasted strongly of damsons. It was delicious, and headily alcoholic. Gina felt so calm and relaxed here, with her new friends in their beautiful house, full of lovely things. Why couldn't she feel like this at Digby House?

'So, Gina, apart from the unwelcome attentions of Mr Sarazan, how's your love life?' Helena asked. 'Have you met Steve yet?'

Gina looked up sharply, wondering if Helena knew or if this was a lucky guess.

'Oh, don't look like that. I only meant that he's a very friendly young man.' Helena laughed. 'Very accommodating.'

'You mean you . . .'

'Oh, come on, Gina. Who can resist the attentions of a hoary-handed gardener, eh? Shades of *Lady Chatterley's Lover*, don't you think?'

'Actually, Lady Chatterley's lover was the gamekeeper,' said Marius.

'Oh, don't be such a pedant, Marius darling.' Helena turned to Gina. 'To even things up between us, Marius has sampled the delights of the Digby House housekeeper, Sally Tobin. I expect you've met her.'

Gina was bemused. 'Does Charles know about this?' she asked.

Helena laughed. 'No, and that's what makes it so much fun, sneaking around behind his back. One time Marius and Sally were making love in the hallway right outside the dining room while Charles was holding a grand and very important dinner party for some of his business associates. Sally had to keep breaking off to go in to clear the dishes and serve the next course.'

Gina was surprised that Marius had shared such intimate details with his wife. Wasn't she jealous? Helena seemed able to read Gina's mind.

'You're wondering how I know all this, aren't you? Well, I was sitting on the stairs, watching. Marius and I share everything. The fact that Charles would have erupted had he found out gave it all that extra *frisson*. On second thoughts, that would have been rather fun, too, don't you think?'

Gina was curious to know more about Marius and Helena's open relationship, but too embarrassed to ask directly. She was fascinated to hear Helena talk of it so matter-of-factly, and couldn't deny that she found the idea appealing.

'Gina darling, you still haven't told us about your love-life. I take it from your response that you've had a liaison with Steve. Anyone else?'

Gina smiled and nodded. The alcohol was starting to take effect, helping to loosen her tongue as well as relax her body. 'Yes. But not with the person I really want. It's funny, I can act like a complete sex-starved harlot with other people, and take sex purely for my own satisfaction and to fulfil my needs: no ties, no commitment. But when it comes to someone I feel something for, mentally and emotionally as well as physically, I become as demure as a nun. I'm so reserved with him – this man in the cast – that I'm not even sure that he's aware that I'm interested, let alone that what I really want is to throw him on to the nearest bed and ravish him until he's like a quivering lump of jelly.'

'Don't give up hope,' said Helena. 'I'm sure you'll get through to him in the end. So what about this other liaison you've had?'

Taking another large, relaxing swig of liqueur, Gina started to tell them about her encounter with Will in the sunken garden. Helena clapped her hands together with delight. 'Go on, more, more! We want all the details.' Gina looked over at Marius, who was sitting in a thronelike oak chair, cupping his glass in one hand and regarding her watchfully. Gina felt the familiar erotic charge racing through her.

As she told them about making love with Will that lunchtime, she steadily held Marius's gaze, gauging his reactions as she offered titbits of her sexual encounter. Listening intently, Helena moved slightly on the sofa, making herself more comfortable and allowing her hand to rest over her left breast. She idly stroked it through her blouse. Gina could tell that Helena was pleased by the attention that was being paid to her husband.

Gina finished her story, and looked across at Helena. 'Look, your glass is empty,' said Helena. 'Fill her up, Marius darling.'

Marius got up from his chair and selected another bottle. As he approached Gina, his eyes were fixed on hers. Holding his gaze, Gina held up her glass. Marius gave her a knowing smile as he filled her glass with the sloe vodka, which was a deeper purply colour than the previous liqueur.

'Oh, this is the same colour as one of my costumes,' Gina giggled, and immediately felt stupid for having said something that sounded so childish and unsophisticated. She covered up her embarrassment by hurriedly taking a large slurp of the liqueur. It was much stronger than the damson gin. She could feel herself becoming slightly warm and woozy with the effect of all the alcohol and the heat of the fire, and so she loosened the top few buttons of her blouse.

'Mariangela Abruzzi is your costume designer, I believe,' said Helena.

'How did you know that?' asked Gina.

'You don't read the women's glossies, do you, darling?' laughed Helena. 'There was an article about her in one of them this month, and it mentioned that *Riding to the Thames* was her new project. Lucky you. Do you get to keep the costumes at the end of the run?'

'I doubt it, knowing Charles,' said Gina, taking another sip of the vodka. It really was very good indeed.

'So tell us more about your amorous adventures,' said Helena. 'Who else have you had a dalliance with?'

Gina laughed. 'Well, I suppose I had one with Miss Abruzzi, of sorts.'

Helena sat up, barely able to conceal her interest. 'Oh yes? Do tell,' she said.

'Well, maybe I misread the signs, but during my fitting with her she was very attentive, and she touched me a bit more than she needed to.'

'Well, who can blame her? Faced with a beautiful woman like Gina, anyone would do the same,' said Marius. Gina looked at the floor and blushed becomingly.

'How did you feel when she touched you?' asked Helena.

'I was a bit confused, I guess,' Gina replied.

Helena looked at Gina penetratingly. 'But were you turned on?'

'If I'm honest, yes, I was.'

'So why didn't you do something about it?' Marius asked, leaning forward eagerly in his chair.

'Um, I don't know.'

'Have you ever made love with a woman before, Gina?' Helena asked.

'No, I haven't.'

'How do you feel about the idea of making love to

158

another woman?' asked Marius, moving his chair a little closer. Gina hesitated. 'Be honest,' Marius instructed.

'I like it,' Gina whispered, embarrassed to have finally voiced a secret thought.

'So if the opportunity were to present itself, you would like to make love to a woman? Would it fulfil another of your needs?' he asked.

Gina nodded. Her heart was thumping so rapidly she thought she could almost hear its beat in her ears.

'Do you prefer the other person to make the first move?' asked Helena.

Gina could feel her mouth drying. She swallowed. 'Well, perhaps, yes.'

'Like this?' asked Helena, getting up from the sofa, moving over to where Gina was sitting. Gina hardly dared draw a breath. Helena sat next to her on the sofa and put an arm up to Gina's neck and started to stroke it very gently. Gina looked across at Marius, who was still seated in his chair. He was regarding her steadily, his interest obvious.

Gina's eyes glazed over as Helena continued her steady stroking. 'How does that feel?' asked Helena.

'Relaxing,' replied Gina truthfully. The rhythm was so soothing. But she hadn't told the whole truth: she was feeling other things as well. Helena placed her other hand on Gina's thigh and started to caress it languidly. 'You have a beautiful body, Gina. I would like to see more of it, if you would let me,' she murmured, her lovely face close to Gina's. Gina could feel the rush of arousal: the rising, driving need for fulfilment. She would not object to whatever it was that Helena wanted to do.

Helena reached over and slowly started to unbutton Gina's blouse, bending her head to kiss the soft flesh as she gradually exposed it. Unable to quite take in what was happening to her, Gina looked over Helena's bowed head at Marius. Surely he would object? But he was smiling, and gently stroking the bowl of his liqueur glass as he watched. When Helena had undone all the buttons,

159

she slowly pushed the two sides of material apart. Gina was not wearing a bra. Her breasts rose and fell with her rapid breaths. Gina gasped as Helena slowly grazed her lips over them, searching for and finding a nipple. She sucked and licked and nibbled and rolled Gina's nipple with her tongue, and Gina brought both her hands up to cradle Helena's head as she kissed her breast. Gina closed her eyes, lost in desire, and wondering what Helena would do next.

She did not have to wait long to find out. She felt Helena's hands stroking her stomach, and then feeling for the fastening at the side of her chinos. A brief unzipping noise, and then Gina felt the release from the pressure of the waistband of her trousers. Still kissing Gina's breasts, Helena reached down and slowly eased Gina's chinos down over her hips. The contact between Gina's tender, aching breasts and Helena's eager mouth was broken as Helena reached down to pull the trousers off over Gina's feet. Gina lay back on the sofa as she did so, feeling overcome by absolute wantonness. She now scarcely noticed Marius's still but intense presence; all she could focus on was the proximity of Helena and the delicious suspense, waiting for her next move.

'You lie back and let me see to you,' whispered Helena, as she crawled back up over Gina's nearly naked and prostrate body and kissed her lightly on the lips. Gina thought how deliciously soft and plump Helena's lips were, so different from a man's. She could faintly taste Helena's lipstick, and could smell her delicious perfume.

Helena looked down at Gina's body. 'Magnificent. You ooze sex, Gina. No wonder Charles is hung up on you.'

She leant forward again, and kissed Gina again, deeper and more hungrily this time. Gina responded eagerly. The softness of Helena's mouth was exquisite. The two women exchanged tiny nibbling kisses, between deeper more probing ones, their tongues delving and exploring.

Gina ran her hands through Helena's hair, feeling the silky softness of her cascading tresses.

Helena lazily stroked Gina's breasts, and then worked slowly down her stomach with faint brushes of her fingertips. She paused when she reached the gentle swell of Gina's stomach, and then leant down and placed a long, slow kiss on Gina's navel, her tongue probing into the small dimple. This was almost too intense for Gina to bear, and she could not stop herself from moving, trying to shift her body so that Helena's searching tongue was guided elsewhere, somewhere lower.

Then Gina felt Helena's hands running up on either side of her hips, brushing over the thin bands of the sides of her thong. She wondered if she ought to bring a halt to this, but other urges were controlling her now. As Gina lay on the sofa, her head thrown back and sunk into a cushion, she felt another, different sensation: light drifts of hot breath on her cheeks. She looked up to see Marius leaning over her. He lowered his head and kissed her gently on the lips. At the same time, she could feel Helena slowly sliding her thong down over her hips.

Gina moaned with mounting desire. She lay in total abandon, with two people worshipping her body, and pleasuring her with no thought of their own needs.

Still leaning over, and kissing Gina deeply, Marius gently placed his hands at the sides of her breasts. She tried to twist her torso to bring his hands into contact with them. He responded by slowly sliding his hands up on to her breasts, brushing them with the palms of his hands, and teasing her hard nipples with gentle strokes of his fingers. Helena stood back and regarded Gina, who now lay naked below her on the sofa.

Gina opened her eyes, to see Helena slowly pulling her blouse off over her head without pausing to undo the buttons. She was not wearing a bra either, and her breasts were small and pert. Helena then stooped and slid her skirt down and off in a single, fluid motion. She was naked under her skirt; her body was a beautiful nut-brown, with an all-over tan which Gina knew must have resulted from hours of wandering round the manor grounds in the nude. Gina looked at Helena, taking in her long, slim legs, her flat stomach, the sumptuous curve of her hips. She was stunning, and now Gina felt nothing but lust.

Helena saw Gina regarding her. 'So, what do you think?' she asked.

'Come here and I'll show you,' replied Gina. All doubts had receded in the wake of the close attentions being paid to her body, and the allure of Helena's beauty. Marius was still lightly brushing Gina's breasts, stopping every now and then to lean over Gina again and kiss her on the lips.

'Will you let me watch?' he whispered to Gina. 'Two beautiful women together. Too much.'

All inhibitions dispelled now, Gina nodded, as Helena lowered herself down into Gina's waiting arms. Gina could feel the fleshy weight of Helena's breasts against her own, and her arms snaked around Helena's waist, revelling in the softness of her skin, and the slimness of her waist. Their legs entwined as they kissed deeply. Marius moved away again and sat back in his chair, and Gina could tell that he was pleased with what he surveyed. Being watched closely made it all the more thrilling for Gina.

As they kissed, the two women began the slow journey of intimate discovery. Gina timidly brought her hand up to touch Helena's breast. She was aroused to feel the soft swell against her palm and then the hard tip of the nipple pressing against her fingers. She caressed it gently, before lowering her head to kiss Helena's breast.

Helena whispered to Gina. 'Let me make love to you on the rug. It'll be more comfortable.' She raised herself up from Gina and slid off the sofa and on to the rug on the floor in front of the fire. She held out a hand and Gina joined her. It was the most natural thing in the world.

The two women lay on their sides, facing each other. Helena drew Gina close and kissed her again, and then pushed her very gently so that she was lying on her back. Still kissing, once again Helena's hand drifted over Gina's body until it reached her lower stomach. Gina could feel her heartbeat thundering. Helena slowly slipped her fingers into the soft curls of Gina's pubic hair, and played with it with her finger tips. Then her fingers slipped lower, over Gina's fleshy mound and towards her innermost place. She stopped. Gina could feel her clitoris hardening with desire under its soft fleshy hood, waiting for Helena's touch. She looked up at Helena, who smiled. 'Shall I continue?' she teased.

'Please,' gasped Gina. Helena ran the tip of her middle finger over Gina's hooded nub and back again, gently and expertly teasing and flicking. Gina could feel the swell of juices in her vagina, and gasped again with sharp desire as Helena slowly slid her finger down over her clitoris once more and then along Gina's moist opening. Involuntarily, Gina parted her thighs, allowing Helena easier access. Helena's finger paused tantalisingly for a moment, and then slipped inside Gina. Wet with desire, Gina urged Helena on: 'More, I need more.' Helena removed her finger and then Gina felt a slight stretching and realised that Helena was now filling her with two fingers, then three.

Helena moved with a gentle rhythm, and then Gina felt another sensation: Helena began to caress her clitoris slowly with her thumb. This was too much, and Gina instantly felt the rushing coursing of her orgasm overcome her. Helena looked down at her tenderly as Gina rode the waves of her climax, arching and shaking and then gently collapsing back on to the rug.

Before she had time to fully recover, Helena was moving over her body again. This time she was covering Gina's breasts and stomach with more light, drifting kisses.

She looked up at Gina. 'Will you let me taste you?' she asked. Gina nodded, and Helena moved lower. Automatically, Gina parted her legs further, and Helena nuzzled her way down her stomach and to the downy hairs. She breathed in deeply. 'You smell so good,' she said, before burying her face in Gina's groin. Gina could feel Helena's silky hair brushing on her stomach, and the hot rush of her breath lower down, and finally her soft tongue, as Helena started to lick Gina's juices from her outer labia.

Then Helena's hands were sliding round by her hips and moving below her, catching a buttock in either hand and raising her slightly off the floor. Helena lifted Gina to her lips and kissed her deeply, probing her inner folds with her agile tongue. Gina gasped as Helena thrust her tongue deep into her vagina, licking and kissing and teasing; she moaned with ecstasy as she felt the pulsing waves of another orgasm mounting.

Then Helena moved upwards, and took Gina's clitoris in between her lips with a gentle kiss. Gina could not keep from writhing with excitement and desire, her bud hardening yet more at Helena's touch. She cried out and arched her back up as Helena brought her to another shuddering climax. Behind her, Gina heard Marius calling out, and knew that his solitary viewing had brought him satisfaction, too.

It was much later. Sated, Gina lay in a state of complete exhaustion. Each of her senses had been overstimulated, tattered, almost worn out. Helena was curled up against her, stroking the soft flesh of Gina's stomach. The glow of the firelight softly illuminated their naked bodies. Marius was still seated in his throne-chair, ever watchful.

'So, Gina. Did you like that?' Helena whispered in Gina's ear.

Gina smiled, and murmured her assent. She was almost too weary, too worn out by their lovemaking to speak. Helena had truly shown her the joys of Sapphic love. Always in control, she had not allowed Gina to reciprocate. 'Another time,' she had whispered. Gina reflected on how different this kind of dominance was from that of Charles. His was to do with taking pleasure for himself, whereas Helena's had been completely about giving.

Helena spoke without opening her eyes. 'Now we've helped you to relax, tell us your problems. Maybe we can help with those too.'

As she lay in Helena's arms, Gina told her two friends all about what she had overheard that day in the library. She was still shocked by the duplicitousness of Charles's plans, even though she knew his character well enough by now; her hurt and dismay was evident in her retelling of the whole sorry story. As she recounted it, Helena first opened her eyes, and then sat upright. She pulled one of the embroidered hangings over her, and sat poised and listening intently. When Gina finally finished, Helena drew in a deep breath.

'Oh dear, he's up to his old tricks again.'

'You mean he's done this before?' asked Gina, aghast.

Marius spoke. 'Well, something in a similar vein, but much worse. Not that I want to suggest that what you're going through isn't bad, of course.'

Gina looked at him expectantly, waiting for an elaboration. Whatever was worse than Charles destroying the prospective careers of seven young actors had to be pretty bad. Marius seemed unwilling to say anything. He looked at Helena questioningly. She leant forwards towards Gina.

'We weren't going to tell you, because we didn't want to worry you unnecessarily. But I suppose it's all rather academic now, in the light of what you've just told us. It's not a pleasant tale. You see, Charles hasn't always lived in Digby House. Up until last year, it was owned by Cecil Doughty, Charles's uncle. Cecil was a lovely old man, one of our best friends. Everyone liked him: he was kind and generous, but a bit eccentric. He never married, and made Charles his heir. But Charles couldn't wait for nature to take its course and for Cecil to die: he wanted Digby House for himself as soon as possible. He got a crooked doctor friend of his to certify Cecil, to have him sectioned under the Mental Health Act; so poor Cecil was bundled off to a mental hospital, with his eccentricity passed off as proof of his insanity.'

Gina was appalled. 'But ... couldn't someone have done something to get the poor man out?'

'We tried, as soon as we found out what had happened, but poor Cecil was so broken by all this that he died only two days after being admitted to the hospital. He just gave up. He couldn't bear to be away from Digby House, and couldn't live with the knowledge of what his own nephew had done to him. And so Charles inherited the lot.'

Gina reeled with the shock of this new information. Charles was not just a bad, unscrupulous man: he was an evil man.

'That man is a complete bastard,' said Marius. 'We can't let him get away with it again, not after what he did to Cecil and now what he's planning to do to you and your friends. He needs to be taught a lesson.'

Helena smiled. 'And we're just the people to do it,' she said.

Gina had refused the Burckhardts' offer of a lift home. They had all had too much to drink to consider driving, and she wanted the walk back to Digby House to clear her head and hopefully to sober up a bit too. Mostly, however, she wanted to be on her own to reflect on what had just happened: the delicious unexpectedness of the lovemaking – lying in a woman's arms, experiencing some of the sweetest orgasms she had ever known – followed by the awfulness of Helena's revelation about Charles. Ignoring Marius and Helena's protestations, she did however accept the offer of a torch. She knew the way back through the woods, and it was a much more direct route than following the winding country lanes.

It was almost one o'clock when she arrived at the front door of Digby House. She hoped that the door wouldn't be locked as she reached for the big brass doorknob. She turned it slowly, and was relieved when the heavy door swung open; with her head bowed in concentration, she turned to close it behind her as quietly as she could. As she turned again to tiptoe across the hallway, she received an unpleasant surprise. Charles was standing not a foot away from her, and she almost bumped straight into him. She had not heard him approaching, and knew with a sinking feeling that she would not be allowed to her room without some sort of retribution having taken place first.

'Good evening, Gina,' said Charles. 'Or maybe I should make that "Good morning", given the time. You do know what the time is, don't you?'

Gina nodded. Charles's voice was a menacing low whisper. 'So, Gina, would you kindly tell me what the time is?'

Gina looked at her watch. 'One o'clock,' she said quietly. She knew that the ritual humiliation was beginning.

Charles took in a deep breath, contemplating what she had just said. 'One o'clock. And tell me, Gina, what time is the curfew here at Digby House?'

'Ten o'clock,' she said, looking at him defiantly.

'So, by my reckoning, that makes you three hours late. Oh dear. That's rather careless of you. Would you mind telling me where you have been?'

Gina didn't see any point in trying to cover up her movements. Charles would find out sooner or later.

'With the Burckhardts.'

'The Burckhardts.' Charles pronounced their name with evident distaste. 'The slut and the lothario. What company you choose to keep, Gina. I'm very disappointed in you.'

'You know, Charles, I really don't care what you think. They're my friends.'

'Well, maybe you will care what I think, when I tell you that I will dismiss you if you disobey me again. I am being lenient with you this time, but you saw what happened to David and Sarah. That punishment awaits you if you defy me again. So don't let me hear again of you associating with the Burckhardts.' Charles almost spat out their name. 'Go to your room, and don't forget this warning.'

Gina felt that arguing back would be counter-productive, as she knew that she had been let off lightly. But Charles couldn't stop her from seeing her friends. That wasn't in her contract, or part of the rules he had laid down on the first day. She brushed past him angrily, and hurried up to her room. She heard Charles going into his study downstairs, and wondered what he was up to at this late hour. Hatching another deceitful plan, perhaps.

As Gina walked along the corridor to her room, she noticed that the door to the room opposite hers was ajar, and a sliver of light was thrown from the room out into the darkened corridor. This was Daniel's room. Gina wanted to talk to someone, and as Daniel was obviously still awake, she thought she would go over and see him. Charles wouldn't hear from his study. She walked over to the door, her hand raised and ready to knock, when she heard a muffled noise from within the room that made her pause. She could hear low moaning: a man's moan, and indisputably a heavy moan of sexual arousal. There was no way that Daniel would be involved with Persis, that was for sure; so she reckoned that his partner must be Sarah, despite her punishment the other night. Gina knew that she shouldn't look, but the urge was too great to resist. She pushed the door very slightly, and it swung half open.

Gina gingerly peered around the door, wondering if Daniel and Sarah would have noticed its movement. What she saw was not what she expected. In the low light cast from the lamp on the bedside table, she saw Daniel standing naked and locked in an embrace with Rory, who was also naked. The two men were kissing with an extraordinary passion, and it looked as if they were trying to devour each other. Daniel's lean and pale body seemed enveloped by Rory's much darker, hairier and more muscular form. Their hands were swiftly caressing each other's bodies, and Gina could see their erections, pressing hard up against their stomachs as they kissed.

Gina was surprised and turned on at the same time. She had never seen two men together like this before, and had not thought that she would find it so arousing. Both men had beautiful bodies. Something about the way they were touching each other told her that they were making love, not just having sex. This was something private, and so she quietly withdrew from the room, and returned to her own bedroom. She quickly stripped off her clothes and stepped into her robe, and then crept past Daniel's still open door along the corridor to one of the bathrooms.

In the shower she mulled over the day's events. She had been surprised by how natural it had felt to be made love to by Helena. She wanted more, to touch Helena in the same way, to feel her and to taste her. As she soaped her body, she felt again the touch of Helena's hands on her breasts. She allowed her hands to drift lasciviously over her body in much the same way that Helena's had done earlier that evening. She also wondered at Marius's self-control, to be able to watch two women making love and to be able to withhold from joining in. And then she thought about the day's other same-sex couple, Daniel and Rory, and her hands slipped lower, feeling her heat and urgency again, a need that had to be fulfilled.

She took the showerhead from the wall and let the warm water play over her stomach and trickle down over her burning sex. Then she shifted so that her legs were slightly apart, and directed the jet of water between her legs. The hot patter of thousands of tiny jets of water against her throbbing clitoris felt so good and, as she pictured Daniel and Rory and wondered what they were doing, the powerful streams of water brought her to yet another climax. She felt her legs buckle slightly under her, and she leant against the steamy tiles of the shower as her orgasm played itself out against the spurting water.

Towelling herself off afterwards, the image of Rory

and Daniel was still strongly imprinted in her mind. She had always thought that everything about Rory was ultra-masculine, completely and almost aggressively heterosexual. It just showed her how deceptive appearances could be. She wondered that she had not seen any signs of an attraction or a flirtation between the two men. How had it happened? When had they signalled their desire for each other? Each day at Digby House was providing a new surprise.

Chapter Nine

Gina came down for breakfast the next morning with a big grin on her face. She had slept well, and had woken feeling full of energy and with a zest for life she hadn't known for quite some time. She wasn't sure whether this was anything to do with her encounter with Helena; or whether it was simply because the sky was already a hot, brilliant blue, the birds were singing and the day seemed full of possibility.

As she walked into the dining room, Matt looked up from his newspaper, and grinned at her broadly.

'Hello there, gorgeous,' he said. 'You look happy.'

Gina beamed at him, secretly pleased that he had not only noticed her, but that he had called her 'gorgeous'. Was this a reflection of what he felt about her, or was he just being friendly?

'That's because I am happy,' she said, going to the sideboard, helping herself to a bowl of fresh fruit salad and putting a big dollop of natural yogurt on top.

She looked over to see Rory and Daniel deep in conversation at the other end of the table. She smiled to herself, and plonked herself down by Matt. Sarah and David and Will arrived just after her. They were arguing about the progress of the English cricket team in the latest Test Match, and barely noticed the others.

'So, how are you?' asked Matt. 'It seems like we haven't had a chat for ages.'

'That's because we haven't,' Gina said, mock-facetiously.

'Where did you get to last night? I knocked on your door to see if you wanted to have a game of billiards after dinner, but you weren't there.'

Again, Gina glowed. Matt had sought her out, and was interested enough in her to want to know where she had been. Surely, if he didn't care, he wouldn't ask?

'Oh, I went out for a walk,' she said, cheeks flushing at the memory of what had followed the walk.

'Must have been quite a trek. I heard you coming in late. I gathered from the fact that you came upstairs almost straight away that Charles didn't give you too much grief. That was unusual for him.'

Gina smiled at Matt. 'That's really sweet of you – that you were looking out for me, I mean. What would you have done if he had started to give me trouble?'

'Oh, I don't know. Swung for him, probably. I'm reaching the end of my tether with that man.'

Gina smiled. 'I don't know whether this is due to the mellow mood that I'm in today, but I've decided that the best way to deal with Charles Sarazan is to ignore him. I'm going to let everything he does ride over me. He's just not worth it, and –'

'Who's not worth what?' a familiar husky voice asked from the other side of the dining room. Gina coldly looked up at Persis, who had just come in. 'Do you know, Persis, I really don't think that this conversation concerns you at all? I guess that you weren't ever taught that not only is it rude to eavesdrop, but that it's also rude to interrupt.'

Persis merely shrugged, muttering, 'Suit yourself.' She walked round the table and sat down on Matt's other side. She put down her coffee cup and a plate with a slice of melon on it, and carefully arranged a linen napkin on her lap. Then she leant over towards Matt, and batted her eyelashes at him. 'Isn't it a gorgeous day,

Matt? Makes you want to take all your clothes off and run around naked. I love being naked, don't you?'

Gina looked away and grimaced. Persis was so obvious it was painful to witness sometimes. And despite the fact that Gina knew full well that Matt disliked Persis, there was still a niggling doubt in her mind that he might yet succumb to her blandishments. Persis was, after all, very experienced at seduction.

'That pretty much depends on where and with whom,' Matt replied.

Persis failed to recognise the dismissive and disinterested tones in his voice, and took his words as encouragement. 'Ooh, do tell. I love being naked outdoors. The heat of the sun on my body is so sexy. Makes me want to, well, get physical, if you know what I mean.'

Matt did not reply, but Persis carried on regardless, speaking loudly enough to ensure that Gina heard as well. 'I couldn't help but notice that you've got such a lovely body, Matt. You must show it to me sometime. In detail. I give very good massages, so I'm told. Maybe I could give you one?'

Persis simpered at Matt, and Gina felt something snap. This was exactly the same line that she had used so successfully on Gina's then-boyfriend the previous year.

'For Christ's sake, Persis. Stop acting like a bitch on heat for once in your life, will you?'

'That's fine, coming from you,' Persis snapped back instantly.

Gina was shocked. What could Persis mean? Did she know about Will? Or Steve? Or even Helena and Marius? No, it wasn't possible. Persis must be bluffing or, if not that, then doing what came naturally to her – being catty.

Persis put her arm on Matt's forearm, and spoke confidentially. 'Really, Matt, I'd watch that woman if I were you. You see what she's like? I've done nothing to offend her, and she's snapped at me twice already this morning. I think I might go and lodge a formal complaint with Charles. In fact, yes, that's what I'll do. Right now.'

Persis put down her napkin by her untouched plate, stood up, brushed the non-existent crumbs down off her dress, and left the table. Gina watched her go in disbelief.

Matt touched Gina's hand, lightly, and yet it sent an electric jolt through her body. 'Don't let her bother you,' he said. 'It's all bluster and, besides, what can Charles do? Tell you both to stop talking to each other? That would be a blessing, I reckon.'

Gina laughed. Matt continued: 'Persis naked. What a thought. Ugh. I think I'd rather see a thirty-stone Sumo wrestler naked than Miss de Gaury. The most attractive thing about that woman is her rear view. From five hundred yards. As she's getting on a plane to take a one-way flight to the other side of the world.'

'You really don't like her, do you?' asked Gina, amused and full of secret relief at having her hopes so overwhelmingly confirmed.

'I can honestly say that I can't stand the woman. If I was stranded on a desert island with Persis, and the nearest landfall was some thousand miles away across the open sea, with coral reefs and man-eating sharks and typhoons in between, I'd start swimming straight away.'

Gina hooted. 'That's a pretty strong reaction.'

'Well, I can't help it. Come on, you're not exactly her number one fan either, are you?'

Gina agreed but, before she could say anything else, Charles came storming into the dining room. His face was dark with anger. Immediately everyone fell silent. They could sense that this was serious.

'Gina. See me in my study, now. The rest of you, start the rehearsals without us.'

Gina and Matt exchanged looks as she unwillingly got up from the table. Surely this couldn't be how Charles would react to a bit of bitchiness between two women, when he had been prepared to overlook her flouting of the curfew by three hours the previous night? Charles irritatedly gestured at her to hurry up. He spoke tersely: 'Come on, come on, I haven't got all day.'

Charles turned around abruptly and left the room.

Gina followed behind, feeling like a disobedient puppy on its way to receive a slippering. As she reached the door, she turned and looked at Matt. He mouthed 'Don't worry' at her. As she walked into the hallway, there was Persis, leaning against the wall, with her arms folded smugly across her chest and a triumphant look on her face.

'Have fun,' she said, as Gina walked past her.

Charles led her into his study, holding the door open for her and shutting it firmly behind her. She stood in front of his large kneehole writing desk, and then decided that this made her seem too much as if she were waiting for punishment, and so she went over to the leather chesterfield sofa and sat down. She settled back into the sofa, trying to appear as nonchalant as possible.

Charles walked over to the fireplace, and took a silver box off the mantelpiece. He took out a large cigar, then fished in his pocket and brought out a penknife. He sliced the end off the cigar with a single, vicious cut, bringing the blade perilously close to his thumb. Then he lit the cigar and walked over to the window, puffing thoughtfully. The room quickly filled with the thick smoke. Gina found this uncomfortable, but said nothing: she suspected that she was supposed to feel discomfort. She was also becoming irritated with his dramatic pauses. Just get on with it, she was thinking. Give me my telling off and let me go.

After a further long pause, Charles turned to Gina.

'I hope that it was worth it the other night,' he said.

Gina was lost. 'What was worth it?' she asked.

'Your early-hours liaison in the hothouse with my gardener. You managed to break two of my rules in one fell swoop. The ten o'clock curfew and no sex.'

Gina shivered. How on earth did he know about it?

Charles saw her bafflement. 'Quite rightly, Persis told me about these grave infringements.'

Persis? But how did she find out?

Charles continued. 'Well, Miss Stanhope, you know the rules, and I must enforce them. You have deeply disappointed me. I allowed you a waiver when you came in late last night. However, now I find that this was not the first time that you have shown a flagrant disregard for the rules.'

Charles took another long, thoughtful puff on his cigar, and slowly blew the smoke in Gina's direction. 'However, I am willing to present you with a choice. I am sure that you will appreciate the special treatment I am offering you, given that you know Sarah and David were offered no such choice.'

Gina looked at him, confused. How had Persis found out? Her mind was racing. Charles's response was too calm, too calculated. She knew that he had reacted in the heat of the moment when he had discovered Sarah and David together. Why wasn't he behaving like that with her? Why was he treating her differently? Why was he so calm? She felt very uneasy.

'So, Gina. I offer you an ultimatum. Either you pack your bags and leave both Digby House and the production immediately, or you allow me to punish you as I think fit. Which is it to be?'

Now things were becoming clearer to Gina. Charles was playing another of his games. They both knew that she could not leave the production as that would jeopardise her place at drama school, and so this offer of a choice was a false offer. There was no choice at all. Not only had she to accept the punishment, she had to 'allow' it. By giving her permission to him, she was being drawn into his kinky games. She would outwardly be a willing participant, even though they both knew that in truth she was there under duress.

Gina looked at Charles, who was gazing out of the window again, seemingly unconcerned, slowly puffing on his cigar. But she could see how tightly he was gripping it, and that his other hand was clenched into a fist. He was feigning indifference, but she knew that he was waiting for her inevitable reply with excitement.

She decided to make him wait. She said nothing. As she sat on the leather sofa, which creaked gently as she shifted on it, she thought about the punishment. She had a pretty good idea about what it would involve. Watching David and Sarah the other night had been an intriguing experience. She had never had any masochistic urges before, but as she watched David and Sarah writhing in their chains, utterly powerless, and as she sensed the dominance and mastery of Charles over them, she had been undoubtedly aroused. She had imagined what it would be like to be in their position. And now it seemed that she was about to find out.

She looked over at Charles, who was still surveying the grounds of Digby House. He had a fine, almost insolent profile, with full lips and a long, straight nose. There was a sort of debased sensuality about his features. She could see that his nostrils were flared, and she thought she knew why: he was aroused. His long fingers brought the cigar to his mouth once more, and she watched as his lips slowly parted and then closed round the cigar. She could imagine those lips on her body, those long fingers exploring her. He was handsome, there was no denying it and, although she despised him, she was attracted to him physically. She felt once more the mixed pangs of desire and repulsion. But somehow even the repulsion made her desire that much keener. But she would not give him the satisfaction of knowing that she was stimulated by the thought of this punishment.

At last Charles turned to her. 'Well, Gina. What is your choice to be?'

'You know damn well,' she said angrily. She didn't mind taking the punishment, but she wasn't going to put up with his games as well.

'Tell me, Gina. I need to hear you say it.'

'You know I can't leave the production. So it's the other option. I won't say "choice", because I haven't got any.'

'The other option,' Charles said, smiling. 'Which is?' He looked at her keenly.

'Punishment,' she hissed.

Charles smiled, and repeated after her, 'Punishment.' He stubbed the cigar out on a cut-glass ashtray, and came around the desk and stood in front of her.

'Repeat after me: I permit you to punish me.'

Gina stared at him angrily. She knew that Charles had placed her in a no-win situation. Better to get it over with. 'I permit you to punish me.'

'Good, good,' said Charles, sitting next to her on the sofa. 'Now say this: I want you to punish me.'

'Get real, Charles.' Gina snorted derisively. She stood up, walked to the door and opened it. 'Let's get this over with. I take it that you want to retire to the torture chamber?'

Charles laughed, almost embarrassed. 'Really, Gina, I'd prefer it if you'd call it the relaxation room.'

'It's academic whatever we call it. We know what goes on in there, don't we?' Gina said as she led the way, suddenly feeling stronger. She had a kind of power over him now. She knew that part of his enjoyment would be derived from her discomfort and unwillingness; so she could ruin it for him, by submitting freely, and by outwardly and perhaps even inwardly enjoying whatever he had in store for her.

She opened the door into the room. She felt for the light switch, but Charles brushed past her. 'There's no electric light in here. I prefer candlelight. So much more intimate, don't you think?'

He took a box of tapers from the small table by the bed, and lit the candles in the chandelier hanging from the ceiling, in the sconces on the wall and in the candlestick on the table.

'It is important that you understand the ground rules. As part of your punishment you must obey my every command, without hesitation. If you hesitate, you will receive additional punishment. Do you agree to these conditions?'

Gina nodded.

'Good. Lock the door and give me the key.'

Gina obeyed, turning the old iron key in the lock and

handing it to Charles. He put it in his trouser pocket, and Gina could see the material stretch over his groin as he did so. His arousal was confirmed to her.

'Now, take your clothes off.'

Despite her dislike for him, part of Gina wanted this. She held his gaze defiantly as she pulled her T-shirt up over her head, and then pulled down her jogging pants. She stood in front of him in her underwear.

'All of them, Gina.'

She reached behind her back to release the clip on her bra, and pulled the straps down over her shoulders. Her breasts fell free, her nipples betraying her own arousal by already puckering and hardening. Then she slipped down her panties and stepped out of them. She stood in front of him, her legs apart, her hands on her hips. She looked at him as if this was the most normal thing in the world, smiling to show him that she wasn't perturbed.

Charles looked her up and down proprietorially, and nodded, seemingly pleased with what he saw.

'Now get on the bed, Gina,' Charles ordered.

She walked over to the big brass bed. It was spread with silk sheets. She sat on the edge of it.

'Lie down, on your back,' Charles said as he lifted the lid of the old sea chest at the bottom of the bed. Gina watched him as he rummaged about in the chest, and wondered what he would bring out of it. She was still sitting on the bed when he looked up, both hands full.

'I said LIE DOWN,' he shouted at her. Gina hurriedly obeyed, taken aback by the sudden vitriol, and cursing herself because she hadn't complied instantly, and so giving him the opportunity to become angry with her. That was, after all, what he wanted. She closed her eyes, and listened as he moved around the bed. She wondered what he was going to do. She had expected the hand-cuffs, the metal loops and the cat-o'-nine-tails, not a soft bed. She felt him tie something soft around her left hand. She looked over, and saw that he was fastening a silk scarf round her wrist and then to the bedhead, pulling her arm so that it was stretched right out from her body.

Then he did the same with her other arm, and then with both her ankles, so that her legs were spread slightly apart. His movements were brisk and businesslike.

When he had finished, he stood back and looked at her.

'You are a beautiful woman, Gina. I have desired you since the first moment I saw you. And now I am going to have you. You are all mine, to do with as I please.'

Gina tried to shift herself, trying to test the strength of her ties. Her arms and legs were fixed so that she was afforded little movement.

Charles saw her efforts, and smiled. 'There is no point in struggling. You can't get free, not until I choose to release you. And now, I have one more adjustment to make.'

Charles came towards her, with another silk scarf in his hands. 'I am going to blindfold you, Gina. It will add to your experience.'

Gina knew that this too was more of Charles's bullshit. What Charles really intended her to feel was even more disorientation, and even more vulnerability: not knowing where or when he would come to her, and what he was about to do to her. Yet another measure to alter the balance of power between them in his favour. But it would not do to attempt resistance, as this was what Charles desired. She raised her head slightly to allow him to slip the band of black silk around her head, and he tied it gently, checking that it was firmly fixed over her eyes. She lay back on the silk-covered pillows, and opened her eyes. The blindfold was so tightly fastened over her face that she could not see a thing. She listened for Charles's movements in the room, but could hear nothing, not even his breathing. The more she strained to hear him, the louder the silence seemed to become. She could hear the blood pounding in her ears, and the rustling of her hair against the silk pillowslips seemed deafening. She wondered if he had slipped out of the room immediately after fixing the blindfold.

She tried her binds once again, hoping this time that

she might be able to work free. She was beginning to feel uncomfortable, not so much physically as mentally. What if Charles left her bound like this for an hour, for the morning, or even for the whole day? She had underestimated him and his ability to confound her expectations. She had thought that she would receive a period of his intense and unfailing attention, intimate and personal, but here she was, abandoned and apparently forgotten.

After a while, it seemed to her that the air around her had become warmer. She was unsure if this was part of Charles's design; or whether, as the sun gained height and strength, the rising temperature outside was leaching indoors. She wondered whether it might be worth calling for assistance, but decided against it. Not yet, anyhow.

Then she heard distant strains of music, so faint that she couldn't tell at first whether she was hearing it or imagining it. Slowly, the music gradually increased in volume. It was a beautifully melodic orchestral piece, rising and falling, flowing and swirling around her. The music soothed her and, as she listened, a faint waft of the heady scent of lilies drifted past, and then was gone. A few moments later, the fragrance returned, stronger this time. The heat seemed to be increasing too. Despite her constrictions, her naked body felt as warm and relaxed as she might have felt whilst sunbathing on a beach or lying on a sun bed. Denied vision, her other senses seemed to be compensating. All her sensations were heightened, amplified. As the music continued, Gina tried to work out how long she had been lying on the bed. It was difficult to estimate time, and she was strangely disorientated.

Then she could smell a familiar spicy aroma above the scent of the lilies, announcing Charles's presence as clearly as if she could see him. She felt the bed lurch slightly, as the mattress to her right side dipped under the pressure. She had heard nothing, but here he was, coming at last to effect his punishment. Then she felt a similar lurch on her left side. She knew instinctively that he had straddled her waist, and was kneeling over her. Gina wondered if he too was naked, and if he was looking down at her prone and tethered body with desire. She felt her stomach contract with arousal. She struggled to bring her body into contact with his, to try to work out what he was doing, but the scarves held her too tightly. She wondered if he would speak, and strained again to hear. This time, she could hear breathing, shallow and rapid.

Her head jerked back into the pillows with the shock as something was pressed against her lips. She hadn't expected the first contact to be there. The pressure was maintained, and Gina realised that it would not cease until she had opened her mouth. She slowly parted her lips, only a very small distance, and felt something being slowly but insistently pushed inside her mouth. And then, almost instantaneously, the taste flooded her tongue and the smell filled her nostrils. It was a strawberry. She opened her mouth further to accept it. It was ripe and full; a delicious taste of summer. Its sweet juices trickled down her throat.

She was surprised by the next sensation as well. She felt something being brushed lightly against her left nipple, and then her right one, before it was placed in the narrow groove between her breasts. She felt a slight pressure, and then a squishing noise, and more of the unmistakable smell of strawberries. A soft spreading motion gently massaged the pulped berry into her skin, stroking the inner sides of her breasts. There was a long pause, and then she felt the brush of hot breath on her skin, and felt the warm moist pad of Charles's tongue as he started to lick the puréed fruit from between her breasts. He licked with long, slow, languorous movements, his tongue moving expertly over her skin, lightly licking and grazing. She felt her nipples harden yet more and her sex quicken.

This was most certainly not what she had expected. She had thought she would be subjected to discomfort and humiliation rather than sensual pleasure. Charles seemed to have an infinite capacity to surprise.

He was moving on. He shifted further down the bed so that he was now straddling her knees. This time he had crushed a fruit into the dimple of her navel, and she could feel his hair brushing against her skin as he leant over her to lick it out. She wondered whether the downward path of travel would terminate in the obvious destination. She wriggled under him, trying to press her stomach up against his mouth, to bring him closer to her. Struggling against her ties only heightened her arousal. It was not only a physical reaction to his stimuli, it was mental too. The idea of being restrained, of being powerless to resist his advances, the thrill of knowing that her captive body was so attractive to him – all played their part. He desired her: he had told her so. Perversely, her dislike for him somehow made her reactions all the stronger.

Charles was now slowly mashing a strawberry on to the soft skin at the top of her right thigh, where it sloped down to meet her groin. She could feel the warm juices slowly trickling down her thigh and into the groove at the edge of her groin, and then down through the edge of her pubic hairs, past her sex and down between her buttocks. Its light passage was ticklish, and yet undeniably erotic as well. She held her breath, waiting for Charles to bring his mouth to the fruit, and near to the source of her unbearable heat. As he did so, she moaned.

Then a strawberry was crushed on to her other thigh, and again she felt his hair brush against her pubic hairs as he leant across her to lick the pulp off her. She was willing him to move his mouth back again, to that central part of her that craved his attentions most. She was moist and ready for him, for his crushed fruit and his searching tongue.

She felt the lurching sensation of surprise as she felt another pressure. Charles was pressing a strawberry against her clitoris, which was still hooded under its rosy cover. The fruit collapsed, and he maintained the pressure, starting a lazy circling movement with his finger against her hard button. She knew that it would not take much of this soft stroking to bring her to an overwhelming orgasm. She wanted to feel his lips and tongue against her there, and willed him to replace his finger with his hungry hot mouth, as he had done elsewhere on her body. She could not take much more of this exquisite teasing.

'You seem to have an affinity with fruit,' Charles's voice purred. 'So let's try another.' Gina held her breath, straining to hear, wondering what he would do now. She heard a fleshy ripping sound, and then a jolt ran through her as she felt something being pressed against her taut and tender clitoris. It felt firm, colder than flesh but warmer than an inanimate object. Charles slid it down from her bud to her opening, and pushed it slowly and yet firmly into her vagina. She was so slick with juices that it entered her easily and, as she took its length, she realised that Charles was fucking her with a banana. He started a steady rhythm, pushing the fruit deep into her and then almost removing it, before pushing it back in again. Gina was shocked, but at the same time she could not ignore the wanton reactions of her body. The banana was as large and hard as any man's penis, and it felt good.

After the earlier long period of silence, Charles was talking now. 'Ah, yes, my lovely Gina, you like that, don't you? Look at you. You're straining up to meet every thrust, aren't you? Does it feel good? Are you going to come for me? Come for me, Gina. Let that orgasm wash over you. You know you want to.'

His voice was insistent, urging and almost hypnotic. Hearing Charles voicing his thoughts spurred Gina on. She loved to hear men talk about sex, voicing their fantasies, especially when they were making love to her. Just the command 'Come for me' was enough to bring her to the brink of her climax. Her back arched up, forcing the banana deeper into her, and her legs flexed and strained with the upswelling sensations.

She cried out, 'Oh yes, oh God yes, do it, make me come.' As she called out, Charles abruptly withdrew the fruit. Gina had never felt such maddening frustration as her near-orgasm faded away, leaving her unfulfilled. The mattress shifted once more as he got off the bed.

After a moment of silence, Charles spoke: 'Success.'

Gina lay on the bed, still held by her silk shackles, limp and defeated. His action had been deliberate. Charles had never intended to let her experience the orgasm that had been building, so deliciously, for so long. He had always been in total control.

She felt his hands at her head, and she automatically lifted her head up from the pillow so that Charles could unfasten the blindfold. He removed it, and she looked up at him angrily. He was fully dressed, and was sneering down at her. He spoke sharply and curtly.

'Do you remember what I said to you the first night you were here at Digby House?'

Gina looked at him uncomprehendingly. He had said many things that night.

'Let me refresh your memory. It was late at night, and you were having an erotic dream, or so you thought. You were enjoying the gentle touch of a hand, a hand that was stroking and caressing your hair and your neck. And then you heard a voice speaking to you. Words filtered through your confused consciousness, and you knew it was me. And what was it that I was saying? "I'm going to make you beg me to make love to you. I'll bend you to my will, and you won't be able to resist." Well, Gina, I seem to have succeeded, don't I? I bent you to my will all right, and you begged. You couldn't resist.' Charles looked down at her, and smiled. 'Most satisfactory.'

'You bastard,' Gina shouted at him. This had all been engineered for her complete and absolute humiliation. He had wanted to make her succumb to him totally so that he could then reject her. How he must have been laughing to himself she writhed in near-ecstasy under his touch.

'Now, now,' tutted Charles. 'Sally will come and untie you when you have calmed down.'

He turned and left the room. Gina hated him more now than she had ever done before.

Sally Tobin arrived some time later and untied Gina without saying a word. Her face registered nothing, which made Gina wonder whether the housekeeper was used to having to perform this duty. Sally went round the room and blew out all the candles, and then left, shutting the door quietly behind her.

Gina lay on the bed for a little while after Sally's departure, trying to figure out what to do. She decided that to brazen it out would be the best plan of action. If she acted as if what had just happened did not bother her at all, she knew it would rile Charles. She must not appear demoralised or defeated. She got up and put her clothes on, and went back into the rehearsal room. She was mildly surprised to see that neither Charles nor Persis were there. She had expected Charles to be present to enjoy the shame and humiliation of her reappearance.

Matt saw her as she entered and he hurried over to her.

'Are you OK?' he asked, his concern obvious and touching.

'I'm fine, Matt. Charles and I had a little session of special instruction, I suppose you might say.'

Matt still looked concerned. Gina tried to reassure him. 'I'm OK, honest. He's a pig, but I'm fine. How are the rehearsals going?'

'Really well. Excellent, in fact. I think we're getting somewhere, despite Persis.'

Just then, Charles and Persis entered the rehearsal room. Charles smiled coldly at Gina. There was no hint in his manner of what had just passed between them.

'Gina, you're here. Good. Right, cast, we're going to rehearse the love scene between Victoria and Felix, Persis and Matt's characters. Go and slip into your costumes,

186

you two. It's not a full dress rehearsal, but you'll need the clothes on that you're going to take off later.'

Matt and Persis left the rehearsal room. Charles was busy organising everyone. 'We need a bed for this too. Will, Rory and David – go to the relaxation room and fetch the brass bed, will you?'

Gina flushed with fury. This was deliberate: another small humiliation. The others might not know what had happened, but they would guess, surely, when they saw the rumpled sheets stained with crushed strawberries, and the silk scarves still attached to the bedhead.

She heard muted swearing and grunting as the three men manhandled the bed frame on to its side and through the door into the rehearsal room. Then Rory and David went back for the mattress. Gina could hardly bear to look. She heard the commotion as they brought the mattress in and set it on the bed, which had been placed in the central stage area.

She heard Will mention pillows and sheets, and looked up. To her relief, the mattress had been stripped, and the scarves removed. Will was carrying the pillows, on top of which were piled some freshly laundered cotton sheets and pillowcases. What a wonderfully efficient housekeeper, she thought, secretly blessing Sally Tobin's name. David and Rory quickly made the bed. Gina looked over at Charles, who merely nodded an acknowledgement at her, before addressing the cast.

'Right. We'll all sit quietly and concentrate as Matt and Persis go through their scene. Remember, this is the culmination of their affair, the first time that they have made love, and it is an immensely special occasion.'

Gina noticed how Persis had become visibly puffed up, self-absorbed and self-important. Gina felt that she couldn't watch the rehearsal of this scene. She had missed it when it had been rehearsed before: that was the morning when she and Sarah had been sent out by Charles. She knew that Persis would be slyly looking across at her during the love scene, basking in her closeness to Matt and in Gina's discomfort and jealousy.

The scene commenced. Persis was overacting as atrociously as ever, and was being overly familiar with Matt, standing closer to him and touching him much more often than was called for in the script. This was all for Gina's benefit, and Gina was well aware of this. Matt looked uncomfortable, but gamely continued. Gina knew he was thinking of the success of the production rather than his own personal circumstances, and was therefore trying to make the best of a bad situation.

Gina also knew that this scene involved Persis undressing in front of Matt, before getting into the bed and inviting him to join her. The lovemaking was explicitly described in the script, the stage directions showing that the scene would carry on for some nine or ten minutes, with the characters conducting a breathless conversation as they made love.

Gina kept her head bowed as she followed the script; the scene relentlessly approached the lovemaking. She wanted to get up and stop this, to save Matt from Persis, but she knew that she couldn't. She did not want to watch, but there was something that compelled her to. She needed to see how Matt would cope with this scene. Would his resolve crumble before the beauty and proximity and availability of Persis's body?

Persis had moved over to the bed, and started to undo the buttons down the front of her dress. She was looking at Matt from under the curling tendrils of her dark locks as she did this, slowly running her tongue over her lips. Matt's character was supposed to be transfixed as he watched her gradually disrobe, and Gina could see that Matt was watching intently. She couldn't tell from his expression what he was thinking, whether he was acting or not. She fervently hoped that he was not being pulled in by Persis, falling for her seductive charms like so many before him.

Gina was also very aware that Persis was dragging this out for an unnecessarily long time. Persis reached the lower buttons on her dress and let it drop from her shoulders. Underneath she was wearing nothing but a tiny white G-string. Gina was grateful for small mercies: she knew that in the production proper Persis would be completely naked. Matt moved towards Persis slightly. Gina looked down sharply at the script, and was relieved to see that this move was merely performed as directed. Persis ran her hands lightly over her tawny skin, provocatively enjoying the feel of her body. Her breasts were tipped with chocolate-brown areolas, the nipples two taut points. Gina was surprised to see that her navel was pierced by a small gold ring. Gina slyly looked round at the other male members of the cast. They too seemed transfixed by Persis's beauty, her seductiveness, her blatant sensuality. Gina felt a sinking feeling. Surely they couldn't fall for this, not after all they had seen and heard Persis do?

Persis moved to the bed and slowly slipped under the sheet, pulling it up around her but leaving her breasts uncovered. Matt walked over to the bed and sat by her, and then gently leant across and kissed her. Gina had to look away. This was too much to bear. She heard the rustle of clothes being removed and dropped to the floor, and then of the sheets being pulled back as Matt joined Persis in the bed. There then followed the creaks of the bedsprings and the coos and gasps from Persis as the scripted lovemaking commenced.

'Sorry, sorry,' whispered Gina, getting up. 'Need the loo.' She hurried past the others and towards the door with head bowed. It was too much. She couldn't stay and watch this.

She spent a good ten minutes in the lavatory, regarding herself in the mirror and wondering if she could ever be a match for Persis. Then she returned to the rehearsal room. To her relief, the scene had just ended.

'That was good, very good,' said Charles, walking over to Matt and Persis, who were still in the bed. 'But there's something not quite right, not quite gelling there yet. You two are lovers, desperately and hopelessly attracted to each other. You can't survive without each other: you are as close as Siamese twins. Your love is desperate, needy and intensely physical. We need to see some of this physicality, this desperation.'

Matt looked at Charles quizzically. He couldn't see what Charles was getting at. Charles walked over to the bay window and gazed out. Then he turned and spoke.

'Yes, I'm convinced that this is the only way. The only way that the closeness of your bond will truly come across to the audience is if there is such a bond in real life as well. I suggest that you two should commence a physical relationship.'

Matt looked at him in disbelief, but Charles ignored him and continued. 'I will make an exception to my rules for this, as it is for the sake of the production.'

'I think that's an excellent idea, Charles,' said Persis, snuggling up closer to Matt and smiling seductively at him. Then she looked over at Gina and smiled – this time a gloating, triumphant smile. She slipped her arm through Matt's.

Matt shook her free roughly and got out of the bed. 'You're cracked, Charles, you know that? You think that you can order me to sleep with Persis?' Gina saw that he had a pair of boxer shorts on, and was secretly thankful that the playwright had stipulated this. She didn't like the idea of Matt being completely naked with that bitch.

Charles laughed. 'Of course I can't force you, Matt. I'm merely making a suggestion. Think of all the great Method actors: think of Robert De Niro learning to play the saxophone for *New York, New York*, piling on the pounds for *Raging Bull*. It's a similar approach. Immerse yourself in The Method. Become the part. Take on Felix's feelings and emotions, take on his appetites. It'll make your performance a hundred times better.'

'No, Charles. The answer's no. There's nothing you can say to make me change my mind. In fact, I don't even know why I'm having this conversation. The whole thing's ridiculous.' Matt turned his back on Charles, walked over to where the rest of the cast were seated and sat down, his arms folded across his chest.

'Well, I am extremely disappointed in you, Matt.

Extremely disappointed.' Charles shook his head. 'We'll break for lunch now. I hope that you will reconsider your rash decision, Matt.'

Gina knew that Charles's disappointment had nothing to do with The Method and the production. He was disappointed because he had failed to control Matt.

During lunch, Sally Tobin came up to Gina as she sat with the others out on the terrace. 'There's a phone call for you in the library, Miss Stanhope.'

'Oh, thank you, Sally. And thanks for this morning.' Gina tried to convey her exact meaning with her eyes, but Sally just looked blankly at her before turning and leaving.

Gina picked up the receiver in the library. She wondered who was calling her. Perhaps it was Kirsten.

'Hello there, Gina,' said a familiar voice.

'Oh, Helena, hi,' said Gina. She felt surprised at her own reaction: not a trace of embarrassment or awkwardness. She was talking to Helena just as she always did, as coolly and calmly as if she entered into lesbian love affairs every day. 'Thanks for the other evening.'

'My pleasure, sweetheart, believe me. Now look, Gina darling, we've decided to have a party on Saturday. I know it's rather short notice, but it'll be getting near the end of your time with dearest Charles then, won't it?'

'Umm, yes. We go to London on Tuesday,' Gina said.

'And am I right in thinking that Saturdays are your free days?'

'You are,' said Gina.

'Right. Ask all the cast, will you? Hell, you can even ask the Gruesome Twosome if you want. Probably best not to stir them up by excluding them. It's going to be a garden party, starting about midday. God knows what time it'll end: probably breakfast time the next day if the last garden party we held is anything to go by. We're having a Nymphs and Shepherds theme. Don't worry if you haven't got time to knock up a costume – just put on a sheet like a toga and bung a wreath of leaves on your head. See you there?'

'You bet. I wouldn't miss it for the world,' said Gina. She had seen what happened during a quiet evening in at Chitherleigh Manor; she wondered what the outcome of a day-long bacchanal might be.

Chapter Ten

*T*here had been great excitement amongst the cast when Gina had told them about the invitation to Marius and Helena's party. Charles had earlier made it clear to them that there was to be no end-of-rehearsals celebration at Digby House on their last night in Devon, and so the prospect of the Nymphs and Shepherds garden party at Chitherleigh Manor was eagerly awaited. The cast all felt that they wanted to celebrate the approach of the end of their time in Devon. They had been rehearsing hard every evening since Gina had revealed Charles's plans; consequently they all felt exhausted, both mentally and physically. A party would do them good.

On the Saturday morning, the cast were discussing the party over breakfast. Costumes were posing something of a problem.

'Oh hell, what am I going to get dressed up in?' Sarah was wailing. 'What do nymphs wear anyhow?'

'Lots of diaphanous veils and not much else, I seem to remember,' said David, hopefully.

'Why not go as a shepherdess?' asked Matt.

'Oh, I don't know. What are you wearing, Gina?' Sarah asked.

'Pretty much what Helena suggested. I'm going to

throw on a sheet and weave a circlet of flowers for my hair. Cheap and cheerful. Besides, it's so hot that anything more than that and I think I'd wilt.'

'A toga. That's a good idea. Do you mind if I copy you?'

Gina smiled at her. 'Of course not.'

'I'm so looking forward to this. It'll be good to let our hair down. We haven't had much in the way of R and R since we last went to the pub,' said Rory.

Gina smiled to herself. She thought back to the special brand of rest and relaxation that she had seen Rory indulging in a few nights ago.

'Have you told Charles and Persis about the party yet?' asked Will.

Gina frowned. 'No. I've been putting it off, hoping that, the longer I leave it, the more likely they are to have a prior engagement. Still, Helena did say to invite them, so I suppose I ought to.'

After breakfast, Gina wandered off to find Charles. Neither he nor Persis had appeared that morning. She tried his study and the library, with no luck. As she walked past the closed door of the torture-room-cum-bordello, she heard what sounded like the low hiss and crack of a whip. She hurried past, not wanting to think about what Charles was up to in there. She left a note pinned to his study door, telling him that he and Persis were invited to the party. She didn't much expect to see him there, knowing what he felt about the Burckhardts, but she felt that she ought to comply with Helena's wishes. Gina remembered the night that Charles had forbidden her to see the Burckhardts again, but she was going to pay no attention to him whatsoever. This was her day off and she was going to have some fun.

The party was due to start at midday. Gina had plenty of time to prepare herself. She went into the grounds to gather the greenery for her headdress. As she was picking some long strands of ivy from one of the pergolas, she looked over and saw that Steve was working in the hothouse. He appeared to be repotting some plants.

194

Gina wondered with a smile whether these were the ones that had been flung to the floor with such abandon the other night. She gathered all the foliage she needed, and then went back inside to take another long shower, her second of the day.

Afterwards, she sat at her dressing table with a large fluffy towel wrapped around her, and spent a leisurely half-hour doing her make-up and arranging her headdress, twining the strands of ivy into a circlet, and then carefully positioning it on her head. She regarded the finished effect in the mirror with satisfaction. The dark, glossy green of the ivy leaves contrasted well with her blonde hair, and the white toga showed off her tan nicely. There was a quick knock on her door and Sarah came in, holding a sheet around her.

'Will you help me with my toga? I can't fix it properly.'

Gina arranged Sarah's toga more neatly, and worked her way around her, fixing the loose flaps of material with safety pins.

'Guess what?' giggled Sarah. 'I'm feeling a bit naughty today. I've not got any undies on under here.'

'Let's hope that there aren't any sudden gusts of wind then,' Gina laughed.

'What do you think I ought to do for a headdress?' asked Sarah.

Gina had a wicked thought. 'There are some lovely plants in the hothouse, really exotic ones. I bet they'd look good.' Gina nodded encouragingly at Sarah.

'Do you think Charles would mind if I picked some of them?' Sarah asked, bothered by the possible consequences.

'I don't reckon he ever goes into that hothouse, let alone knows what's in there. You should go and have a look. And anyhow, Charles won't find out. He's otherwise occupied at the moment.'

Sarah smiled happily. 'OK, I'm off. Don't let the others go without me, will you?' She hurried out of the room.

* * *

The seven friends had hired a minibus and driver from a local firm to take them to the party, and had booked a return trip too, at a time to be determined later that evening. It all depended on how good the party was. At one o'clock in the afternoon, six of the seven partygoers were gathered at the front of Digby House. The minibus was there, its engine running. Rory looked at his watch.

'Does anyone know where Sarah is? We can't keep this good man waiting indefinitely.'

'I think I know where she might be,' said Gina. She hitched up her toga sheet and started gingerly off up the gravel drive towards the hothouse. She had decided to go to the party barefoot as she was sure that nymphs didn't wear shoes, but was beginning to wonder whether this was such a good idea.

As she approached the hothouse, she started to sing loudly to announce her presence to the occupants. It had the desired effect. Sarah appeared at the door, her toga falling rather becomingly off her shoulder and her cheeks flushed. She was holding a wilted trail of foliage in one hand.

'Come on, Sarah, they're waiting.'

Sarah gave a sheepish smile. 'Sorry. I sort of lost track of time.'

'I take it that you found what you needed in the hothouse,' said Gina impishly.

Sarah giggled. 'The gardener was ever so nice. He gave me these: they're passion flowers.' As they walked back towards the minibus, Sarah handed Gina the greenery. 'You couldn't make it into a circlet for me, could you? I'm all fingers and thumbs when it comes to things like that.'

Sarah squealed with delight as the two women rejoined their friends. 'Look at your costumes,' she said, tugging at the short hem of Matt's Greek-style tunic, which he had made from a cut-up sheet. Gina thought how handsome Matt looked, especially with so much of his body on display.

Daniel was dressed with a sheepskin rug tied over his

back and a short pair of horns fixed to his head. 'I've always been a sheep rather than a shepherd,' he said by way of explanation.

The three other men were dressed in more normal clothes, although they had made an attempt to replicate a vaguely agricultural look by tying baler twine around their waists and ankles, and sticking strands of straw into their hair and out of their clothes. Rory was chewing on a long piece of grass.

'You three look more like scarecrows than shepherds,' giggled Sarah.

'At least they've made an effort,' said Gina. 'Marius and Helena won't mind. It's the thought that counts.'

When they arrived at Chitherleigh Manor, the party was already in full swing. There were people roaming about in the wild expanses at the front of the manor house. The sound of a string quartet could be heard coming from behind the house, and Gina led her friends round the building to the garden at the back. There were crowds of people there, drifting by in groups, lying on the lawn, even seated in the low boughs of the apple trees. Everyone was in costume. The women had obviously taken to the Nymphs theme with gusto. Almost to a one they were wearing outfits of varying degrees of transparency, made from curtain netting and fine muslin, ruched and draped around them. The men were dressed in a greater variety of costumes, and Gina noticed with a grin that a couple of men were in drag, and had come dressed as nymphs.

Helena was lying in a hammock, being gently rocked by one young man and fanned by another. The two men were wearing loincloths and not much else. Their skin was covered in some kind of gold paint, and it glittered and sparkled in the strong sunlight.

'Darlings,' Helena exclaimed as she saw Gina and the others. She indicated to one of the young men to help her out of the hammock, and came over to greet her guests.

'Gina, darling,' she said, kissing Gina on both cheeks

197

and then putting her arm round her waist and giving it a squeeze. 'Welcome to our rural idyll. Chitherleigh Manor has become Arcadia for the day. You must introduce me to your lovely friends.'

Gina introduced everyone, and then she noted with mock-regret, 'I don't think that Charles and Persis will be joining us.'

'Oh, that's too bad,' said Helena with an equal lack of sincerity. 'But look how wonderful all your costumes are. You've made such an effort. How terrific. Drinks are on a couple of trestle tables over there by the dovecot, and there's food in the kitchen. Help yourselves and have a good time, my darlings.'

Just as she had finished speaking, Helena was whisked off by some of her guests. Gina was left wondering where Marius was. She couldn't see him. Rory, Will, David and Daniel immediately made a beeline for where the drinks were, taking Sarah with them.

'This is quite some place,' said Matt, looking around him, and then turning to her and smiling. Gina was pleased that he had stayed with her rather than disappearing off with unseemly haste to search out the alcohol. 'Do you know many of the people here?' he asked. Gina scanned the scene, and recognised a few people from the carnival crowd, and some of the locals from The Three Horseshoes. 'Not really,' she said.

'Not that it matters. We can talk to each other all day, can't we?' Matt asked. 'You look lovely in your costume, by the way.'

Gina blushed. This was what she had longed for: at last she had Matt's undivided attention. Like Sarah, Gina had decided to go without underwear to the party, and she wondered whether Matt had tried to guess what she was or wasn't wearing under her sheet. The toga was tied over one of her shoulders, just covering her breasts, and although she had fixed it at her side so that two edges of the sheet crossed over one another, as she walked the material fell apart, revealing the long, golden length of her leg right up to near the top of her thigh.

She saw with pleasure that Matt had noticed, and then demurely adjusted her toga, holding the two flaps together to cover herself up.

They walked over to a stone bench, and sat side by side, talking for a long time. Matt was very attentive, asking Gina about her family, her work and her home. She noticed that his eyes would often stray to her legs or the exposed parts of her breasts, and at one point he shifted closer to her on the bench so that his knee was touching hers. She wondered if this was accidental and if he would move his leg, but it remained where it was, pressed against hers. The heat from his body felt as if it was burning through the thin linen of her sheet. Matt asked Gina about her plans for the future, about what she wanted to do when she finished at The National Academy of Dramatic Arts.

'If I finish,' Gina corrected him. 'Don't forget, I might not even get in, if Charles has his way,' she said.

'I used to read palms, you know, tell people's fortunes. It was a bit of a party piece of mine. I could do yours, if you like,' said Matt. 'Maybe that'll tell us.'

Gina didn't believe in palmistry and she also felt that, in the unlikely event of Matt having the gift of prognostication, she wasn't sure that she wanted to know what lay in store for her. But the overpowering urge was to give her hand to Matt. She wanted him to hold it and to feel him tracing the lines of her palm with his fingers.

She held out her hand to him, almost like a supplicant. He took it with both of his own, and gently laid it palm upwards on his left hand. Then he started to stroke her palm with his fingers, with a light, gentle circling motion. She looked across at his bowed head, so close to her own, and regarded his profile. He hadn't shaved that morning and she could see the pronounced stubble on his cheeks and chin. She loved these contrasts between men and women: smooth against rough, muscles against softness. He looked up at her.

'You have a very strong love line. Very strong. It's a powerful force in your life.'

'Love. Hmm,' said Gina. She couldn't think of the last time she had been in love. She thought she knew when the next would be though, if things went as she hoped.

'Well, some palmists prefer to call it a lust line,' he said with an ironic smile.

'Which do you prefer?' asked Gina, gazing at him steadily.

'It depends on the person I'm doing the reading for,' he said, returning her gaze just as steadily.

'So, what would it be in my case?' she asked.

He traced the lines on her palm with his finger. 'This branch of the line here tells me that you are very physical, that you love sex; this one joining it shows that you pursue your desires and needs vigorously. But this fine line here shows me that where the attraction is very strong you become shy and reticent, expecting the other person to approach you. But once you overcome that shyness you are a wild sensualist. So, all in all, I think it would probably be lust.'

If this is bullshit, it's very convincing bullshit, she thought. He certainly seemed to have judged her character correctly. Matt looked at her, holding her hand and stroking it steadily. She felt sure that the pressure against her leg from his was increasing too. The area of contact between their flesh had spread from a small point at the knee to the whole of the upper leg from knee to thigh. Her heart raced, and she tried to keep her breathing as steady as she could, wondering what he would do next. This was too delicious.

Matt slowly lowered his hand with hers in it until the back of his hand was resting on her thigh. Then he started to slowly move his hand backwards and forwards, very gently, over her linen-covered flesh, bearing her own hand along in his. Gina couldn't believe it. This signal was unmistakable, unambiguous. At last.

'Hello, my little lovebirds,' said a voice behind them. Gina looked round quickly, not immediately recognising the voice. It was Marius. He was carrying a rough earthenware jug, which Gina could see was full of wine. 'Can I interest you in some more wine?'

'Oh, thanks,' said Matt, letting go of Gina's hand to reach over and raise his glass for Marius.

'And who are you?' asked Marius. 'I haven't yet had the pleasure.'

You're not the only one, thought Gina ruefully.

'Matt Burton. I'm one of Gina's fellow actors.'

'Delighted to meet you, Matt,' said Marius, putting down his jug and giving Matt's hand a firm shake.

'Me too,' said Matt. 'Gina's told me all about you.'

'Oh has she now?' asked Marius, cocking an eyebrow at Gina. Matt missed the look that passed between Marius and Gina, as he was too busy gazing about him. 'This is a fantastic place,' he said.

Marius started to tell Matt about the history of Chitherleigh Manor, and Gina felt herself becoming detached and disinterested and, above all, frustrated. Just as she was about to get somewhere with Matt, Marius had unwittingly intruded.

Some time later that afternoon, Gina was sitting on the stone steps leading down from the manor house to the croquet lawn. She was feeling very drunk and, as sometimes was the case when she got drunk, a little maudlin. After a while spent reluctantly listening to Marius's history lesson, she had left the two men and had gone to refill the jug. In the process of so doing she had managed not only to spill red wine all over her toga, but on her return Matt and Marius had gone. She thought that Marius might have taken Matt off to show him round the house. She had spent a good half an hour wandering around looking for them, but to no avail. She had lost Matt somewhere in the throng. She was so frustrated as they had seemed to be getting on so well, and at last their relationship had moved up a gear from friendship to flirtation. Her maudlin state also led her to start worrying about the production, its impending debut, and probably almost instantaneous cancellation.

201

Helena came and sat next to her. 'What's up?' she asked.

Gina didn't feel like telling Helena about her little hiccup with Matt. 'Oh, Helena, sometimes it just all seems so hopeless. Thanks to Charles, the production is bound to be pulled almost immediately, and I can kiss my place at The National Academy goodbye, that's for sure.'

Helena patted Gina's arm reassuringly. 'Hey, look. Don't worry about the production. And I mean that. Don't worry.' Something about the way Helena said this, her absolute conviction, told Gina that she should believe her.

'Oh hell,' said Helena. Gina glanced over to where Helena was looking, and saw that Charles and Persis were walking across the lawn towards them, formally linked arm in arm. Persis looked stunning. She was dressed in a gorgeous outfit of finely pleated white organdy, which was carefully designed to resemble the costumes worn by ancient Greek women depicted on vases and in statues. The pleats clung to and accentuated her curves, and a pale-blue silk band was tied in a shallow X-shaped cross above and below her breasts, emphasising them. The dark points of her nipples were visible through the sheer material. Charles was wearing an oriental-looking costume, with baggy trousers and an intricately embroidered waistcoat over a collarless linen shirt. He held a hooked staff in his other hand, and wore a cap made from sheepskin.

Helena got up to greet them. 'Charles. Persis. I'm so glad that you could come,' she said, stretching out her hand to them. Gina thought what a good liar Helena was.

Charles smiled thinly. 'Hello, Helena.' There was a pause. Charles made no attempt to speak.

'I love your outfit, Charles. What is it?' Helena asked, trying to instigate some sort of conversation. Ever the perfect hostess, Gina mused.

'It's an early-twentieth-century Kurdish shepherd's

costume. I would have thought that would have been obvious to anyone with a modicum of taste, intelligence or education,' said Charles in dismissive tones. He looked down at Gina. 'Have you been drinking?' he asked sharply.

Before Gina could say anything, Helena replied almost instantly. 'Of course she bloody well has, Charles. This is a party, or had that escaped your notice?'

Charles ignored Helena, leant over Gina, and spoke in a low and menacing voice. 'You know the rules, Gina. After the other day, I would have thought that you would be the last person to break them again.'

Helena interrupted. 'Christ, Charles. You just love bullying people, don't you? Well, you can't do it here. Gina and the others are our guests, in our home; if we choose to offer them alcohol and they choose to accept it, it's absolutely no affair of yours, no matter what egotistical control-freak trip you happen to be on. Got that?'

Gina was surprised by the speed with which the old animosities had been resumed.

Charles stared icily at Helena, his eyes narrowed to mean little slits. 'You haven't changed, have you, Helena? Still as shrewish as ever, I see.'

'And you're still the same pompous, arrogant, controlling, conniving shit, Charles.'

'I don't much care to stand here and listen to this,' Charles said, tight-lipped.

'No, and guess what? You don't have to. Why don't you do us all a favour, take your friend, and leave?' Helena was squaring up to Charles like a boxer. She had no fear of him.

Charles glared at her, so close that they were almost eyeball to eyeball. Helena did not flinch or back down, and Gina knew that she was witnessing a colossal battle of wills. After what seemed like an eternity, Charles did what Gina had considered the unthinkable thing. He turned away from Helena, and moved across to Persis, who had neither moved nor spoken during this debacle.

'Let's go, Persis. We are clearly not welcome here.' Attempting to salvage some shreds of dignity, he proffered his arm to Persis, and they walked away.

Helena watched them leave, and then looked at Gina and grinned. 'Oops. So much for being polite to my guests. Still, good riddance to bad rubbish, as they say. Now we can really start to enjoy ourselves. What do you say?'

'I say yes!' cried Gina, jumping up. She had never seen Charles look so disconcerted or so vulnerable. Helena was a wonder.

Helena took her by the hand. 'Come with me,' she said, putting her arm through Gina's. 'Let's go for a walk.' Helena steered her towards the far end of the orchard. When they were away from the other party-goers, Helena leant confidentially towards Gina and asked, 'Now, what about that nice young man I saw you with earlier. Is he one of your lovers?'

Gina laughed. 'No,' she said.

'But you wish he was. He's the special one, isn't he? I can see that from the way you behave when you are around him. Your body language is very telling.'

'Oh. Is it that obvious?' Gina asked.

'As clear as if you had his name tattooed in a heart on your arm, Gina darling. But I'll tell you something else. I've been watching you both through the afternoon, and it's also obvious that your feelings are reciprocated. I've seen how he is with the other women here, and he's very different with you. And, when he's not with you, he's watching you. In fact, there he is, over there.'

Gina caught her breath. So Matt had reappeared from wherever it was he had got to. She didn't dare turn her head to look: she felt it would be too obvious. 'He's talking to a lovely young lady wearing next to nothing, and he's all but ignoring her. He's looking over her shoulder at you.' Gina looked down at her feet and smiled to herself.

'Oh look, there are my darling attendants,' said Helena. She turned to Gina. 'You will excuse me, won't

204

you? I've got a little unfinished business with those two beautiful boys.'

Gina watched as Helena walked slowly towards the two men who had earlier been swinging her in the hammock. As Helena reached them, she gave first one and then the other a long, hungry kiss. Then, putting her arms around their waists, she walked off between them towards one of the wildflower meadows in the distance. Gina turned to see where Matt was. She would go and join him, and with any luck they would take up where they had left off earlier that afternoon. She scanned the groups of people in the direction that Helena had been looking, but couldn't see him. She cursed. He must have wandered off again.

Cross, she decided to go for a walk along the river at the bottom of the orchard. Matt didn't seem to be too bothered about seeking her out or staying with her. Perhaps he was just stringing her along. Her instincts told her otherwise, but her instincts weren't infallible.

As she approached the river, she heard the murmur of voices above the gentle rippling noise of the water. She stopped by a large willow and peered round the thick trunk towards the source of the noise. She didn't want to intrude if it was a lovers' tryst or an emotional heart-to-heart. Experience had taught her that these were the kind of events which tended to increase in frequency the longer a party had been running, and in direct proportion to the amount of alcohol consumed.

What she saw surprised her, but she didn't look away. She too had consumed enough alcohol to be feeling distinctly horny, and the flirtation with Matt had left her hoping for fulfilment.

Standing on the flat grassy bank near the river were Sarah, Rory and Marius. A large cotton blanket was spread beneath their feet. Sarah's head was turned towards Marius, and they were kissing passionately. Rory was standing in front of Sarah, nuzzling the top of her breasts, and his hands were sliding between the two flaps of material of her toga.

Gina watched in fascination as, still kissing him, Sarah felt with one hand for the front of Marius's costume. She pushed her hand down past the waistband of his leggings, fumbled inside, and then pulled his prick out of his trousers. Gina watched, fascinated. His penis was long, hard and circumcised. Marius's eyes were shut in blissful anticipation.

Rory saw what was happening, hurriedly undid the baler twine that was holding up his trousers, and pushed them down. He was wearing a thong underneath, and he slipped out of this too. Then he reached down and took Sarah's other hand, and placed it round his thick cock, now almost fully erect.

Sarah looked down, and smiled. She started to masturbate the two men very slowly, working up and down their pricks with long, slow strokes. Then she dropped to her knees, so that she could see them more closely. Her long, slim arms were working busily, and Gina thought that she was clearly experienced in this art. The two men threw off the rest of their clothes, and soon were both completely naked, flanking the kneeling Sarah. Gina knew that they were excited, both by what was happening to themselves and by what each could see Sarah doing to the other, and it did not take long for Sarah to bring them towards ejaculation. Rory came first, his milky semen shooting upwards in three rapid spurts. Marius was not far behind, and he came over Sarah, leaving a long wet stain on the material over her left breast and glistening on her neck.

Gina watched in transfixed silence from beyond the tree. If this last fortnight had taught her anything, it was that she liked to watch. She thought of Martin in the heat of her garden back home in London; of Sally and Steve glimpsed through a window; of the punishment meted out to David and Sarah; and of the snatched view of Rory and Daniel making love. She brought her hand to the front of her toga, resting it gently over the mound of her pubis. She could feel the springiness of her hairs beneath the linen, and the heat of her arousal, but she

206

was not going to touch herself. She needed to see what else might happen without distracting herself.

The two men collapsed on to the cotton blanket after coming, recovering their sapped strength. Sarah was obviously impatient for her own gratification. She ran a finger up the splash of semen on her neck, collecting it, and then lay down on her back between the two men. She slipped her hand in between the flaps of her toga; the slow, rhythmical movement of her hand underneath the material showed that she was touching herself, using Marius's semen to lubricate the passage of her fingers. Sarah shifted her legs so that they were bent at the knees and then spread them as wide as she could. The toga slowly fell back down her thighs to around her waist. Gina could see Sarah deftly working her fingers around her clitoris, and in and out of her pink, moist vagina. Sarah was now fully exposed to the world, but did not seem to care, so driven was she by her quest for satiation.

Gina heard a sudden noise: a woman giggling and then hurried footsteps. Helena appeared from the direction of the orchard with her two young men in tow. Their gold bodypaint had all but rubbed off, and they were somewhat dishevelled. In contrast, Helena was looking radiant. She paused when she saw her husband and the two others by the riverside: a vivid tableau of lovers caught in flagrante delicto. Sarah's hand froze at her crotch, and then she quickly scrambled to her feet.

'Darlings,' Helena said. 'How delightful. A little afternoon love by the river. May we join you?'

She walked over to Sarah and kissed her full on the lips. Sarah made no attempt to pull away: instead, she put her arms around Helena's waist and pulled her closer as she returned her kisses. Gina watched excitedly as the two golden men came over, stood on either side of Sarah, and began to touch her through her toga. One of the young men slid the hem of Sarah's toga upwards, feeling for her sex and, as he did so, Sarah placed a hand on Helena's breast, caressing it through her costume. Aroused again and with their cocks already stiffening,

Rory and Marius scrambled to their feet. Rory stepped up behind Helena, and started to fondle her body through her costume. Marius moved behind Sarah, and slid his hands up and round to cup and massage her breasts as she kissed Helena.

Gina was torn between the desire to see more and the need to find Matt. She wanted to experience some afternoon delight too, but only Matt would do right now. She turned and left the Saturnalia by the river. As she walked back towards the house, she could hear Sarah's gentle purring moans rising in volume.

Much later that evening, Helena spoke to Gina as she and the others were waiting in the minibus for the stragglers.

'Have you seen your would-be lover yet?' she asked.

Gina shook her head. 'Only briefly. I think he's left. I've looked everywhere for him.'

'Never mind,' said Helena, giving her a reassuring smile. 'You'll have lots of opportunities, don't worry. And, talking of opportunities, why didn't you join us earlier on?' Gina looked up. Helena laughed. 'I saw you by the tree. I thought that you might come over and join us. Or perhaps you were too preoccupied with thoughts of someone else?'

Gina nodded. Despite being turned on by what she had witnessed down by the river, she had had no desire to join in. Matt was the one she wanted.

'Oh, here he is,' said Helena, stepping out of the door of the minibus to allow Matt to get on. Matt came and sat next to Gina, even though there were several other spare seats.

'I was looking for you,' he said. 'I thought you'd gone off with someone.'

'That's funny. I was thinking the same about you,' Gina replied.

'We must have been circling round the house and each other all night, never quite meeting up. What a pain in the arse,' Matt said.

'Goodbye, darlings,' Helena called out as the minibus started up. 'See you all at the first night.' Each member of the cast called out their thanks and goodbyes.

Gina thought about reaching out for Matt's hand in the dark but, when she looked over at him, he was gazing out of the window into the blackness. She hoped that something might happen between them when they got back to Digby House, but Charles was there to greet them, sour-faced and looking at his watch. It was well past the curfew time, but he said nothing. He followed them all up the stairs and silently stood watching them as they went into their rooms. When Gina came out ten minutes later to go for a shower, he was still standing there; a mute, brooding presence. On her return, she locked her bedroom door, just in case. Throughout the night, she could hear the floorboards creak on the landing as he shifted from foot to foot during his long vigil.

On Sunday, rehearsals continued as usual. Charles seemed disinterested in the proceedings. He stood at the back of the rehearsal room, leaning against the wall, and gave no direction at all. Most of the time he appeared to be staring through the actors and out of the window behind them. The cast exchanged glances, shrugged shoulders, and got on with their work. They were used to rehearsing without Charles by now, and the play was continuing to come together very well. Their after-hours rehearsals had paid off. Unsurprisingly, Persis had not deigned to attend any of them, and so Gina and Sarah had shared her part. The cast agreed that the play ran much more smoothly without her. Everyone had learnt their lines perfectly, and the movements of the cast around the stage and each other were now perfectly choreographed. If Charles had noticed these differences, he said nothing.

Gina regarded Matt thoughtfully as he ran through one of his scenes with Persis. As well as being unbearably handsome, he really was a very talented actor indeed, she thought. Quite the stuff of which matinée idols were made, in fact.

At about twelve o'clock, Charles left the room without saying anything. He did not return. Over lunch, Persis disappeared and then came back to announce that Charles would not be joining them again that day, though she offered no explanation. She also announced that the second costume fittings would take place that afternoon. She handed round sheets with timings for the fittings. Gina's appointment was at four o'clock.

During the afternoon rehearsals, Gina wondered how she would behave with Mariangela this time. She had had her experience with Helena since she last saw Mariangela. During her initiation into lesbian love, she had been passive, allowing Helena to explore and pleasure her without giving much in return. Now she was ready to experiment some more. She too wanted to fully discover the innermost secrets of a woman's body, to explore and satisfy Mariangela, to feel her moving in the throws of passion while her deft hands and mouth worked their magic. She needed sex, and she felt predatory. This would be the perfect opportunity to vent the sexual frustration she felt over Matt.

Time seemed to drag, and four o'clock approached slowly. At last it was time, and Gina walked to the doors of the same reception room that Mariangela had used before. She wondered how she would control this meeting. Mariangela seemed a dominant woman, but Gina was determined that she would be the one instigating the seduction this time. She smiled to herself, thinking how surprised Mariangela would be. She knocked boldly on the door. To her astonishment, a man's voice answered. Probably Mariangela's assistant. She was annoyed, as the presence of another meant that this meeting would not go as she wished.

She entered the room, and saw a young man standing by the clothes rack.

'Hello, I'm Gina,' she said. 'I've come for my fitting with Miss Abruzzi.'

'Oh, I'm sorry. Weren't you told? Miss Abruzzi is unable to attend today, so I'm standing in for her. I'm Piet, her assistant.'

Gina felt a sharp pang of disappointment. She wouldn't be getting to know Mariangela better now after all, or to experiment with the new-found facet of her sexuality. Still, there would be other opportunities, she felt sure.

At supper that evening Charles was again absent. Persis seemed lost without him and, when David asked her where he was, it was obvious that she didn't know. During the meal, Sally entered the room and coughed to gain everyone's attention. The cast looked up expectantly, waiting for the announcement.

'I've just had a telephone call from Mr Sarazan. He asked me to tell you that he's been called away on urgent business, and that he won't be back for the rehearsals tomorrow or on Tuesday morning. He wishes Miss de Gaury to act as his deputy in his absence. He will see you all at The Redditch on Thursday, at ten o'clock in the morning.'

The cast exchanged knowing looks around the table. Charles's directorial absence and the substitution of Persis in his place was a final attempt by Charles to sabotage the production. He was as intent on dooming it to failure as they were on saving it.

Chapter Eleven

*I*t was midday on Tuesday and, as Gina drove away from Digby House, she felt a weight lifting. Despite his absence on the cast's last two days there, the atmosphere that Charles engendered was cloying, dark and unhappy; she was relieved to be leaving. She would miss the others, especially Matt, but they were meeting up again in a couple of days for the two and a half days of final rehearsals at The Redditch.

Five hours later, Gina was pleased to get home at last. She parked her car in the street outside her house and lugged her suitcases out of the boot and up the steps. The front garden was looking rather overgrown, and was in dire need of some attention. Gina didn't mind, though. There was nothing like a spot of weeding to calm her rattled nerves. She often meditated when she was gardening, as she found it a good time for calm introspection.

She unlocked the various locks on the front door, and then slowly pushed it open. There was quite a mound of post on the mat. She bent to scoop up the letters, placed them on the table in the hallway and then went back for her suitcases. She dumped them in the hall and went to have a look around the house, to check that everything was in order.

Some of the houseplants looked forlorn and droopy, and Gina realised that she had neglected to ask Kirsten to pop by and water them. She had been so excited about her trip to Devon a fortnight earlier that she had forgotten about these little details. Funny that, she thought. Had she known then what she knew now, she might not even have gone to Devon, let alone have been excited by the idea. But no, she didn't want to think like that for, if she hadn't gone, she wouldn't have had the chance to get to know Matt.

She went into the kitchen and filled the kettle. A pot of fresh coffee would sort her out. She walked through to her office. Everything was as it should be. Through the sliding doors she could see the garden, lush and overgrown. The roses needed dead-heading, and the hollyhocks and delphiniums had flopped badly and required staking. There were lots of weeds to be pulled up too, and the lawn needed mowing.

She went back to the hall table and picked up her post: lots of junk mail, flyers for the opening offers at a new local pizzeria, two old copies of *The Stage*, some bills, a bank statement and a few personal letters. She took them through to the kitchen and started to go through them as she waited for the kettle to boil. One of the letters was addressed in a hand that she didn't recognise. She looked at the postmark: Devon. It was a thick envelope, made from good-quality paper, and she could tell from the feel of it and the way it rustled that it was lined with tissue paper. It was either from Charles, or from Helena and Marius. There was only one way to find out. She opened it, and a clutch of tickets fell out as she pulled out the letter. She picked one up and looked at it. It was a ticket for the first night of *Riding to the Thames*. She smiled, and unfolded the letter:

Darling Gina,
Here are thirty tickets for *Riding to the Thames*. Knowing Charles, I rather doubt that he will bother to issue any of the cast with complimentary tickets

– what a sod. Anyhow, I decided to remedy that particular situation myself. Can't have you without all your friends and family out there to see your moment of glory! I've given the same number of tickets to all the others, apart from Miss de Gaury, so you should have a good solid core of enthusiastic supporters in the audience. We'll be there too, cheering you all on. Break a leg!

Much love,

H.

How sweet of Helena. She was such a kind and thoughtful woman, thought Gina. The kettle came to a boil and clicked off. Gina got up to make the coffee, deciding to allow herself half an hour to relax before she started the unpacking, washing and tidying that inevitably followed any period of time spent away from home.

Gina went out with Kirsten that evening to the local pub. She told her friend everything about her fortnight in Devon: the house, the rehearsals, her various sexual adventures, and her experiences with Charles. But mostly she spoke of Matt and of her feelings for him, and Kirsten was typically brusque.

'If he didn't leap on you when he had the chance at the Nymphs and Shepherds party, it doesn't sound to me like he's going to make a move at all. You should have joined in that orgy: four men and two women! Wow! I'd have gone for it if I'd been there. It's typical. You get all the breaks, you jammy old bag.' Kirsten laughed. 'Mind you, after what you've told me about Charles Sarazan, I'm not so sure I want you to give him my phone number after all.'

Kirsten gradually convinced Gina that she was wasting her time hankering after someone who obviously wasn't interested in her. The two women talked for the rest of the evening about nothing but men and women, relationships and sex. As Gina let herself into her house at half past eleven that night, she was feeling charged, earthy and distinctly in need of physical release. She had an idea.

The heatwave had not yet broken; it was another hot, still night. Gina opened all the windows and slid back the glass doors to try to get some kind of through-draught circulating round the house. She went into her bedroom, switched on the bedside lamp and started to undress slowly, hoping that Andy was out there watching. She would do a special striptease, just in case.

She undid the mother-of-pearl buttons of her silk blouse one by one, feeling her fingers working between her breasts, brushing against her deep cleavage as she worked her way down. Then she slipped the blouse off her shoulders and let it fall to the floor. She admired herself in the large mirror on the front of her wall-length wardrobe, opposite the bed. Her breasts were cupped in a black lacy bra, giving her a full, ripe cleavage. She could see the darkness of her areolas through the lace, and the points of her nipples. She turned to the side, admiring the way the undersides of her breasts shelved out so distinctly, and the fleshy curve of their upper parts.

Gina put her hands on the waistband of her calf-length skirt and slowly wiggled her way out of it, exaggerating her movements, and pushing it down over her hips, her suspender belt and the tops of her stockings, before it then fell freely to the floor. She had small black lacy panties on, and she could see the darkness of her pubic hair through the lace: a tempting inner place. She looked at herself in the mirror again. Her body was trim and toned, and the black underwear looked stunning against her tanned body. She ran her hands over the tops of the stockings, enjoying the smooth sensuous feel of the fine material. She turned, and looked over her shoulder at her back and bottom, enjoying the sight of her small firm buttocks separated by the thin strip of black lace. Gina loved looking at her body, and sometimes this was the only stimulus that she needed to pleasure herself.

She heard a cough, and turned to the direction from which it had come; pleased that once again, her ruse had worked. There was Andy, and next to him was another young man, with a mop of dark hair falling across his face. He was broader and blockier than Andy, but just as fit. Andy grinned at her. 'Hello, Gina.'

'Well, this is a treat. Hi there, Andy,' she said, as she walked nonchalantly over to him and tilted her head upwards to kiss him on the cheek. She could see that, beneath his fringe, the other lad was ogling her so hard that he looked like he might burst a blood vessel. 'And who is your friend? You should introduce us,' she said, as she held out her hand to the young man. Her heart was pounding, but she mustn't let them know. She must remain in control.

'This is Phil,' said Andy. 'He's at college with me. We've just got back from a week's surfing holiday in Cornwall.'

Gina shook his hand, smiling to herself at the incongruity of this introduction. It wasn't every day that she greeted a complete stranger in her underwear. Teasingly, she said, 'Oh, but that's not fair, I must give you a kiss too.' Inexperienced and unused to such blatancy, Phil swallowed hard as she moved towards him and went up on tiptoe to kiss his cheek. As she moved away again, she looked down and saw with satisfaction another reason for Phil's awkwardness: his jeans were bulging promisingly at the front. He, meanwhile, had his eyes firmly fixed on her cleavage.

'Tell me, Phil, how old are you?' Gina asked.

Phil answered in a hoarse whisper without removing his eyes from her breasts, 'Nineteen.'

'Oh, that's nice,' Gina purred. 'I expect Andy has told you that we are very good friends. I'd like it very much if you and I were friends too. Would you?'

Phil nodded, silently and vigorously. She moved towards him again, and cupped his face with her hands, whilst his hung, seemingly useless, by his waist. She kissed him lingeringly on his lips.

Unbidden, Andy moved close behind her as she kissed Phil and put his hands around her waist, and then ran them up and down her sides, his fingers gently drifting over the outer sides of her bra as he did so. He kissed the back of her neck. This drove her wild, and she broke from Phil and slowly arched back against Andy, her head thrown back against his shoulder.

Phil quickly recovered from his apparent passivity, and cupped her breasts, cushioned in their black lacy cage. With a slow rotating movement he traced small circles on the bare flesh of her cleavage with his thumbs. Then he leant forward and buried his face there, breathing her scent in deeply before starting to cover the exposed part of her breasts with small, grazing kisses. The tiny pricks of his stubble on her breasts tantalised her: so different from her own smooth soft skin.

Andy's hands were now about her waist, moving down to her hips and back up again, playing gently with the lacy band of her suspender belt, then lower to the thin thongs at the sides of her panties, and then to the silky stocking-tops, before reversing the journey back up her body.

Phil undid the clasp of Gina's bra which was nestled at the base of her cleavage. Slipping his hands inside to hold her breasts, he pushed the lacy cups of her bra back, and the straps slid off her shoulders. His hands were cold against her hot flesh, and the roughness of his palms chafed against her nipples, causing them to pucker and harden yet more. He cupped her breasts, caressing them, and he leant forward to kiss her, more demanding this time, greedily crushing her lips with his.

The touch of two pairs of hands on her body, the feeling of two men making love to her was electrifying. She was enclosed by these two young, tall and very obviously aroused men, and their closeness was almost overwhelming: Phil caressed her breasts while Andy was pressed hard up against her back, sandwiching her deliciously.

Gina felt Andy's hands moving from her hips to the

217

gentle rise of her stomach. With one hand he caressed the shallow dimple of her navel, while gradually slipping the fingers of his other hand under the lacy material of her panties. She quaked with anticipation as she felt the slow downwards trace of his fingers there: light touches on her skin and then on the upper margins of her pubic hair. She started to grind her buttocks slowly against him, feeling the straining hardness of his excitement against her.

Phil kissed her hungrily before lowering his head to plant more long, lingering kisses on her breasts. Gina's nipples were so hard and tight that she needed relief; so she arched her back, pressing back against Andy, and thrust her breasts forwards at Phil, twisting at the waist to try to direct a nipple to his mouth. He slowly kissed his way around the dark circle of her areola, teasing her, before taking her nipple in his mouth. Her vagina instinctively contracted with desire at the contact. He started to gently suck, whilst kneading her other breast in his hand. He ran his tongue over and around the taut, sensitive tip, and then began to suck again, harder this time and taking more of her breast into his mouth. Then he broke away from her.

Phil stood back from her, breathing rapidly and heavily, and looked at her as she stood pressed back against Andy. Gina knew that Phil was taking it all in: Andy's hand down the front of her panties, her legs long and slim in their sheer black sheaths, her breasts high and full, one wet from his kisses, her lips slightly parted with desire. Without taking his eyes off her, he hurriedly threw off his T-shirt and jeans. He was stocky and well-built, with a broad chest and thick thighs. His cock stood proud and hard, and tapped against his belly, just under his navel, as he moved. He knelt in front of her and slowly moved his hands over her stockinged legs, lingering at the soft naked flesh of her thighs. His eyes were fixed on her lacy panties, and on Andy's hand inside them, which was moving slowly and deliberately over her tangle of curls.

Then Andy took his hand out of her panties, and Gina groaned in frustration: he had been so close to touching that part of her which ruled everything right now. As Phil leant closer and kissed his way across the tops of her thighs and then over the front of the lacy material of her panties, she felt Andy move away from her, and saw in the mirror that he was quickly taking off his clothes. His tan was complete apart from a tiny area where he had worn swimming trunks. Gina realised that this was the first time that she had seen his cock, which she already knew the feel of so well.

She reached down to Phil, and indicated that he should get up. He stood in front of her and she looked him up and down, almost purring in appreciation, before reaching down to grasp his hard cock with her left hand. Andy moved round to face her also, and with her right hand she reached out for him, and took his circumcised prick, and started to massage it backwards and forwards in time with the rhythm she was working on Phil. Phil's eyes were shut, his head slightly thrown back and his nostrils flared, while Andy was intently watching Gina's hand, curled around his own engorged prick. She smiled to herself, feeling giddy with the power and control that she exerted over these two young men. She thought back to how she had seen Sarah do the same thing a few days ago. But it felt much better to do it than to watch. She could feel their cocks twitching and thickening, and she had plans for these two.

'Andy, take my panties off,' she ordered. He hesitated for a moment, not wanting the lascivious movement of her hand to stop, but she let her hands fall to her sides as she waited for him to obey. He dropped to his knees, and gently eased the tiny scrap of lace down over her hips.

'Phil, lie across the bed, on your back,' she commanded. Phil scrambled on to the bed and lay down, his rasping breath coming in short jerky snatches, so great was his desire. She moved on to the bed, and straddled him on all fours. She knew that beneath her lay a young man who could hardly believe his luck, a young man who was about to have his fantasy of being seduced by an older woman fulfilled. She smiled, and lowered herself over him so that the tips of her breasts were brushing across his chest, and kissed him. He responded passionately, but she broke away and started to kiss his neck, his shoulders and then his chest. She paused to suck lightly on his nipples, teasing them with her tongue, before moving down to his navel. She could feel the urgent twitching of his prick as it jerked back and forth against his stomach, brushing her chin.

'Oh, please,' he moaned, and she knew that more than anything he wanted her to take him in her mouth. Instead, she moved back up his body with her trail of kisses, and could feel him tensing with frustration. Kneeling over him, she looked down at his hard cock, and watched intently as she slowly lowered herself on to it. He moaned quietly. He was thick, and she could feel herself being stretched as she slid down over him.

Gently she started to work herself up and down on his pulsing prick, feeling that wonderful sensation of being fully filled with a large, turgid cock. She looked over to the mirror, and could see that Andy was standing behind her, masturbating as he watched her sinking down over Phil's cock. Phil held her at her waist, and soon he started to thrust upwards to meet her movements. She placed a hand on either side of his head, and leant right forward on her hands and knees so that she could feel the pure intensity of his fucking, ceasing her own rhythm to enjoy the urgency of his movements.

Then she felt the mattress give slightly, and looked up to see that Andy had moved on to the bed in front of her. He was kneeling just behind Phil's head, and was grasping his erect penis in his hand, gazing down at it as he masturbated slowly. He slowly pushed his hips forwards and, holding his cock, brushed it slowly backwards and forwards over her lips. She could smell his arousal, and with her lips she could feel the slippery lubrication on the end of his cock.

'Eat me,' whispered Andy, and she slowly opened her mouth to take in his hard, salty length. Andy started to fuck her mouth with the same rhythm that Phil was thrusting into her from below. She could feel the muscle and the veins of his penis against her lips and her tongue, and as he drew his cock back from her mouth she expertly flicked the end with her tongue. He gazed down at her as he pushed his penis back in again, her mouth stretching into an O around it. Gina could feel him hardening, and guessed that he was not far from coming.

Andy slowly withdrew his cock from her mouth and got off the bed. Gina was surprised at his control, that he had chosen to delay his orgasm. She looked in the mirror, and saw him get on to the bed, straddling Phil's legs as he knelt behind her. She felt the pressure of one of Andy's hands on her back, pushing her down slightly, and she looked in the mirror to see him pumping his penis with the other hand. She could feel Phil hardening inside her, and from his distracted moans she knew his orgasm was imminent. Suddenly she was aware of a pressure against her small, puckered opening. She looked in the mirror and saw Andy rubbing his cock between the cheeks of her buttocks. This was something of a surprise. She hadn't expected so young a man to have such unorthodox sexual tastes.

Her eyes widened as he increased the pressure, pushing gently into her tight orifice. He slid into her, his cock filling her as she was already filled with Phil. This sensory overload, of being taken by two men at once, moving in her with different rhythms, brought her to her peak. Her orgasm came, unexpected in its intensity, causing her to flop forwards over Phil like a rag doll. Phil shuddered, and gave a loud moan as he came, his prick twitching inside her. Almost instantaneously, with his hands on her hips, Andy pumped his final, thrusting strokes deep into her.

They lay there afterwards, calm and quiet in their release, the two young men nestled around Gina on the bed, both touching and stroking her, while she listened to the soulful call of the owl outside. Sleep soon came, and as she drifted off she dreamt that she was lying in Matt's arms, that it was Matt and Matt alone who had just been making love to her.

It was Thursday morning. Rehearsals at The Redditch were due to start at ten o'clock, but Gina had been awake since six and ready to leave the house by seven. She sat at the kitchen table, sipping her third cup of coffee that morning. She was nervous and apprehensive about the following few days. Rehearsing in a small room using the minimum of props was one thing: rehearsing on a proper stage, involving full props, scene changes, complicated exits and entrances was something else. Also, Gina had never played to such a large auditorium before, and wondered whether she would be able to project her voice right to the back. But, despite her worries, Gina was also exhilarated. This was as close to the big time as she had ever come.

She looked at the clock again. It was time to take the tube out to Richmond. She gathered up her script, and her shoulder bag containing her sandwiches for lunch, some wet wipes, a towel and some spare clothes to change into after the rehearsals. Locking up the house, she wondered how she would be feeling when she unlocked it again that night.

Ten minutes later, walking down the steps into the tube station, Gina noticed a brightly coloured advertising poster. It stopped her dead in her tracks. It was for *Riding to the Thames*, and there, amongst the others, was her name: Gina Stanhope. She felt a thrill of excitement, of pleasure, and of pride. But she was also puzzled. It seemed strange for Charles to be advertising the play if he was planning on it being a failure. On the escalator down to the trains, there were more posters. It seemed as if every other advertising space on the walls was taken up by the bright-red posters for the play. Walking on to the platform, she saw two women standing by one of the posters, discussing the play.

'Oh, I want to go and see this. They were talking about it on the radio this morning, and it sounds really good.'

Gina glowed with pride as she walked past the women.

On the rattling tube train, she sat opposite a young man who was reading a newspaper. Here was another pleasant surprise for Gina. On the back page was a full-page advertisement for the play. Gina was intrigued now. Who was providing all the publicity?

Once in Richmond, she rummaged in her shoulder bag for her street guide. She had never been to The Redditch before. She was glad that she had chosen to walk to the theatre from the station as it gave her time to go through her mental relaxation exercises, trying to calm the rising panic she felt in her tightly knotted stomach. She arrived at the theatre at a quarter past nine. It was a massive Victorian red-brick building, intricately decorated with theatrical motifs around the windows and doors. The name of the play was spelt out in three-foot-high letters over the grand entrance. Gina grinned. Following the signs, she walked around the back of the building to the Stage Door. Gina took a deep breath and pushed it open.

A smiling young woman in paint-spattered dungarees greeted her from the Stage Door office, pushing back the glass screen that separated them. Gina introduced herself.

'The others are in the Green Room, if you would like to join them. Second door on the right,' the woman said, pointing up the corridor. 'I'm Abby, by the way. Assistant Stage Manager and general dogsbody.'

Gina smiled, nodded a hello, and walked along the corridor to the Green Room. Even backstage, the theatre was a lot plusher than any she had worked in before. As she approached the Green Room, she could hear familiar voices. She opened the door, and was relieved to see the friendly faces of Matt, Will, Daniel, Sarah, Rory and David.

'Hi there,' said Matt, getting up and coming over to her. He gave her a kiss on the cheek, and Gina felt her stomach give a little leap.

'I'll get you a coffee,' said Rory, going over to a professional-looking espresso machine. Some bone-china cups and saucers were stacked by the machine, and next to them sat a plate of chocolate éclairs and florentines. Gina was even more impressed. At other theatres, the best she had ever had was instant coffee out of a polystyrene cup, and some stale digestive biscuits, if she was lucky.

'Persis not here yet?' she asked, as Rory handed her a small cup of strong black coffee.

'What do you think?' laughed David. 'The Queen Bitch will keep us waiting for her grand entrance, no doubt.'

The Green Room door opened, and everyone fell silent, in case it was Persis. Abby stuck her head round the door. She grinned at them all.

'If you're ready, I'll show you round backstage and then to your dressing rooms. Charles wants you on stage at ten prompt, he said.'

The cast gathered up their coats and belongings, and followed Abby down the corridors and in and out of rooms as she showed them round the bustling backstage area, and introduced them to various backstage crew members. It didn't surprise Gina to find out that she was sharing a dressing room with Sarah, whereas Persis had one all to herself. Still, she didn't mind as it was nice to have company, someone to talk to before the final call on to the stage and to help to keep those gnawing, fluttering butterflies at bay.

She was chatting to Sarah as they poked around in the dressing room, looking in drawers and cupboards and unpacking their few possessions, when an announcement rang over the tannoy.

'Cast of *Riding to the Thames* to the stage, please.'

They made their way to the stage. Charles was already standing on the main stage, looking out to the auditorium. As the cast gathered behind him, he ignored them. They waited for him to turn, but he remained steadily regarding the sea of seats.

Matt spoke. 'We're ready, Charles.'

Charles answered without turning. 'But I, my dear Matt, am not.'

Gina was quite happy for Charles to continue with his self-indulgent grand gesture. It gave her time to take in her surroundings. Her first impression of the theatre would stay with her for a long time, she knew. Gina gazed around her. The theatre was huge, much bigger than she had expected, even though she knew it was a 750-seater. The auditorium was as elaborately decorated as the foyer, and at the sides of the two balcony levels were rows of boxes, each one framed by swags of red velvet curtain. On the stage, the set was already built and furnished for the first act. Gina wondered how the set changes would work, but knew that she would find out very soon. They only had two and a half days to rehearse here, after all, before the first night on Saturday.

Charles took in a deep breath, and then turned to face them.

'Good morning, cast. I hope you approve of my choice of theatre.' The cast murmured their assent. Charles nodded and continued, 'I'm sure we are going to have a huge success on our hands.'

Matt muttered under his breath, 'You two-faced bastard.'

Charles did not hear. He clapped his hands together. 'Right. Take five minutes to familiarise yourself with the stage, the set and the props. We'll go from the top and run right through, including set changes.'

As he was speaking, Persis appeared through a door at the back of the auditorium and slowly walked down towards the stage.

'Sorry I'm late, Charles darling,' she said. She offered no explanation and Charles did not seem to require one. How different it would have been if I'd been late, thought Gina.

* * *

During a break in the rehearsals, while the set was being rearranged, Gina wandered off for a quick look at the front-of-house area. The foyer was carpeted with a sumptuous red carpet, and was a glinting grotto of gilt and brass. A wide, curving double staircase led up to the auditorium. Three large crystal chandeliers hung down from the high ceiling, which was decorated with stucco swags and ornate plasterwork, all gilded to match the walls. Typical Victorian excess, she thought to herself.

She wandered through to the bar, a low-ceilinged and intimate room. The metal shutters were drawn down on the bar, and she could hear someone moving around behind them. The clink of bottles suggested that they were restocking the shelves. Walking back into the foyer area, she bumped into a man clutching a clipboard and with a walkie-talkie clamped to his belt.

'Hello there,' he said. 'You must be with the cast. I'm Geoff, the Front of House Manager.' Gina introduced herself, he held out his hand and they shook. Gina instantly liked the look of Geoff. He had a friendly smile and an easy manner.

'Oh, maybe you could tell me,' said Gina, a sudden thought coming to mind. 'How are the tickets selling?'

'Really well, so I'm told. I'll take you over to Maisie. She's the box-office supremo, the woman with all the facts and figures to hand.' Geoff led her over to the box office and introduced her to a short, bespectacled woman, who smiled a friendly greeting.

'I can tell you, I've been working in the box office here for seven years now, and I've never experienced anything quite like this before,' Maisie said.

'Like what?' asked Gina, intrigued.

'Don't take offence, Gina, but for a new play by a new playwright, with an unknown cast and director, it's quite extraordinary. The tickets are selling like hot cakes. There's no big name to draw the punters, and I don't really understand it. Still, mine not to question why. But there is one thing I did want to ask. All the crew here are curious to know: why the strange rehearsal arrangements? Two and a half days is cutting it a bit fine, don't you think? Why aren't you spending a longer period rehearsing here?'

'Oh, it's a long story,' sighed Gina. As she was speaking, one of the phones in the box office rang.

'Excuse me,' said Maisie. 'Duty calls.' Gina heard her take a booking for forty-five seats. The caller wanted tickets for the first night, but Maisie said that it was sold out. Gina couldn't suppress a whoop of delight as she hurried back to the stage.

An hour and a half later, at the end of the first complete run-through, the cast stood waiting for Charles's reaction. They knew that it had gone really well, apart from Persis's contribution. Instead of projecting her voice, she had merely shouted. The others had waited for Charles to intervene, but he had let it pass without comment or correction.

Charles seemed preoccupied. He was frowning. Gina thought that it might be because he had not expected the run to go nearly as well. He had underestimated how hard the cast had worked during their additional rehearsals, and how much better the performance had become as a result. Gina turned to Matt and grinned. He gave her a thumbs-up sign in reply.

Charles finally spoke. 'That was good,' he said. 'Rehearsals recommence at two o'clock.' He walked quickly off the stage.

In the Green Room during their lunch break, the actors flicked on the television to catch the lunchtime news. They watched in silent and surprised fascination as a feature on the 'Arts Roundup' section mentioned *Riding to the Thames*, telling people to hurry up and buy tickets to see this hot new play. 'Word of mouth is that this is going to be a scorching production,' said the presenter. Persis got up and rushed out of the room.

'I don't get it,' said David. 'Where is this word of mouth coming from? This morning's rehearsal is the first that anyone other than the cast has seen. How can it be so popular already? Normally you have to wait for the rave reviews before the audience numbers start to pick up.'

Gina told them about the advertisements that she'd seen on the underground. Sarah added that she'd come in by bus, and that there were lots of adverts for the production both inside her bus and on the sides and backs of other buses she'd passed during the journey. And then there were the newspaper and radio advertisements.

'Charles is hardly going to promote a play he wants to fail, is he?' asked Daniel. 'So who is? The theatre?'

'Not very likely. They're merely hiring out the theatre space to Charles. It's not an in-house production so they won't be the ones responsible for publicity,' said David.

'How very strange,' said Matt.

Gina remembered something Helena had said the other day, and suddenly she had the blinding realisation of just who was responsible for this. 'He needs to be taught a lesson,' Marius had said, and then Helena had added that they were just the people to do it. What an appropriate way for Helena and Marius to take revenge on Charles, given their involvement in the arts. Gina wondered how much they were spending. It must be an awful lot of money. She only hoped that she and the others could do the Burckhardts justice.

After lunch, Gina was walking from her dressing room back to the stage when she heard a familiar voice coming from behind a closed door. She looked up. It was the door of Charles's office – a temporarily converted dressing room. Charles's voice was angry, and from the lack of any response she could tell that he was on the telephone.

'What the hell do you mean you can't cancel the advertisements?' A pause. 'No, I did not place them.' Another pause. 'Look, you half-wit, I am Charles Sarazan, the director and producer of the play. If I don't want these advertisements run, then you pull them, OK? That is all the authorisation you need.' There was a much longer pause. 'Well if you aren't going to cancel the advertisements, would you kindly tell me who placed them, so that I can go and wring their bloody necks.' There was another pause, and then Gina heard the phone being slammed down. Charles muttered angrily to himself. 'Jumped-up little jobsworth. "Confidential information". Who the hell does he think he is?' Then she heard him heading towards the door, and so ducked into an open doorway nearby. Charles would wring her neck if he knew that she had overheard.

The next day, and only the second day of rehearsals in the theatre, it was time for the first full dress and technical rehearsal. Paul Lane, the lighting designer, had spent the morning making the final adjustments to the lighting and tutoring the technicians in its deployment. Up in the control box, Abby and the Stage Manager were preparing the sound effects and music cues. Gina and Sarah shared a dresser, Kate, and she had spent the morning unpacking, and checking and ironing their four costumes with an accompanying and mounting chorus of appreciative 'oohs' and 'aahs'.

The full run took just over three hours and, bar Persis's excesses, it went very well. The backstage crew were experienced and undertook their duties smoothly; the lighting crew picked up every cue, and the costume changes went perfectly. The cast were seized by an excited euphoria. They knew that this production could be very, very good. The play was well written, the characters believable and engaging, and their acting had improved by leaps and bounds. Conversely, Charles's direction had become laxer and laxer, but this had ceased to matter. The production had taken on a momentum of its own, and the cast's self-belief powered it on, in spite of what they knew of Charles's plans.

'OK cast,' said Charles. 'Very good. Relax tomorrow morning, and be here at midday for the final dress rehearsal. It's the first night tomorrow and, as you all know, the press will also be attending. I expect that they will have a lot to write about this production.' Gina was watching him closely. He smiled as he uttered this last sentence. She suspected that he was up to something. Smiling was not something Charles undertook often or lightly. He dismissed the cast with a casual wave of his hand.

Chapter Twelve

The next morning, as Gina came in through the Stage Door, Abby leant out of the hatch of the Stage Door office and called after her.

'Gina, Charles wants to see you in his office, straight away.'

Gina wondered what this would be about. She walked down to Charles's office, and knocked on the door.

'Come,' called Charles.

Gina entered. Charles was busily tapping away on a laptop computer. 'You wanted to see me?' she asked.

Charles looked up at her. 'Ah, Gina. Yes. Bad news, I'm afraid. Poor Persis has come down with laryngitis overnight. Her throat has just about closed up and she can't say a thing. I've been trying to figure out what to do. Been kicking myself for not thinking about understudies until it was too late.' He shrugged his shoulders.

You lying bastard, Gina thought angrily. This was just another of Charles's many attempts to ruin the production. She was certain that, as they spoke, Persis was sitting at home in perfect health. She wondered what Charles had bribed Persis with to make her agree to drop out. And what about the understudies that he had threatened David and Sarah with, the night that he had taken them to the torture boudoir? Much as she had suspected then, the understudies had never existed. Just another of Charles's deceits.

Charles continued. 'I've thought it through carefully. I've decided the best thing is for you to step into Persis's role. Sarah can take your part as well as her own, as the characters that you have been playing up until now are only on the stage at the same time once. That's not a problem, as Sarah's original role in that scene was a non-speaking one. We can lose that easily. I'm sure you won't find it too difficult to take on Persis's role – you've seen it rehearsed enough times. I've already told Sarah. She seems remarkably calm.'

Charles smirked, and then he gestured at Gina to indicate that she was dismissed. She wanted to say something, but bit her tongue. She would put all her energies into the part instead. Gina went into the Green Room. Sarah was already in there, and had obviously told the others.

'Jesus, he doesn't give up, does he?' exploded Matt, as he saw Gina coming in, grim-faced.

'We might have expected this, I suppose,' David said fatalistically.

Gina realised that things could slip badly, and that it was up to her to prevent it. The morale of the cast was dependent on her.

'Look, I know Persis's part, no problems. Sarah knows mine, don't you?' She turned to Sarah, who nodded uncertainly. Gina continued. 'There's no need to worry. I know we've only got one rehearsal, but we can do this with our eyes closed, can't we?'

'Yes, you're right,' said Matt. 'We've done it without Persis enough times already. And look on the bright side, Sarah. You get to wear Gina's gorgeous costumes.'

Sarah immediately perked up. This obviously hadn't occurred to her. 'Hey. We'd better round up Kate and check that we can fit into our new costumes,' she said.

An hour and a half later, the call went out over the tannoy for the final full dress rehearsal of *Riding to the Thames*. During the rehearsals, Gina was concentrating so hard on remembering the script and finding her way around the stage in her new part that she didn't have time to think about being worried or nervous. That was, not until it was time to rehearse the love scene with Matt.

She suddenly realised what she was going to have to do: stand naked in front of Matt, and he would look at and appraise her body. She had been naked before him the night of the skinny-dip, but that was under soft flattering moonlight, not the harsh glare of stage lights. But she had no time to prepare, or to do anything about it. The action was progressing inexorably towards the love scene.

She left the stage on cue, and waited in the wings, stepping into the beautiful flowing chiffon dress and allowing Kate to button it up and arrange the folds of cloth around her, like a bridesmaid fussing around the bride before she steps into the church. She could smell Persis's perfume on the dress, and she pulled a face.

Kate noticed. 'Hey, are you OK?' She looked at Gina with concern.

Gina nodded. 'Yes, honestly, I'm fine. Just a touch of nerves.'

'I'm not surprised,' said Kate. 'Full dress rehearsal also means full nudity. Rather you than me. I couldn't do it.'

Gina smiled to herself. If only you knew, she thought. She looked over to the other wing and saw Matt changing into his costume for the next scene. The stage lights went down and the slow mechanical hoisting of the set change started. The backstage crew could be heard quietly scuffling about on the stage, changing the props. It was time. With the stage lights down, she took up her position at the centre of the stage. In the dimness, she could see Matt already in position.

Gina was surprised to find how easy it was to fall into character and to be flirtatious and brazen in front of Matt, and in front of all the other watching cast and crew members. The slow, ritual teasing and flirting of the two characters seemed to be so natural, it hardly felt as if she was acting. She was so focussed that no one else existed apart from Matt.

Before she knew it, she reached the point in the scene where she had to take her clothes off. She remembered how Matt had watched Persis, and could hardly bear to look up at him, but she had to for the sake of the part. Matt was gazing at her with an intensity which she found unsettling. He watched her closely as she unbuttoned the dress, dropped it over her shoulders, and then slowly stepped out of it. She stood, allowing him to look at her body at length, then turned, went to the bed, and slipped under the covers.

She couldn't wait for him to join her in the bed, and she hoped that her desire was not too obvious. He quickly undressed down to his boxer shorts: the playwright had obviously thought the audience less able to cope with male nudity than female. Matt came over to the bed. Gina was breathing rapidly now, glad that she could disguise her own desire as being that of her character.

The bed shifted slightly as Matt sat on it, and again as he leant over her. His closeness was almost unbearable. Then he kissed her. Gina felt her whole body tingle: this was their first kiss, something that she had wanted to happen from almost the first moment she had seen him. Although the kiss was closely scripted, Gina could not help but think that there was something more to this than just a stage kiss. His lips seemed to linger on hers for longer than was needed. Then Matt pulled back the covers and slipped into the bed with her. Gina was praying that she would not forget her lines, that the overwhelming and intimate presence of Matt would not prove too distracting, that she could resist the urge to reach for him right there and then.

He looked deeply into her eyes as they went through their lines. When they had to kiss again, he pulled her close to him under the sheets. She almost called out with delighted surprise. He was stirring against her. He wanted her. But the scene was moving on, and the dialogue was tricky and involved, so Gina had to concentrate hard on getting her lines right. All the time she was aware of the presence of Matt next to her in the bed. She willed herself not to become distracted.

Gina felt Matt move against her again, and his hand slipped round her waist once more and pulled her close, as scripted. Her breath was coming in short ragged pulls, but she hoped that Matt would think that this was merely nervousness due to her newness in the role. Her hands were pressed against him, and she could feel the short soft curls of the hair on his chest and the strong, rhythmical surge of his breathing as he cradled her. She could feel something else too: against her groin was the unmistakable hardness of his manhood under his boxer shorts. Placing a hand on her lower back, he pulled her even closer to him, and then shifted so he was over her, his legs straddling hers.

This was the part that Gina had dreaded: the part where they had to pretend to make love. Gina wondered how she could go through the motions without becoming carried away, especially as it was obvious to her that Matt was aroused. He spoke his lines and then leant down to kiss her again, and she responded with a vigour which was no act. Then he started to move rhythmically over her, as if they were actually making love. She could feel his penis pressing hard against her, straining now. She longed to release it, but could not. She was still not completely sure if it was her he desired or if this was purely the physiological reaction of his body to certain stimuli.

He spoke the line which was her cue, and she looked up at him and arched her back, pressing up into him, against his hardness, as she faked her orgasm. She called out his name. As she sighed and moaned, she could hear laughter. The crew and the rest of the cast were snickering in the wings. She realised that, in her excitement, she had forgotten to call Matt by his character's name.

Gina felt slightly dazed as the lights dimmed and the

scene changed again. Matt gave her an affectionate pat on the rump as she got out of the bed. 'I really enjoyed that,' he said, smiling. 'I mean it.' She hurriedly left the stage, and went to her dressing room. Her next scene was in about ten minutes, and she wanted to splash her face with cold water. She was hot and bothered, for sure.

At the end of the rehearsal, the cast were ecstatic, hugging and kissing each other. It had gone perfectly and, what was more, they had all enjoyed themselves: a sure sign of a good production. Charles, who had said nothing throughout the entire rehearsal, gave a weak, strained smile.

'Beginners' call is at five to eight,' he said, and left.

Walking back to her dressing room, Gina wondered whether she was right about Matt. Was he really attracted to her? After all, she knew that men could get involuntary erections, nothing to do with lust or desire. Was that what Matt had been experiencing?

Gina spent the rest of the afternoon reading quietly in her dressing room, trying to make sure that she knew Persis's part perfectly. Sarah had gone shopping: she said that it was the best method of relaxation that she knew. Gina could hear the busy noise in the theatre, as the cleaners polished and swept, the bar staff tidied the bar areas, and the backstage crew made their final checks. Nearer the time, she could hear giggles as the young ushers arrived. They were mostly teenagers making some pocket money from an evening job in the theatre.

There was a quiet knock, and Matt stuck his head round the door. 'Can I come in?' he asked.

'Of course,' said Gina, delighted that Matt had sought her out. She curled up on the chaise longue so that there was room for him too.

'I just wanted to pop by to say I thought you were great this afternoon,' he said.

Gina smiled uncomfortably. Did he mean her perform-

236

ance in general, or was he being oblique, and specifically referring to her performance in the bed?

'It can't have been easy for you, but I think you did very well. You were certainly very composed during the love scene.' He looked at her and smiled.

'Well it was all due to your reassuring presence,' she said. They exchanged a long look, and Gina felt that the unspoken words were understood.

He reached out and stroked her arm. 'I'm looking forward to tonight. I can't think of anyone I'd rather have as my leading lady,' Matt said.

Sarah came in, her timing immaculately bad. 'Oops. Not interrupting a beautiful moment, am I?' she asked with a grin.

'Of course not,' said Gina, cursing silently. She wanted more time alone with Matt. Things were starting to go right, at last. 'We were just discussing our parts.'

There was another knock on the door, and Abby came in with a handful of cards. 'These have arrived for you both,' she said, putting the pile down on one of the dressing tables. Sarah leapt on them, sorted them into two piles, and then handed Gina hers. 'Have you heard the news?' Abby asked. 'The tickets have been selling so well that you've got a full house for the next three and a half weeks at the latest count, and they're still selling. And you won't believe it: there's a plane circling overhead, trailing an advertising banner for the play.'

'Hey, that's fantastic,' said Sarah, settling into a chair and starting to open her cards. Gina realised that she and Matt were not going to get any more time alone together, and he seemed to sense the same thing.

He got up, and smiled at Gina. 'I'll leave you to it. See you later.' Gina watched him go, marvelling at the near-perfection of his rear view.

'I dare say you will,' said Sarah happily, not looking up from her cards. She was visibly buzzing with the heady mixture of excitement and adrenalin. She continued to rip open the envelopes, but Gina left hers sitting on her lap. 'Go on, open them,' said Sarah impatiently.

'No, I'm going to save them until just before curtain-up,' Gina replied.

There was another knock and Abby came back in, with a huge cellophane-wrapped bunch of flowers cradled in either arm, one for Sarah and one for Gina. Sarah squealed with delight. Gina had never seen such lavish bouquets before. She opened the small card perched in between the flowers, and read the message:

Pleased to tell you that Charles is backing a smash hit, and Cecil is avenged. Break both legs!
All love, Helena and Marius.

Now all Gina had to do was acquit herself well.

It was almost time. Gina had managed to eat some food earlier on, but her throat was so tight with nerves that she had found it difficult to swallow it down. She was already in her first costume, and her hair had been put up in an elegant French plait. She applied her stage make-up, trying to dull out all thoughts of the people who were even now arriving at the theatre, milling in the bar or finding their seats. Most of all, she tried not to think about the reviewers who would be sitting in the front rows, scrutinising her every move, and making notes on every aspect of her performance. She wondered if tonight was the night that the tutors from The National Academy of Dramatic Arts would be in the audience.

Gina opened her cards. The biggest one was from Kirsten, and there were lots from other friends. Two more bouquets of flowers arrived for her, one from her ex-colleagues at the clothes store, and the other from Andy. Sweet lad, she thought with a smile.

The tannoy crackled into life. 'Five-minute call for *Riding to the Thames*. Five minutes please. Five minutes.'

Gina looked across at Sarah, who smiled back nervously, and said, 'Oh God. That means there's only ten minutes until the curtain goes up.' She was looking very apprehensive.

'This is it, Sarah,' said Gina. 'In just over three hours, it'll all be over, and we'll be wondering what all the fuss was about.'

They walked to the backstage area, joining the other actors en route. There was a light, joking atmosphere, an overreaction to the adrenalin which was rushing through them all. The excitement was palpable. Daniel was juggling with three apples. 'Displacement activity,' he said to Gina. 'If I concentrate on this I can't get nervous.'

The cast gathered behind the curtain for a last-minute group huddle. They stood in a circle, with heads bowed and holding hands, each silently thinking of success, willing it to happen. 'Let's make it a good one,' said Matt; then they broke the contact, slapped each other on the back, shook hands, and hugged.

The tannoy crackled again. 'Beginners' call for *Riding to the Thames*. Beginners' call, please. Beginners.'

They heard a creaking and realised that the fire curtain was being raised. Gina looked at Abby in panic. Surely it wasn't time for curtain-up yet? Beginners' call was a full five minutes before curtain-up.

'It's OK. There's a slight hitch with the pulleys. They're just raising the fire curtain to loosen them and put on some oil,' Abby whispered to her.

Sarah took the opportunity to go up to the stage curtains and peek out at the audience. She parted the long red drapes a few inches, and then gasped. 'Oh my God, there are so many people out there.'

David laughed. 'What did you expect? It's a full house.'

More creaking indicated that the fire curtain was being lowered again. Charles walked on to the stage. He signalled to the backstage crew to join them. When everyone had gathered in silence, he cleared his throat and then spoke in a low voice.

'Good luck.'

There were angry gasps as he turned and left the stage.

Gina couldn't believe what Charles had just done. Although she was not superstitious herself, she knew that a lot of theatrical people were. Wishing them 'Good luck' was tantamount to calling the worst of all bad luck down on them.

Matt stepped into the spot Charles had just vacated. 'Look, everyone, ignore him. Let's do this for us, for each other. Oh, and break a leg.'

Everyone grinned. They could hear the bell summoning the last stragglers in the audience from the foyer and the bars. It would be curtain-up any minute now.

Gina, Rory and Daniel took up their positions on the stage behind the curtain. The house lights went down and they heard the expectant murmur of the audience gradually quieten, then cease. There was a drawn-out creaking noise as the fire curtain was raised once more and then the heavy stage curtains were slowly drawn apart. This was it. Gina looked out. She couldn't see anyone in the pit of blackness that faced her, but she knew that 750 pairs of eyes were on her. She took a deep breath, and spoke the first line of the play.

The excited buzz backstage during the interval was electric. Gina knew that she was part of something special. All the promise of the later rehearsals had reached fulfilment. The play was superb, the production was excellent, the sets, lighting and costumes were first class, and, most important of all, the acting was of uniformly high standard. Everyone had pulled out the stops, and given it an extra effort that had never been apparent during the rehearsals. The last-minute swap seemed to have had no adverse effect at all. Gina and Sarah were coping with their parts as if they had always played them.

Abby went out to the bar to eavesdrop on people's conversations. She came back wearing a Cheshire Cat smile.

'They're raving about it. I saw Michael Glubb out

there, so I sidled up past him. I heard him say "very impressive" to his companion.'

Everyone cheered. Michael Glubb was a theatre critic for one of the broadsheets, and was well known as a stern and rigorous reviewer. If Michael Glubb could be pleased, then the play was guaranteed success.

The bell went for the end of the interval, and the tannoy announcement reiterated it. The cast reassembled in the wings, ready for the beginning of the next act. Gina jogged up and down on the spot, trying to dispel some of the nervous energy she felt coursing through her. She looked across at Matt, who winked at her. She winked back, and then laughed. She couldn't have dreamt of a better outcome.

It was time for the love scene. Gina slipped into her costume, a dreamy calmness coming over her. She hardly thought of the play, or of the audience. All she could think of was that soon she would be lying naked in a bed with Matt. She wished that she could freeze that moment for ever.

Stepping on to the stage, she felt a charge, and not just from herself. The audience were watching with expectancy too. They knew from the development of the play that a love scene was imminent, that this would be the culmination of the affair between Matt and Gina's characters. They had been moving inexorably towards this since almost the first scene. Gina felt that she could sense the audience willing her on. Their concentration was so complete that there was barely a cough or a shuffle emanating from the auditorium.

She moved towards Matt. He looked so good, dressed in jeans and a torn white T-shirt, stretched tight over his chest. She placed her hand on his pectorals, and could feel his heart thumping beneath. Their flirtatious conversation commenced, and Gina held Matt's gaze as she spoke her lines, every word her character spoke echoing her own thoughts and desires.

As she slipped out of her dress, the audience gasped,

surprised by her nudity. She looked at Matt for reassurance, as she had not expected quite this reaction. He was looking at her intently, and she could see that his pupils were dilated. She knew then that he desired her: in the bright spotlights an actor's pupils were usually contracted to a small, sharp point of black in the centre of the irises. Matt's chest was rising and falling rapidly, and she could see his fast pulse throbbing in the vein in his neck. The heat from the spotlights, combined with that generated by the audience, and this outer warmth added to the delicious feeling of inner warmth that Gina was experiencing. Drawing out her part, she stood for much longer than scripted to allow Matt to fully appreciate her. Then she turned and walked slowly and seductively to the bed. She slid back the sheets and got into the bed, waiting for him to join her.

Matt hurriedly threw off his clothes until he was only in his boxer shorts. Gina knew instinctively that she would be able to see the obvious signs of his arousal, and sure enough there was a prominent bulge at the front of his boxers. Gina hoped that under the loose material it was not too obvious to the audience. He came over to the bed, sat on the side, and then leant over and kissed her. Matt kissed her hungrily, almost bruising her lips against his, and even more ardently than he had kissed her during the rehearsals. Then he pulled back the sheet and joined her in the bed.

As Matt spoke his lines, he was rustling about with the sheets and looking up when he was supposed to be looking at her. Gina was unsure why, but thought that perhaps it was nerves. Then Matt turned and pulled her close to him to kiss her again. This time Gina was truly shocked. Matt was naked. Whilst rustling with the sheets, he had also removed his boxer shorts. And now only was he naked, but she could feel that he was fully hard, his cock twitching against the soft mound of her belly. She tried desperately to remain calm, and to remember her lines. He pulled her close and kissed her and again she was shocked, for this kiss was not scripted

One of his hands slid under the sheets and caressed her soft skin at the side of her waist, before sliding upwards and cupping her breast. Her nipples immediately reacted to his touch, stiffening so much that they were almost painful.

Matt broke away from their kiss to allow her to speak her lines and, as she was doing so, his hand roamed over her body, stroking and caressing her. She felt the contraction deep in her stomach, a violent spasm of need and urgent want, and felt herself becoming moist. She tried to keep her voice steady as his hand gently traced a line down her stomach and between her legs. His hand found her downy cleft, and she could feel his fingers gently stroking and probing her by-now slippery wetness, the centre of her desire.

As Gina finished her lines, Matt pulled her close and kissed her yet again, another unscripted kiss. Gina could not now conceal her arousal. She kissed him with a demanding ferocity, and pressed herself against him. She cared little about the audience, even about her performance: all she wanted right now was Matt.

Now it was time for their scripted lovemaking. Matt shifted on the bed so that he was kneeling on all fours over her, with his legs straddling hers. The sheet was up over his back, shielding their nakedness from the audience's gaze. She looked down beneath the sheet and could see his cock hard up against his stomach, throbbing with his desire. He leant down over her and kissed her hungrily again. Then, with his left hand around the base of his cock, he guided his penis towards her pulsating sex. Distracted, and yet desperately trying to remain composed, Gina spoke her last line before the lovemaking commenced.

'Take me.'

No sooner had she spoken these words than Matt pressed his solid, straining penis against the entrance of her slick vagina and, after a slight moment's resistance, slid powerfully into her. Gina gasped. He was filling her completely. He pressed his mouth to hers again, before murmuring in her ear: 'Gina.' He started to thrust with a slow steady rhythm, moving in and out, plunging so far in again each time that she felt she would not be able to take all of him. His hand had moved down to where their bodies were linked, and he started to massage her clitoris with his thumb, rolling and pressing it gently with a rhythm matching that of his thrusts. Gina felt the sudden oncoming rush of her approaching orgasm. The knowledge that they were making love in front of 750 people drove her over the edge, and 750 people watched as she thrashed and cried out with the most powerful orgasm she had ever experienced. They were both so aroused that Matt started to come almost immediately after her, pumping into her with long, slow, juddering thrusts. He collapsed over her, kissing her sweat-drenched neck, as the stage lights dimmed.

As the final curtain fell, the applause from the audience was thunderous. Gina looked across at Matt in near-disbelief. This was truly beyond her wildest imaginings. He came across to her and kissed her gently on the lips and then moved closer for a longer, deeper kiss. She put her arms around his neck and pulled him hard up against her, feeling the security and comfort of his firm muscular body. The rest of the cast gathered on the stage for the curtain call, but it was as if they did not exist. The curtain rose, but Gina and Matt were still entwined and too engrossed to notice. As the audience saw them kissing, a cheer went up.

There were eight curtain calls before the audience would finally let them go. A call for the director went up, but Charles did not appear.

Gina hardly registered a thing as she walked off the stage. It felt as if she was floating. Everything seemed so unreal, so heightened. But, above everything else, blotting out all thoughts of acceptance to drama school and of critical success, was the thought of Matt, of his body moving against and into and with hers under the thin cotton sheet.

She felt an arm slip round her waist, and looked up. It was Matt. People were coming up to them, slapping them on the back and shaking hands, kissing their cheeks, but Matt never relinquished his hold on her.

Abby came rushing up. 'My God, that was fantastic. Unbelievable. We were going to have a party in the Green Room, but I don't think there's enough space. We'll have it on the stage. I'll get the stagehands to clear it,' and she went dashing off again.

Matt finally released Gina as she reached her dressing-room door. 'See you in a bit,' he said, and kissed her once again, slowly and lingeringly.

Gina sat at her dressing table in a daze. Sarah was babbling on ten to the dozen at the other dressing table as she wiped off her make-up, but Gina hardly heard her. She was lost in her thoughts and in her happiness. There was a knock at the door. Sarah leapt up to open it, and shrieked with delight as she saw Marius and Helena standing there.

'Come in, come in,' Sarah squealed excitedly.

Marius produced a bottle of champagne and two glasses, and Helena held out two more. 'You were fantastic, both of you,' she beamed.

Gina hugged them both. 'Thank you so much for everything,' she said.

Helena kissed her on the cheek. 'No, thank you, Gina. If it hadn't been for that lucky meeting in the woods, we might never have had this perfect chance to settle old scores. And you were brilliant.'

Marius looked at Gina and winked. 'You were superb, very convincing. Especially the love scene.' He eased the cork out of the bottle and filled the four flutes with the sparkling champagne.

'Have you seen Charles?' asked Gina. He had not been in the backstage area after the play had finished.

'No, and I don't care to. He must have realised by now that he's been pretty comprehensively trounced. I doubt you'll be seeing him again tonight,' said Helena.

'Here's to your success,' Marius said, raising his glass.

'Success,' the four friends toasted.

Gina felt she had to say something. 'I hope that you didn't spend too much on all this. I know how expensive advertising is, and all those tickets as well . . .'

Marius merely laughed. 'Gina. One thing my business experience has taught me is the truth of that old adage: You've got to speculate to accumulate. The result of our little investment is more than worthwhile, and we consider it money well spent. And, besides, we didn't buy many of the tickets. We didn't need to, as they were selling so well by word of mouth.'

'You will come to the party, won't you?' Gina asked. 'We're going to wait up for the notices in the early-morning editions of the papers.'

'We'd be delighted,' said Helena.

Fifteen minutes later, when Sarah and Gina had changed out of their costumes, cleaned off their make-up, and showered, they all wandered over to the stage area. The party was already pretty wild: a natural extension of the adrenalin which had been present in the theatre since before the first curtain went up. There was a big table on one side of the stage laden with drinks, and on another were plates piled with slices of pizza.

'I thought you'd all be hungry. We haven't really had much of a chance to eat, have we?' said Abby.

Up in the control box the Stage Manager had put on a tape of dance music, and soon the whole stage was a throng of people dancing, chatting, laughing and having a good time. Charles was conspicuous by his absence.

At four o'clock in the morning, Abby and Geoff went out to buy the early-morning editions of the papers. They returned ten minutes later with a pile of newspapers. Abby called for quiet.

'Right. I'm going to read these out one by one, with no censoring. What they wrote is what I'll read.'

'Oh no, please,' said Sarah. 'What if they've written something really horrible?'

'They won't have, silly,' said Will. 'It was fantastic, we all know that. Go on, Abby.'

Abby pulled up a chair from the side of the stage and clambered up on to it. Geoff handed her the first newspaper, folded back to the relevant page. She cleared her throat, and read the review. When she finished, everyone cheered. The same thing happened with each review, for each one was glowing, and some almost ecstatic.

After Abby had finished, the reviews were passed round so that people could read them again. Certain phrases seemed to swim before Gina's eyes as she scanned the newsprint:

A great new talent has sprung on to the London theatrical scene. Gina Stanhope played Victoria with uninhibited passion, conviction, energy and a rare understanding.

Rarely have I enjoyed a night at the theatre so much. It would be difficult to find fault with any aspect of this production – apart from the fact that it had to end after some three hours of sheer pleasure.

Matt Burton gave a sensitive and intelligent performance. An actor of great promise, I think we will undoubtedly be seeing much more of him in the future.

The director and producer of this new play, Charles Sarazan, is to be congratulated. His vision in producing a play by an unknown playwright, and in casting it with as-yet-untried actors was a daring gamble which paid off royally. He has an undoubted knack for spotting bright new talent, and has a deserved success on his hands.

Gina Stanhope was a revelation – more so when you learn that she stepped into the part of Victoria not eight hours before giving her stunning first performance.

Do anything you can to get hold of tickets for this exciting new production!

Gina had to pinch herself. She could scarcely believe it. The play was a success and, moreover, she was a success.

At half past eight the next morning the party was still going on, although people were sitting and talking now rather than dancing. The newspapers lay strewn across the floor, which was also covered with empty wine bottles and discarded plastic cups. Matt was sitting on the floor, resting against a pillar; Gina was sitting between his legs, leaning back against his chest. Matt's arms were about her, and his face was buried in her hair, nuzzling the nape of her neck. Gina was happier than she had ever been in her life.

'I've been wanting to do that with you for the last two weeks,' Matt whispered in her ear.

She turned and looked at him, grinning with disbelief. 'So why didn't you?' she asked.

'I thought I might blow my chances if I came on too strong,' he replied.

Gina threw her head back and laughed. 'Oh my God, I don't believe it. I fancy you and daren't make a move; you fancy me and daren't make a move. You mean we were both tiptoeing around each other when we could have been at it like jack rabbits?'

'Thank heavens we've cleared up that little misunderstanding then,' Matt laughed, kissing her again.

Above the murmurs of conversation, a phone rang somewhere. Abby scooted off to answer it. She came back and hurried up to Gina. 'A Miss Nelson from The National Academy of Dramatic Arts would like to speak to you.'

Gina cast a look at Matt, and got up and went to the office. She picked up the receiver. 'Hello?'

Miss Nelson was brisk and businesslike, exactly as she had been on the day that she had headed the interviewing panel. 'Miss Stanhope. I have just read this morning's papers. I don't think there will be any need for one of our tutors to visit your production. I am pleased to confirm your place at the college, and look forward to welcoming you here in September. My congratulations.'

Gina slowly walked back to rejoin Matt. 'More good news?' he asked, and she nodded. He looked at her searchingly. 'Look, do you want to slip away for a while? We don't have to be back here until this afternoon. Come home with me. Please.'

Gina held out her hands, and he took them. She helped to pull him up, and then kissed him. 'I'd love to,' she said.

BLACK LACE NEW BOOKS

Published in March

THE CAPTIVATION
Natasha Rostova
£5.99

It's 1917 and war-torn Russia is teetering on the brink of the Bolshevik revolution. The Princess Katya is forced to leave her estate when a mob threatens her life. After a daring escape, she ends up in the encampment of a rebel Cossack army. The men have not seen a woman for weeks and sexual tensions are running high. The captain is a man of dark desires and he and Katya become involved in an erotic power struggle.

ISBN 0 352 33234 4

A DANGEROUS LADY
Lucinda Carrington
£5.99

Lady Katherine Gainsworth is compromised into a marriage of convenience which takes her from her English home to the Prussian Duchy of Heldenburg. Once there, she is introduced to her future in-laws but finds they have some unconventional ideas of how to welcome her into the family. Her father-in-law, the Count, is no stranger to the underworld of bawdy clubs in the duchy and soon Katherine finds herself embroiled in political intrigue, jewel theft and sexual blackmail.

ISBN 0 352 33236 0

FEMININE WILES
Karina Moore
£7.99

Young American Kelly Aslett is due to fly back to the USA to claim her inheritance according to the terms of her father's will. As she prepares to fly home she falls passionately in love with French artist Luc Duras. Meanwhile, in California, Kelly's stepmother is determined to secure Kelly's inheritance for herself and enlists the help of her handsome lover and the dashing and ruthless Johnny Casigelli to assist her in her criminal deed. When Kelly finds herself held captive by Johnny, will she succumb to his masculine charms or can she use her feminine wiles to gain what's rightfully hers?

ISBN 0 352 33235 2

Published in April

PLEASURE'S DAUGHTER
Sedalia Johnson
£5.99

1750, England. After the death of her father, headstrong young Amelia goes to live with her wealthy relatives. During the journey she meets the cruel Marquess of Beechwood, who both excites and frightens her. She escapes from him only to discover later that he is a good friend of her aunt and uncle. The Marquess pursues her ruthlessly, and persuades her uncle to give him her hand – but Amelia escapes and runs away to London. She takes up residence in an establishment dedicated to the pleasure of the feminine senses, where she becomes expert in every manner of debauch, and is happy with her new life until the Marquess catches up with her and demands that they renew their marriage vows.

ISBN 0 352 33237 9

AN ACT OF LOVE
Ella Broussard
£5.99

In order to be accepted at drama school, Gina has to be in a successful theatrical production. She joins the cast for a play which is being financed by kinky control freak, Charles Sarazan, who begins to pursue Gina. She is more attracted to Matt, one of the actors in the play, but finds it difficult to approach him, especially after she sees Persis, the provocative female lead, making explicit advances to him. Gina learns that Charles is planning to sabotage the production so that he can write it off as a tax loss. Can she manage to satisfy both her craving for success and her lust for the leading man?

ISBN 0 352 33240 9

To be published in May

SAVAGE SURRENDER
Deanna Ashford
£5.99

In the kingdom of Harn, a marriage is arranged between the beautiful Rianna and Lord Sarin, ruler of the rival kingdom of Percheron, who is noted for his voracious sexual appetite. On her way to Percheron, Rianna meets a young nobleman who has been captured by Sarin's brutal guards. Their desire for each other is instant but can Rianna find a way to save her young lover without causing unrest between the kingdoms?

ISBN 0 352 33253 0

THE SEVEN-YEAR LIST
Zoe le Verdier
£5.99

Julie – an ambitious young photographer – is invited to a college reunion just before she is due to be married. She cannot resist a final fling but finds herself playing a dangerous erotic game with a man who still harbours desires for her. She tries to escape a circle of betrayal and lust but her old flame will not let her go. Not until he has completed the final goal on his seven-year list.

ISBN 0 352 33254 9

If you would like a complete list of plot summaries of Black Lace titles, please fill out the questionnaire overleaf or send a stamped addressed envelope to:-

Black Lace, 332 Ladbroke Grove, London W10 5AH

BLACK LACE BOOKLIST

All books are priced £4.99 unless another price is given.

Black Lace books with a contemporary setting

ODALISQUE	Fleur Reynolds ISBN 0 352 32887 8	☐
VIRTUOSO	Katrina Vincenzi ISBN 0 352 32907 6	☐
THE SILKEN CAGE	Sophie Danson ISBN 0 352 32928 9	☐
RIVER OF SECRETS	Saskia Hope & Georgia Angelis ISBN 0 352 32925 4	☐
SUMMER OF ENLIGHTENMENT	Cheryl Mildenhall ISBN 0 352 32937 8	☐
MOON OF DESIRE	Sophie Danson ISBN 0 352 32911 4	☐
A BOUQUET OF BLACK ORCHIDS	Roxanne Carr ISBN 0 352 32939 4	☐
THE TUTOR	Portia Da Costa ISBN 0 352 32946 7	☐
THE HOUSE IN NEW ORLEANS	Fleur Reynolds ISBN 0 352 32951 3	☐
WICKED WORK	Pamela Kyle ISBN 0 352 32958 0	☐
DREAM LOVER	Katrina Vincenzi ISBN 0 352 32956 4	☐
UNFINISHED BUSINESS	Sarah Hope-Walker ISBN 0 352 32983 1	☐
THE DEVIL INSIDE	Portia Da Costa ISBN 0 352 32993 9	☐
HEALING PASSION	Sylvie Ouellette ISBN 0 352 32998 X	☐
THE STALLION	Georgina Brown ISBN 0 352 33005 8	☐

--------✂--------------------

Please send me the books I have ticked above.

Name   ....

Address   ....

           ....

           ....

           .... Post Code   ....

Send to: **Cash Sales, Black Lace Books, 332 Ladbroke Grove, London W10 5AH, UK.**

US customers: for prices and details of how to order books for delivery by mail, call 1-800-805-1083.

Please enclose a cheque or postal order, made payable to **Virgin Publishing Ltd**, to the value of the books you have ordered plus postage and packing costs as follows:

UK and BFPO – £1.00 for the first book, 50p for each subsequent book.

Overseas (including Republic of Ireland) – £2.00 for the first book, £1.00 each subsequent book.

If you would prefer to pay by VISA or ACCESS/MASTERCARD, please write your card number and expiry date here:

....

Please allow up to 28 days for delivery.

Signature   ....

--------✂--------------------

WE NEED YOUR HELP ...
to plan the future of women's erotic fiction –

– and no stamp required!

Yours are the only opinions that matter.

Black Lace is the first series of books devoted to erotic fiction by women for women.

We intend to keep providing the best-written, sexiest books you can buy. And we'd appreciate your help and valued opinion of the books so far. Tell us what you want to read.

THE BLACK LACE QUESTIONNAIRE

SECTION ONE: ABOUT YOU

.1   Sex (*we presume you are female, but so as not to discriminate*)
Are you?
Male   ☐
Female   ☐

.2   Age
under 21   ☐   21–30   ☐
31–40   ☐   41–50   ☐
51–60   ☐   over 60   ☐

.3   At what age did you leave full-time education?
still in education   ☐   16 or younger   ☐
17–19   ☐   20 or older   ☐

4   Occupation _____

1.5 Annual household income _____

1.6 We are perfectly happy for you to remain anonymous;
     but if you would like to receive information on other
     publications available, please insert your name and
     address

     _____

     _____

     _____

     _____

SECTION TWO: ABOUT BUYING BLACK LACE BOOKS

2.1 Where did you get this copy of *An Act of Love*?
     Bought at chain book shop   ☐
     Bought at independent book shop   ☐
     Bought at supermarket   ☐
     Bought at book exchange or used book shop   ☐
     I borrowed it/found it   ☐
     My partner bought it   ☐

2.2 How did you find out about Black Lace books?
     I saw them in a shop   ☐
     I saw them advertised in a magazine   ☐
     I read about them in _____
     Other _____

2.3 Please tick the following statements you agree with:
     I would be less embarrassed about buying Black
     Lace books if the cover pictures were less explicit ☐
     I think that in general the pictures on Black
     Lace books are about right   ☐
     I think Black Lace cover pictures should be as
     explicit as possible   ☐

2.4 Would you read a Black Lace book in a public place – on
     a train for instance?
     Yes   ☐   No   ☐

SECTION THREE: ABOUT THIS BLACK LACE BOOK

3.1 Do you think the sex content in this book is:
    Too much   □   About right   □
    Not enough   □

3.2 Do you think the writing style in this book is:
    Too unreal/escapist   □   About right   □
    Too down to earth   □

3.3 Do you think the story in this book is:
    Too complicated   □   About right   □
    Too boring/simple   □

3.4 Do you think the cover of this book is:
    Too explicit   □   About right   □
    Not explicit enough   □

Here's a space for any other comments:

SECTION FOUR: ABOUT OTHER BLACK LACE BOOKS

4.1 How many Black Lace books have you read?   □

4.2 If more than one, which one did you prefer?

4.3 Why?

SECTION FIVE: ABOUT YOUR IDEAL EROTIC NOVEL

We want to publish the books you want to read – so this is
your chance to tell us exactly what your ideal erotic novel
would be like.

5.1   Using a scale of 1 to 5 (1 = no interest at all, 5 = your
      ideal), please rate the following possible settings for an
      erotic novel:

          Medieval/barbarian/sword 'n' sorcery   [
          Renaissance/Elizabethan/Restoration   [
          Victorian/Edwardian   [
          1920s & 1930s – the Jazz Age   [
          Present day
          Future/Science Fiction   [

5.2   Using the same scale of 1 to 5, please rate the following
      themes you may find in an erotic novel:

          Submissive male/dominant female
          Submissive female/dominant male
          Lesbianism
          Bondage/fetishism
          Romantic love
          Experimental sex e.g. anal/watersports/sex toys
          Gay male sex
          Group sex

5.3   Using the same scale of 1 to 5, please rate the following
      styles in which an erotic novel could be written:

          Realistic, down to earth, set in real life
          Escapist fantasy, but just about believable
          Completely unreal, impressionistic, dreamlike

5.4   Would you prefer your ideal erotic novel to be written
      from the viewpoint of the main male characters or the
      main female characters?

          Male   ☐   Female
          Both   ☐

5.5 What would your ideal Black Lace heroine be like? Tick as many as you like:

Dominant	☐	Glamorous	☐
Extroverted	☐	Contemporary	☐
Independent	☐	Bisexual	☐
Adventurous	☐	Naïve	☐
Intellectual	☐	Introverted	☐
Professional	☐	Kinky	☐
Submissive	☐	Anything else?	☐
Ordinary	☐	_____	

5.6 What would your ideal male lead character be like? Again, tick as many as you like:

Rugged	☐		
Athletic	☐	Caring	☐
Sophisticated	☐	Cruel	☐
Retiring	☐	Debonair	☐
Outdoor-type	☐	Naïve	☐
Executive-type	☐	Intellectual	☐
Ordinary	☐	Professional	☐
Kinky	☐	Romantic	☐
Hunky	☐		
Sexually dominant	☐	Anything else?	☐
Sexually submissive	☐	_____	

5.7 Is there one particular setting or subject matter that your ideal erotic novel would contain?

_____

SECTION SIX: LAST WORDS

6.1 What do you like best about Black Lace books?

_____

6.2 What do you most dislike about Black Lace books?

_____

6.3 In what way, if any, would you like to change Black Lace covers?

_____

6.4   Here's a space for any other comments:

_____
_____
_____
_____

Thank you for completing this questionnaire. Now tear it out of the book – carefully! – put it in an envelope and send it to:

    Black Lace
    FREEPOST
    London
    W10 5BR

No stamp is required if you are resident in the U.K.